Praise fo

ANGEL DE LA LUNA AND THE

"Angel de la Luna is a beautifully told, and at times, heartbreaking coming-of-age and coming-to-America story. Evelina Galang is a masterful storyteller and through her brilliant voice and craft, Angel and her family become ours too."
—EDWIDGE DANTICAT

"Angel de la Luna is pure poetry, a heartrending story told by a young girl whom I would follow anywhere. The voice is pitch-perfect; the music a constant. In this collision of cultures and languages, of the deepest sorrows, M. Evelina Galang has found resounding beauty. I want to shower her and her book with rose petals!"**—CRISTINA GARCIA,** author of *King of Cuba*

"Remarkably complex and eminently readable, M. Evelina Galang's *Angel de la Luna* speaks of people separated by time and distance; it speaks of the tension created by Filipino and American cultures; it speaks of comfort women and the horrors they faced at the hands of Japanese soldiers during World War II. Only a writer of Galang's talents and accomplishments could tackle such important subjects with grace and dignity. *Angel de la Luna* is a novel of great beauty and strength."
—PABLO MEDINA

"A richly detailed novel full of music and color, *Angel de la Luna and the 5th Glorious Mystery* tells a story of difficult journeys: from innocence to experience, from life in the Philippines to life in the United States, and from longing through anger and back to love again. Just as Angel finds strength in the stories of other women who have endured the hardest of circumstances, readers will find strength in the unforgettable Angel as she discovers her own life's rhythm."

—**SHERI REYNOLDS**, author of *The Rapture of Canaan*

"A story of teenage rebellion, *Angel de la Luna and the 5th Glorious Mystery* is also a novel of adult grace. Its particular triumph is to give an intimate voice to radical themes: a young woman sees the immigrant's American dream through the lens of Third World activism and gives us startling ways of looking and words for seeing the world."

—**GINA APOSTOL**, author of *Gun Dealers' Daughter*

"A poignant and well-crafted coming-of-age novel set in Manila and Chicago, *Angel de la Luna and the 5th Glorious Mystery* is about a Filipino family's and, in a larger picture, their native country's, fractured past and present. Above all, it is about the indomitable spirit of a young woman, which guides her out of grief and longing and fuels her with renewed strength to continue her struggle against injustices."

—**R. ZAMORA LINMARK**, author of *Leche* and *Drive-By Vigils*

ANGEL DE LA LUNA AND THE 5TH GLORIOUS MYSTERY

ANGEL DE LA LUNA
AND THE 5TH GLORIOUS MYSTERY

A NOVEL BY M. EVELINA GALANG

COFFEE HOUSE PRESS
MINNEAPOLIS
2013

Coffee House Press books are available to the trade through our primary distributor, Consortium Book Sales & Distribution, cbsd.com or (800) 283-3572. For personal orders, catalogs, or other information, write to: info@coffeehousepress.org.

Coffee House Press is a nonprofit literary publishing house. Support from private foundations, corporate giving programs, government programs, and generous individuals helps make the publication of our books possible. We gratefully acknowledge their support in detail in the back of this book. To you and our many readers around the world, we send our thanks for your continuing support.

Visit us at coffeehousepress.org.

LIBRARY OF CONGRESS CATALOGING-IN-PUBLICATION DATA
Galang, M. Evelina, 1961–
Angel de la Luna and the 5th Glorious Mystery :
a novel / by Evelina Galang.
pages cm
SUMMARY: As a baby in her mother's womb, as a schoolgirl in Manila, and as a reluctant immigrant to Chicago at age sixteen, Angel burns with a desire to be an activist, but learning truths about her mother and grandmother help her find peace.
ISBN 978-1-56689-333-6 (pbk.)
[1. Mothers and daughters—Fiction. 2. Family life—Philippines—Fiction. 3. Family life—Illinois—Chicago—Fiction. 4. Human rights workers—Fiction. 5. Filipino Americans—Fiction. 6. Immigrants—Fiction. 7. Philippines—Fiction. 8. Chicago (Ill.)—Fiction.] I. Title.
PZ7.G129646ANG 2013
[FIC]—DC23
2013003663
PRINTED IN CANADA
FIRST EDITION | FIRST PRINTING

For all my girls—especially my nieces—
Nina, Mia, Julia, Anna, Ligaya, Nika, and Carmen.
And to my nephews—
Manolo, Mikey, Schottie, Noah, and Mason,
because you should know the stories too.

MANILA, 2000

ONE

The day my father, Ernesto de la Luna, disappeared he gave me one thousand pesos. "I'll be home in three days," Papang said, counting the money. "But just in case. Take care of your ináy, Angel."

It's been two weeks. My mother is out of her mind.

This morning, St. Magdalena's school bus pulls up to our house. The roosters crow and traffic gathers beyond Mabini Street, everyone fighting for space. Drivers honk horns, long bellows sing from diesel trucks. An old vendor rolls his heavy cart up the hill and caws, "Mais! Mais!" The lamps along Mabini shut down one by one.

We climb aboard the empty bus—my grandmother Lola Ani, my little sister, Lila, and our ináy. I lift two plastic supot of chicken and rice and put them on an empty seat. The driver loads our maletas into the back of the bus. We're not sure how long we'll be gone. A day, a week, maybe a month. The bus is so big and white and we are tiny in its space, sitting away from one another, each gazing out a different window.

As the bus eases onto Mabini, Lola Ani makes the sign of the cross. We pray for safe travel. We pray for good health. We pray for Mother Superior for loaning us this bus. We pray for Papang. We bless ourselves and our family and we bless the drivers who will be traveling on these roads. My family's voice comes together. It is the only sound I hear beyond the chugging engine.

"Angel," my mother says. "Text your papang again. Tell him we're coming na."

"But Ináy . . . "

"Don't answer back. Just text him, ha?"

I look to Lola Ani. She turns away from me, arranging herself in her seat. "Opo," I answer, pulling out my phone.

"Good girl," Ináy says. "Tell him aalis na tayo."

The bus idles at a stoplight like it's waiting for me to text my father. My thumbs tap the keys, swift like drumsticks on a snare. All the while I stare at the back of Ináy's head, the way it bobs like a blossom on a vine, gingerly holding on, as if the wind will blow her petals out the bus window. I feel the blood spinning in my belly, threatening to spoil my breakfast. Two thumbs hit send, a beep sounds. Ináy sighs. "That's my good girl."

When the light goes green we shoot down narrow streets, weaving our way to the superhighway. Though it's early, before long we're stuck in traffic, idling behind a carabao-driven cart. A mountain of hemp baskets, bags, hats, and mats piled onto the cart obstructs our view. A vendor perched on top waves the heat away. His cart is surrounded by odd-plated vehicles, by the smog of diesel fuel. Slowly, the sun tries to burn the vast Manila haze hovering over us.

If Papang were here we'd be riding in his van. He knows how to drive on seven thousand islands, knows all the long and shortcuts. He goes ikot-ikot in the traffic as if the car is his dancing partner. He says even if it takes him longer to get there, it's better to keep the car moving. It makes the customers think they're getting somewhere rather than sitting still in traffic. His clients come from all over the world. Americans are loudest, he says. They talk nonstop about nothing. He pretends he can't speak English sometimes so they won't talk to him. But then they just talk louder, like yelling will give meaning to their noise. Papang pretends to care. He nods his head and gets them places without a fuss.

Driving is what Papang does for a living, but really he's a musician. He plays rhythm and blues through the night, till the sun burns through smog. He smokes cigarettes, drinks whiskey, and is known all over Makati as the Beat Man. "A heart that won't quit," Ináy once said. "That's what drew me to your father."

When I was still too young for school, I'd sit in the front seat while Papang drove his clients from one end of Manila to another. He took them to business meetings and restaurants in Makati. Sometimes he took them to resorts in the provinces. After he'd drop them off, Papang and I would listen to the blues, and he'd teach me how to hold his sticks and how to beat the drum. "The trick, Angel, is not to think. Just feel it. Listen to the way the tires roll, or the way the wind blows. Listen to the engine when it's idling. You can hear the traffic breathing if you are very still. It has a heartbeat." And then he'd thump his chest and chant,

3

"Pintig. Toom-toom. Pintig. Toom-toom. Pintig." I'd join him, eyes closed, hand on my heart, beating to the count, my whole body vibrating with each syllable—pintig, pintig, pintig.

The cell phone bee-beeps. Lights neon green. Asks, *Nasaan ka?*
Here, I text back. *My mother is losing it. My papang is gone.*
Yeah, pero nasaan ka? Karina asks me again. Sometimes she irritates me, and it doesn't matter if we're best friends. She is slow.
On Mother Mary's school bus. Going to the province to find my papang.
Must be nice, Karina writes me*, related to Mother Mary Superior.*
And when I don't answer her, the phone bee-beeps again. *Hope you find your papang.*
Me too.
I prop the window open and dust from the road drifts in along with traffic horns and motors rumbling. Beyond the glass the palengke sprawls with bright bushels of kangkong, green leafy spinach, and pechay. I see mangoes and bundles of lychee, red as rubies. Before St. Magdalena's, we used to walk through the palengke to get to class. Holding Lila's hand, I'd guide her past the hot reds and greens of the vegetables and past the fish packed in ice. We knew everyone in the stands. Sometimes we'd get treats on our way to school. The year Papang made lots of money driving foreign clients around Manila, we stopped going to public school. We stopped sitting in crowded classrooms with boring teachers. We stopped working after school. We stopped walking all over Manila. Instead, we attended St. Magdalena's

School of Holy Angels where the nuns take their girls to the Cordillera Mountains on field trips to get closer to God. Papang drove us to school. We ate our lunches in the courtyard gardens. Afterwards we'd stroll arm-in-arm with our batchmates, exchanging stories of aswangs, fairies, and other spirits.

The bus races down a boulevard; the sky lightens to gray. Behind the cityscape an orange red fights its way past the oppressive haze, colors the sky. At a stoplight, a series of jeepneys with brilliant purple-and-orange banners rippling from the back zooms past, honking and chanting in one miraculous voice.

"Naku!" I shout.

"What is it?" Lila asks. "What's the matter, Ate Angel?"

I say, "Didn't you see that?" and when she says, "What?" I tell her, "It was nothing." Not a flash of white, not a van going so fast it blurred before you, not our papang zipping through the streets of Manila, his silver-blue van buried deep in the pack of jeepneys, heading off to some protest.

I see Papang's van rushing through every stoplight, rushing past us even when traffic is still.

"Ano, Angel," Ináy calls, "Wala pa bang sagot ang papang mo?"

Of course there is no answer. What does she think? I close my eyes, hold my breath, listen to the traffic's beating heart.

"Pero didn't I hear your cell phone beep?" Ináy asks.

"Si Karina," I tell her. "Walang sagot si Papang."

Were Papang here, he'd flip that radio on, and the van would pulse with the bass of pop radio. He'd nod his head and drum the steering wheel with his fingers and reach out and tap Ináy like she was the snare on his drums. She'd roll her eyes, but secretly she'd love it and in the end the four of us would be stuck there in traffic, dancing in our seats, being our own rock band.

But not today. Today the ride is so quiet I can hear Ináy shiver when she sighs. I feel her sadness and think about ways I want to go to her, but I cannot. I look over at her, the way her body has wilted. She has thrown her legs on the back of the seat before her, and her arms sprawl on either side of her, sighing like a teenager. I motion for Lila to sit with Ináy, but Lila says, "No, Ate Angel, she wants you. You sit with her."

"No, she doesn't," I say. "You're the baby. She wants you."

When Lila refuses to go to our mother, I shift my way down the bus aisle, walking my hands across the railing overhead. Under my feet the bus rumbles, hitting every stone and dip in the road. I fall into the seat behind her, and I lay my head on her shoulder. "Ináy," I say. "What if Papang was in that accident?"

"What accident?"

"The one in the news. The crash," I say.

"No. Can't be. Maybe he has no load. Maybe the battery has died."

"But, Ináy, it's been two weeks."

"Siguro," she tells me, "those clients from Hollywood are working him too hard. Baka when he comes back he'll have earned our passage to America."

I shake my head and feel the tears rising, threatening to come out. "Pero, Ináy, remember how two weeks ago you said he was with us. You said he was there in your room. What did you mean?"

6

"That was a dream. But this is the truth, anak, you'll see. He's coming home, and when he does we'll be that much closer to America."

"But we're not going to America. Papang is missing, Ináy."

And that's when she screams at me as if I am responsible for losing him. Her arms fly up, her face grows red, and Lola Ani has to run to the back of the bus to hold onto her, to calm her. She fights my grandmother, pushes her, and Lola Ani almost hits her head on the corner of a seat.

I pinch my arm. Wake up, I think, wake up. It's as if I've gone to sleep and someone has kidnapped every single person in my family and replaced them with a stranger. Some alien beings who look like my relatives, sound like my relatives, but are not my relatives. My nails dig into my skin, but when I open my eyes, I am still here, sitting alone in the middle of the bus, my family scattered about like fallen fruit, my papang not among them. "Wake up," I say out loud. Gumising ka na. Tama na ito.

TWO

Two weeks before Papang disappeared, he drove us down the narrow mountain passage of the Cordillera Mountains, winding dirt roads, paikot ikot on round sharp corners, zooming past cars on one-lane roads, practically leaping over carabao-driven carts. The skies had grown dark that afternoon, and the rain came down in sheets across our wide windshield.

"Dahan-dahan, mahal," Ináy warned him. "Baka maaksidente tayo."

He told her to stop worrying. He told her to trust him. "Mahal," she answered. "I trust you naman. It's the other drivers. It's my stomach."

He told her to focus on a point far away, like another mountaintop, like a cloud in the sky, or the place where the sun would be if it was shining. But Ináy moaned and shook her head. I gave her a bottle of water. Lola Ani handed her a salted egg. She refused us both, closing her eyes and leaning back. Lila tried to kiss her, but even this she waved away. I knew what was coming. She told us that the world was framed with lights cracked and wavy, dotted with black spots. Her vision was going away, she said. She tossed her feet onto the dashboard, then she sat up again and fiddled with the radio. Static spat from the speakers, cranky and mean. We had lost reception. "Slow down, my love," she said again. "I'm really feeling sick."

He said to think of something beautiful. "The ocean," he suggested. She shook her head and reminded him that the ocean had waves and the thought of all that motion made her stomach fall and rise, made her head spin. "Say a prayer to Mama Mary," he told her, handing her his rosary. But the circular motion of the beads running through her fingers and the repetition of the prayers, over and over, just made her dizzy.

And before we knew it, she was spitting up her food into plastic bags for the rest of the trip, and for the next forty-eight hours.

When we got back to Manila, Ináy went straight to bed and Papang and I snuck up to the roof and set up our drums. We hauled out the tom-toms and snares; we balanced the cymbals and centered the bass before his low metal stool.

Papang gave me his old pieces because, he said, I had the kind of beat you don't learn. "You inherit it; you create it." He said it came with the blood. Slowly, he added shiny black and silver pieces to his set and I inherited the old ones. So far I've got my own tom-tom, snare, and two sizes of cowbell.

He rolled his sticks across the tight skins of each drum. He crashed the cymbal and told me to follow his lead. Papang beat the drum, keeping time with his whole body. The whole set breathed with each stroke and a wind pushed Papang's hair away from his face. I hit the snare drum. I slammed the tom-tom. I told him, "Tomorrow I am trying out for the school band. Not the orchestra," I said, "Not the jazz band but a rock band— Holy Rock 'n' Roll!"

"That's the band? Holy Rock 'n' Roll? Very cold."

"No, Papang," I banged the drum. "Cool." I crashed the cymbals. "Cold is the temperature. Cool is the way things are." I rolled my eyes at him. "So corny, Papang." I kicked the pedal.

"Listen first," he said, tapping at the bass drum. "Hold those sticks like I taught you."

The rhythm of our sticks fell into a pattern and our drums began to sing. The bass thumped and beat—pow pow—while the cowbells rang. It was thunder, it was rain, it was a battery of pebbles falling to the earth. I closed my eyes and did my best to play like him, to match the passion of each beat. This is what it felt like: like all the hearts in the world beating, vibrating so loud I felt it in my chest, so many feelings released all at once—the tension in my bones and all the breath I'd been holding—flying out of me like a school of tiny silver fish leaping from the sea. For a moment, I forgot that I was fourteen. My heart expanded like a balloon and light shot from my fingertips, my toes. Shafts of light blasted from my ears. I was a star bursting. I was Manila Bay. It felt like that— like the sound began inside me and filled up the room.

And then my mother summoned me and ruined everything. "Ate Angel," my sister whispered in my ear. Her voice was small like a thought. "Ate, Ináy wants you to come to her. Masakit pa rin ang ulo niya."

"Ate," Lila said again. This time she put her hand on my shoulder and squeezed. "Please come now. Please."

Papang stopped in the middle of a drum roll. "Go, Angel," he said, "you heard your little sister. Your mother has a migraine. Go." And just like that the rhythm stopped. The light went dark, and I felt my heart go small.

Inside her dark room she had blocked the sun with drapes lined in heavy plastic. The air con kept the noise out, muffled the chaos from the streets. I crept on my tiptoes, my hands held up in the air. I crawled under the blanket next to my mother, and I kissed her clammy cheek. She was so beautiful, even when sick. Her eyes fluttered at the recognition of my kiss. She rolled her head left and right, as if the movement would slide the pain out of her. Taking my hands in hers, she squeezed.

"Anak," she whispered. "Why do you suppose God does this to me? Ang sakit!"

Her breath smelled like bile from her belly. "Sumuka ka ba?" I asked her, even though I knew she had.

She nodded. "I got so sick. Lila cleaned it up already. Can you still smell it pa?"

"Don't worry about that, Ináy," I said kissing her hand.

The door slid open and Papang greeted her quietly. "Ano, sweetheart?" he asked. "Can I come in?"

When Ináy heard Papang enter, she sat up like she'd been waiting for him forever. I climbed out of bed and stood near the window so they could have this moment alone. I cracked the curtains open and afternoon sunlight forced its way into the room. Below I saw the beggar children on the other side of Mabini, working the sidewalks like a band of thieves.

I turned to my parents who were locked in a soft embrace. They whispered so quietly I could not make out their words.

He kissed her on the forehead. "Come on, anak," he said. "Make your mama feel better."

After he left, I approached her. "You have to tell me what to do," I said. "I'm still not sure."

"Just follow your intuition, anak," she said. "Hold your hands over me and see where they lead you."

I dipped my fingertips into the ointment, and I began at her feet, rubbing and pulling on her toes. Her feet were bony and her toes were long like fingers. The arches had fallen from all the walking and the bottoms of her feet were covered in calluses. It was hard for me to find flesh soft and untouched.

"Why do you start there when you know it's my head that hurts?" she wanted to know.

"You said to follow my intuition, di ba?"

She let out a long sigh. "Oo ngâ, I did," she said.

I massaged each of her hands, kneading the fleshy palms, pinching down on pressure points. The ointment smelled of mint, of camphor, of healing. Her breathing was shallow and restless. The headache surged and she squinted. My hands hovered over to see where I should go next, floating from the top of her head through her shoulders and chest, lingering at her heart and passing over her belly, her pubic bone, and limbs. I knew I was supposed to feel a jolt or a buzz or something, but I felt nothing. I tried again. I let go of my ideas. I stopped thinking. I imagined there was heat and I let it guide me and hold me. I put my hands down on her eyes.

"That's good," she said. "Now let them rest. What do you feel?"

"Nothing. I feel like my hands are over your face."

"I feel heat," she said. "I feel a light buzzing. You don't feel it?"

"A little," I said, lying, and then I felt the subtle movement of air. The right side of her head seemed to pulse a little faster and angrier than the left. Soon, her breathing slowed and I watched the fall and rise of her chest. I placed my hands under her head and cradled her like that. I closed my eyes. I thought nothing. I waited. From the start she had said that I was born like her, hands reaching out of her womb, grabbing at the doctor and nurses. I was a gift from God. That hilots are born this way—not head first into the world but hands. But I didn't believe her. This felt weird to me. But I obeyed her and placed my hands on her as if to heal her. I did it because I was her anak and she asked me to. I didn't believe in magic. But I wanted her to feel better. I wanted the anger to leave her body. I said a prayer. I whispered to my angel and asked her to guide me. I sat like that for almost an hour until my mother told me her headache had gone away.

The next morning Ináy was still sick. Papang wanted to cancel his business trip to Baguio. I heard them talking. I could smell her sour stomach.

"You have to go. The money is too good."

13

"The money is nothing if you're like this."

"Go. I'll be O.K."

The voices went blurry. They were whispering, and I imagined he was holding her, rocking her, maybe he was pushing the hair from her face. And then she told him, "Angel can stay with me today. She can heal me."

But I was trying out for the band.

"What about Lila?"

"Your mother can take her to school," Ináy told him. "You go to Baguio, mahal."

But what about the band? And anyway, I would rather be at school reading about the Glorious Mysteries or drawing murals of Philippine history for art class. There were so many words to discover, to taste, to gather into sentences. So many ways to say the word beautiful and I wanted to find them. Please don't make me stay, I prayed.

I heard them sigh and knew they were falling back to sleep, stealing one last nap before the day began.

I wish they had stayed in bed all day. I wish I had gone to school. I wish, I wish, I wish.

Later that night, when Lila and I were lying in our bed and Lola Ani was combing her silver hair, I saw the moon rising big and fat just outside my window. The kuliglíg chirped high-pitched and light. A basketball slapped at the pavement somewhere on our street, and the voices drifted in and out of our room. Suddenly, we heard moaning so terrible and deep we thought an animal had charged into our little house. It was a lion's roar. We ran from our bed into her room and found Ináy on the floor, shaking, weeping, going mad. She pulled at her hair as she called Papang's name. There was nothing we could do, and even though Lila and I did not know what was happening, we followed the rhythm of her cries, we shook, we fell to our knees and embraced her.

"Bakit, Ináy?" I begged her. "Anong nangyari?"

"Ináy," Lila shouted. Her lips trembled. Her hair fell into her eyes. "Natatakot ako, Ináy." She wrapped her arms around our mother and held her tight as if that might have kept her from leaving us, but Ináy took a breath and made herself large and hard to hold.

We were calling her name like she was calling our father's. The three of us latched onto one another and it seemed the whole house was sighing. The curtains blew though the windows were closed. The walls shook. The moonlight knocked at the glass and the whole world seemed to shift below our bodies.

Lola Ani entered the room and grabbed hold of my mother's wrists. She didn't say anything. She wore no expression. She might have been picking objects up from the floor and putting them in their place, when she brought Ináy to bed. That tiny brown woman with frail bones and wrinkled skin dragged my mother from the floor and tucked her in. She let my mother cry. She had Lila and me sit at the foot of her bed and pray.

"What happened?" I asked her.

"Nothing," Lola Ani said. "Wala."

But Ináy was sure that Papang was with us. "Nandito siya!" she yelled. "Nandito siya!"

"Where?" Lila wanted to know. She ran to the window to look for his van.

"Lila," Lola Ani called her back. "I asked you to pray, anak."

Lola Ani was so calm, so steady. She didn't believe Ináy when she said Papang was in the room. She did not not believe her. She just tucked us in our mother's bed and watched us through the night.

That night we caught Ináy's dreams as they spilled from her. We drank them like water. Before I knew it, Lila and I were dreaming our mother's dream. I heard my mother's voice soft like a lullaby, and then she cried, "No! Mahal! No!" And her body churned like a storm brewing in the sea and then she broke into sorrowful cries. We were all clamoring, calling out for Papang, our faces wet with so many tears.

I'm not sure how she knew. She just knew. And just like that Ináy was lost—lost in her grief, lost in the house, lost to the days and to Lila and me. She grew thinner and her clothes flowed like a stream of water. We couldn't see her body anymore—just the sleeves of her nightgowns or the hem of her skirts, just the oversized hat that she wore to hide her swollen eyes. My sister and I woke up night after night and found Ináy floating above our bed, her spirit hovering toward the open window, yearning to roam night skies. Lola Ani held her down, reached up and pulled her legs from the ceiling and tucked her back into our bed. Sometimes Ináy floated away at daybreak and our old grandmother had to climb ladders and rooftops, crawling up branches of guava trees to reach her, singing soft prayers as she tugged at our ináy and brought her back to earth.

THREE

We retrace Papang's route, driving through green mountains, stopping at sleepy villages scattered across the Cordilleras. The old bus grunts, winding up roads, a fat white elephant with little energy. This is the same passage we took just weeks before he disappeared, on our way home from the provinces.

We rise above the sea, so high our roof nearly hits the clouds. Beyond the ridge of mountains a valley of green leaves balances on trunks thin as pencils. I brush a tear away.

We stop at every roadside shack and talk to vendors selling corn, nuts, bunches of fruit, homemade candy. We snake through crowded little towns on dirt roads and idle in the middle of town squares. Lila and I wait on the bus with Jun-jun, the driver, while our Lola Ani speaks to locals. Worry fills her tiny body, spills out in her words as she waves her hands up to the sky. Electricity sparks and sputters from the ends of her brittle white hair. She nearly lights the air on fire. She drags a hanky across her forehead and Papang's name, Ernesto de la Luna, falls like sweat from her temples. She draws figures—what looks like my father and several passengers—in the sky. The locals nod, answer her with slumped shoulders and downcast eyes. They light up cigarettes and blow smoke to the wind, squint like they are listening, like they can make sense of Lola Ani's body talk. But it is my mother, Milagros de la Luna, who questions them directly, speaking in the dialect, charming farmers, roadside vendors, and tricycle drivers with the cadence of her voice. She is the one who slips them first an embrace and then a few hundred pesos in search of her missing husband. Perhaps they are mesmerized by the way her body hovers ever so slightly above the dusty roads. Perhaps they are hoping to catch a glimpse of her face behind her movie star sunglasses and her floppy straw hat. Slowly, our mother comes back to us, her feet softly touching ground, her voice calm as mountain wind. She is now at work, searching for her husband. She is coming back.

At sundown, the bus pulls into my father's barrio, a little town near Luna just north of Bagiuo. On these streets the only lights are the moon and the stars and an occasional window in a house. The people wander up and down the main street, bouncing basketballs, making tsismis on church steps, or playing mahjong in the bodega of a house. Our white school bus climbs up the hill like it's running out of gas. When they see us, the people chase the bus, tapping on the glass, greeting us.

The door slides open and voices explode like a rush of air. We get off one by one and everyone surrounds us, holding us, twirling us about. The young ones file one after the other and taking Lola Ani's hand, they bring it to their forehead. "Bless, bless, bless," Lola Ani whispers. Lila and I grab the hands of everyone around us, elders we know and love and elders who are strangers and we make mano too, placing the tips of their fingers upon our foreheads. Respect. Respect. Respect. "Bless, bless, bless," they whisper back.

No one asks about Papang. No one pokes their head into the bus or calls his name. I look into the eyes of my lola's old sister, Lola Kula, and my cousin, Ate Rosalie, and I can see that they have been thinking about this moment for a long time. When Lola Kula reaches my Lola Ani, they collapse into one body, breathing together and crying wildly, loud sorrow spilling out of them. My mother stands there with her hands in her pockets. Silent. I call out to Ináy, but she doesn't answer. Doesn't feel me watching her, wondering how we can be here, in my father's barrio and he is not with us. No one calls his name. My cousins tackle me and I am lost. They shout in my ears, pull at my arms, tap me on the back, but I cannot feel a thing. I cannot breathe much less smell that night air or their skin, soft with sweat and tinged in dirt. I feel nothing.

The next morning my cousins and I roam the dirt path to the dagat to bathe. Behind me, Lila and Bebet flit about like two blue dragonflies. In front of me, Charing trails Ate Rosalie and her baby, whispering something I cannot hear. They strut back and forth across the road, their hips zigzagging like a metronome keeping time. Everyone wants to be like Ate Rosalie. Her hair shimmers like a waterfall streaming down her back. And she is strong, a graduate of St. Magdalena's school of holy aktibistas. Until her pregnancy, had been campaigning with our grandmother's youngest sister, Mother Mary, Holy Angels' Mother Superior. Now Ate Rosalie carries her baby on her hip and wanders the roads of the Cordillera Mountains like she owns them.

"What are you talking about?" I ask, chasing after them.

"Just this campaign," Charing says.

"What campaign?"

"Nothing," Ate Rosalie says. She wipes the snot from the baby's nose. "We're not talking about anything." She squints in the sun and her face squishes up like a heart that is shutting down. "You marching with Mother Mary?"

"No," I say. "Why would I?"

"Wala. You're a St. M girl, why wouldn't you?"

"I'd love that," Charing says. "How many marches have you been in?"

"Plenty," Ate Rosalie says, smiling now. "One day I'll take you to the city and we'll bring down the government."

Her words spear me in the stomach and I don't know why. She hands the baby to Charing, lights up a cigarette, and blowing smoke to the sky, she walks away.

"I want to march," I shout. And then I think about what I should have said; I was protesting the streets of Manila long before I was born. All my life, I have been told that during the

People Power Revolution in 1986, my ináy carried me in her womb. I was a big girl, swimming in a sea too small to hold me. Her body rocked back and forth, taking little strides forward. She had to keep her feet wide to stay standing, to keep from toppling over and losing me all together. When she shouted, "MA-KI-BA-KA!" and they shouted back, "HUWÁG-MA-TA-KOT!" I kicked her belly hard. When she invited the others to join the struggle like that, with her brown fist in the air and her feet solidly planted on Philippine soil I wanted her to know I was one of them. I was not afraid. MAKIBAKA! I wanted to shout back. But I didn't have words. I only had my body, small and not yet ready for this world. I kicked at her. I punched. I yelled back and the sea inside her belly filled my mouth. I nearly drowned and fighting to breathe, I kicked so hard I almost broke her. She fell in the middle of the march. She hit the pavement and a thousand resisters came running to her aid.

I was almost born that day. I almost died that day.

Ate Rosalie chases after Lila and Bebet who are wrestling like they are fighting, but laughing all the while. "Come on," she says to them. "You'll get left behind."

The water in the dagat is so cold and clear, I can see to the bottom, where the coral begins, where the sand has been swept by the waves. We swim like fish. I float on my back and the small ones cling to my limbs, floating too, watching the clouds move above us. Lila and Bebet grab handfuls of sand from the bottom of the dagat and rub their faces and arms and legs. They place giant pieces of seaweed on their heads and shoulders giggling, they sing corny love songs to each other. In the water, our T-shirts balloon and make us appear like fat people with tiny heads and limbs. We swim underneath the green waters. We surface and hold onto each other.

It seems like we are treading water for hours, circling each other like a school of fish. I float on my back, watching the sun sinking into fat white clouds and struggling its way back out. Lila and Bebet circle me. "What are you two doing?" I ask.

"Nothing," they giggle back at me. "Wala, Ate."

But the two bob in the water, mouths to ears. Charing floats on her belly and when she stands she stops a second to listen to the two. "Bebet," she says. "That's enough. Don't scare Lila."

"I'm not scared," she answers. "Is it true?"

And Charing looks at me and says, "He's telling her about the lolas."

"Our lolas?" Our grandmothers?

"No, the Comfort Women, sa gera," she says, like I should know. And then she dives into the water, casting her body far from me.

The children's voices are so low now and every now and then their mouths sink into the edge of the sea and the ocean swallows their words. But I hear them—two girls swimming in the dagat, four soldiers and two long bayonets, fishing in that same ocean. Tell me, I say, but they swim away.

"Our secret," Bebet says. "You have to be ten to understand." They hold their breath, cling to each other—a shoulder, a leg, an

23

arm. Lila's fingers go to her lips as they shiver blue. She wipes her face with the back of her hands, pushing the ocean away so she can hear. I move closer to her, ask her if she's O.K. and when she nods, I shoot my body through the sea and rise up, blasting water at them.

When I look to the shore I see Ate Rosalie standing with her arms crossed against her chest. She doesn't swim with us, but stays in the shallow end, wading to her knees, wrangling her boy out of the tide. When she was in Manila she never saw us. But sometimes we'd see her on TV at a rally, shouting through a bullhorn and casting angry looks into the lens, her boyfriend, J.R., always fighting by her side. After she got pregnant, he disappeared like a ghost into nowhere. She said he loved her so much, he couldn't take it. He was dying, she said, but no one believed her. I wave to her madly, jumping out of the water and calling out her name. Her smile turns crooked and thin.

Later that night God sends us a message. Go find him. Bring him home yourself.

The cousins are gathered around the television, lying on top of one another, on bellies and chests and the fat flesh of arms. I sit with my mother watching a telenovela where women leap into their lovers' arms, where sisters slap sisters in the face, where husbands cheat with laundry maids. Ináy curls up like a kitten, tucking her thin legs beneath her. She pulls out her cell phone and texts Papang, *Come back na mahal.* I close my eyes so I can hear the whispering at the kitchen table. "Ináy," I say, shaking her leg gently, "Ináy, give me your phone na." But she only sinks deeper into her cushions.

Our old grandmothers sit at the kitchen table, a light bulb swinging gently over them. Who should go get him? Who should stay here? They fear my ináy will collapse.

Lola Kula has heard that bodies were found in the crevices of the Cordillera mountains—several Americans and a Filipino, tossed about and planted deep into the mountain's side. "Could it be Ernesto?" she asked my lola, "Baka anak mo iyon, Ani."

"Baka walang signal," Ináy says. She scrolls through the pad, looking for messages from Papang. Her fingers pound at the keys. *Answer me na, mahal! Nasaan ka?*

"She should stay here with Angel," Lola Kula says. "She should rest. She will need her strength."

"Lola," I call from the sala, "Si Ináy—"

"Not now, anak." Lola Ani waves a hand in the air. "We are thinking."

"But La," I say.

"Not now, anak."

Lola Ani sips from a tall bottle of orange soda. "She should see her husband. She should know firsthand."

I turn away from the telenovela and watch the grandmothers. They sit for the longest time, just looking at one another, that bald light bulb swinging over them. Each woman waits for the other to understand, to do what is right. I hold my breath. I count to ten. I wonder why their silence scares me.

They cannot be talking about my papang. Papang is a good driver. He would never miss a turn, no matter how sharp, no matter how slippery, he would swerve like a dancer shifting his weight in the middle of a crowded floor. He would scare every-one around him and maybe teeter a bit, but he would land with all four tires on the ground.

My mother marches into the kitchen and leans across the table. The old women watch as she places her thin arms between them, her beautiful face bright as the full moon. She tells them, "He is my husband. It's my right." And then Ináy holds her phone up to the window and hits the send button with her thumb, calling Papang home.

At dawn fog has swallowed us up. We can't see five feet before us. The school bus charges up the narrow passage so close to the mountain, I can touch the rock wall out my window. But we are moving fast. "Dahan-dahan!" Lola Ani warns Jun-jun. "They get too cocky, these drivers," Lola tells us. "They think they can just feel their way up the mountain—di ba—even Ernesto used to be the same way."

"Yes, ma'am," says the driver, "Opo, ma'am." But his foot is heavy on the pedal and the bus grinds so loud I am sure he can-not hear her calling over it. I am sure that like Papang, he is feel-ing his way up this mountain. He drives by sound. There is nothing on this road but our bus, the birds in the trees, and wind, and in the distance we can hear a choir of roosters cawing to each other—but here there is no other car, no van, no truck. You can tell from the lack of motors roaring. Sometimes we round a cor-ner and instead of slowing down, I can feel the bus accelerating. What's wrong with him, I think, doesn't he know why we're here?

When we get to the next village, the sun is just coming out of sleep and darkness has moved a few shades toward light. The bus pulls up to the city hall, a painted cement building growing out of the mountain's side like a tumor. No lights yet, no people. We wait on the bus.

Across from the municipal building, a street vendor sets up her stall. My mother goes to her and the old woman tells her that, weeks before, a blue van carrying foreigners and one small driver from Manila flew down the mountaintop during an unexpected storm somewhere on Kennon Road. Witnesses say the rain fell hard and softened into mud, and the blue van slid down its side like a boy's toy, tumbling and rolling down until it crashed into a forest of trees.

Hours later, the barangay captain arrives, unlocks the doors and my ináy and Lola Ani follow him through the iron gates and into the building.

FOUR

Lila and I wait for Ináy on the bus. I place my arm around my little sister and she begins to cry. "Don't," I whisper. "You don't know what's going to happen." She looks up, her small face fat with tears and I see Papang there—his mouth and his eyes and his big ears.

The tiny stones hitting the sides of the bus sound like maracas shaking. A gust of wind blows through the aisles, howling as it enters, leading us to look up at the sky where the clouds no longer float, but move with that same wind. I imagine Ináy's sleeves hanging from her thin arms, lifting her up into the sky, her body swimming past the clouds, shooting like a star into the universe while Lila and I stay grounded on this school bus, shut in by steel walls, dirty glass windows, and the smell of diesel exhaust.

If Papang is among the dead, she will explode like one of those telenovela women, falling to the dust and pounding a fist to her heart. The sound of her grief will ring throughout the Cordillera Mountains. It will take an army to keep her from flying off to space.

If Papang is among the dead.

Lila buries her face into my belly. "Stop it," I tell her, "you're making my shirt wet with all your luha. Tama na." I wipe her face dry with my sleeve. Up front, Jun-jun has fallen asleep and is snoring. I put my arms around Lila and hold her tight. I tell her everything is going to be just fine and that Papang is probably going to surprise us with something big. And when that doesn't seem to make her feel any better, I take my hands and drum on her legs and then on her belly and I dance in my seat. Lila breaks into a smile and taps on my arm, drums on the seat before us, a beat uneven and misplaced, but full of heart.

Outside, a large open truck full of soldiers packed like farm animals barrels past our bus. The men have long rifles slung around their shoulders, and they squat in the bed of the truck. "New People's Army," I say to Lila.

"I know," she says.

Soon, Lola Ani and Ináy march out into the light and the wind picks up again and blows their hair straight on end. Their clothing moves like sails. Ináy is quiet. She is calm. I breathe, I sigh. "See?" I tell my sister. "o.k. lang."

My mother finds a seat away from us. She pulls a sweater from a plastic bag and wraps it around her bony shoulders. Even though the sun is slipping behind clouds, she unfolds her big black shades and places them on her face like a movie star.

The sun goes down fast now and the van zips around the hills, up a one-lane mountain road. "Too fast," Lola Ani says. "Baka may mabangga tayo."

But Jun-jun tells her not to worry. "You know how it is," he says. "Too slow and the bus will not go up." Everybody drives these mountains like they are on a race with God.

"Dahan-dahan," she says again.

Looking out the window, all I see are the vast crevices between the rocks. It's like the bus is an ant clinging to a hill. Any moment, a breath may shift the sands, cause us to tumble and fall into the cliffs below. My ears pop. The mountains exhale cool winds that skim my temples, pop my eardrums. Lila taps me on the shoulder and when I turn to her, she's pinching her nose and blowing like her head is a balloon filling up with air. She motions me to follow her. Mountain air invades my body, swells my heart, pops my ears again.

Lila leans her chin onto my shoulder and places her hand on me.

"Mahal kita, Ate," she says.

"Yeah," I tell her, turning back to check on our mother, "I love you too."

We have stopped where the mountains slope and roll across the country. Lila and Lola are peeing. I look down at the gravel and see a stream coming from behind the bus. In the distance, I hear the rumble of a truck on gravel and suddenly another jeep of rebels zooms past us, men and women in bandanas, dark fatigues, and rifles, raising their fists to the sky in greeting as they pass. Ináy and I ignore the shouts, choosing instead to watch the mountains turn one into the other, like bodies turning in their sleep. Above us large birds soar, gliding on slight wind. When I look at my mother, she is gazing at me and I say, "What is it Ináy?"

She doesn't say anything back, she just keeps looking at me. So I ask her again and this time she pulls drumsticks out of her back pocket, Papang's drumsticks.

"Where did you get those?" I ask her. "Didn't Papang bring them on his trip?"

And she smiles at me then and nods. "Anak," she says. "These are yours now." And then I hear it, the rattling branches in a nearby tree, the sound of crickets syncopated and just a little offbeat. "Mine?" I say. And there is the thumping of the heart. Pintig, I hear my papang calling, pintig. Pintig. Doom-doom. Pintig. Doom-doom. Pintig. I hear it so loud, resounding everywhere as my mother pulls me to her, not a word between us, not a whisper.

The sun sets so fast, it spills red across the horizon and tints everything, even our faces, our hands, our feet. In one quick moment, the darkness descends and I cannot distinguish the shapes of things.

FIVE

I am not sure when it happens, only that there is a moment where I am taken from my life and put into a movie house. I am sitting on a soft red seat in an audience among strangers.

The movie takes place in my father's barrio. The filmmakers must have traveled here with Papang, and falling in love with the scenery—the rich tropical foliage, the hilly streets, and the quaint church with its stone courtyard, lost kittens, chickens and local carabao—they must have insisted on coming back here to shoot this picture, to use my family and to make us stars.

The movie isn't in English or Tagalog or our dialect, it's in a foreign foreign language and the lines are translated in English subtitles.

In the next few weeks, every relative travels to Lola Kula's house. The women spend days cooking and cleaning and getting the sala ready for my papang. The church ladies arrive too, bringing flowers shaped in horseshoes and circles and gigantic wall hangings. There are so many big arrangements of brightly colored gardenias and roses and sampaguitas that we nearly choke from all that sweetness. Outside, the men cleanse four piglets by starving them for one week. Then they slice the vein in their necks and the pigs squeal, "Ayaw ko! Buhay ko!" Cries so deafening and sad, I cannot stand to watch the life drain out of them. And later, when the pleas have died, the men hoist the baboy onto spits and roast them over hot coals.

For weeks the kitchen smells of blood stew and pinirtrong bangus, chicken adobo and sinigang. We steam rice cakes and cassava cakes. We glaze bananas in sweet brown sugar. We shave coconuts to their core. If you did not know any better, you'd think this homecoming is a happy reunion of lost sons and broken-hearted mothers, of lonely wives and warrior husbands. You wouldn't know how sad we really are.

When Papang arrives, they place his coffin in the middle of the sala, and dress him in the clothes he wore when he married my mother, a beautiful embroidered barong tagalog made of fine piña weave and a linen pair of black pants. Lila calls me to him, asks me to help her and the ladies, but I can't. "Tell Lola Ani I'm busy," I answer. "Tell her I'm cooking." From the kitchen, I watch them turning his body, pulling the clothing over him, moving him into a bed made of narra wood, strong and heavy. Lila tells me later that they have placed a dark veil over my father's face. The face, they said, is too disfigured to reconstruct. I am sure this is a mistake. They have the wrong man, I say. I am sure that is not my papang, though he seems to fit well in the clothing and everyone talks with him as if he is here.

On the first night, the town's women open up our front doors and for days the people come into our house and fill up each room, sitting among the flowers and the food and the body and they talk about their lives, they talk about how sad it is to lose a man so young and they talk about my mother as if she too has died. Lila helps Lola Ani with whatever she asks. All day and night Ináy sits in the love seat just in front of the casket. She doesn't move. She doesn't speak. When the women bring out their rosaries, she closes her eyes, but I know she's not praying. She's barely breathing. I hold my hands over her. I place my palms on her heart, over her head, on her back and I wish the heat would ease her pain. I close my eyes and try to think of nothing, I listen for my own heart, but all I hear is the rhythmic shooshing of voices, the click-tick-tick of the house clock and the clamoring of spoons and forks. Nearby, an engine hums and I think that Papang's van is in the house. I am trying to do as Ináy asks, to follow my intuition, but I am powerless. I am not a hilot. Each day comes and goes and it is as if my mother is in a coma. We watch the neighbors approach my father, place their hands inside the coffin. They talk to him and joke around with him, but he, like my mother, remains motionless.

Today a thousand roosters strike their song before the sun arrives. They are a chorus, off tune and well meaning, echoing from valley to valley. In the corner of the bedroom, a window has been propped open and from it comes an inkling of morning. Beyond the roosters there is the hush hush hush of the walis against concrete sidewalks. There is the opening and closing of gates and the kuliglíg who have stayed awake, chirping. No light comes from the opening, only a warm sweet breeze and these sounds of morning. My sleeping cousins surround me.

Last night, we all climbed into bed and fell about each other like pillows.

"Does your father come to you in dreams?" asked Charing. She swung her long black hair out of her eyes and revealed a dark mole on her neck. "I would be so scared."

"I'd say, 'Kamusta po, what it's like over there,'" said Bebet.

"No, you wouldn't," Lila said. "You'd run scared."

Bebet made a mean face and growled. "No, I wouldn't." Then Lila pinched him. "Aray!"

"Don't talk like that about my papang."

Ate Rosalie hushed us all. "Good night, Uncle," she called, "If you don't mind, huwág na. It's too late to visit na. Matulog na kami!" And then everyone laughed and someone put a hand on my belly and shook. I didn't say anything at all.

"You don't believe in those things, Angel. Do you?" Ate Rosalie cradled her son in her arms and the boy's laway drooled all over her exposed skin.

I couldn't tell them. They'd never sleep. Since we have arrived, I have seen that same white light that darted through traffic the day we drove out of Manila. I have seen it zipping through the crowded house. Sometimes that light is in the kitchen, or hovering in the sala. Sometimes it dances by the window and shoots across the room. I am so sure it is Papang. No face. No voice.

No scent. But the light. And when I really hurt, I close my eyes and sometimes I still see the light. And I focus on the heart sound and everything quiets around me—even the voices in the house—even the music and the movement of the people and I hear the house singing the way my papang's drums used to sound. Syncopated and blues-like, a beat that dragged and moved the body to dance.

I know that Papang is with us now. I knew that he was in that room, even as they were asking, last night.

And all night, the questions ran in circles and the sweet breath of my cousins' stories wove our arms and legs together like one gigantic human quilt. At first our words were fast and shallow, our questions laced with high-pitched giggles. Later, as the night wore on, our voices died and silence took over. Our breathing grew long and deep, and one by one we came together, all those legs and arms belonging to one enormous body. Now the cocks are crowing, and everyone except me remains asleep.

On the other side of the bed, Lila cradles one of the cousins as if she is the mother and the child is her baby. The room smells of the faintest traces of wet diaper, of babies' sweat, of faces pink and warm with sleep. I ease my way out of a tangle of arms, hold my breath, and step carefully onto the wood parquet floor, only to find more sleeping bodies.

Downstairs, Lola Ani is walking out the door, a basket hanging from the crook of her arm.

"Where are you going, Lola?" I ask, rubbing my eyes.

"To see your Lolo. Do you want to come?"

"But it's so dark. How will you find your way?"

"This day is long, anak. I won't get another chance. If I'm going to go, I'll have to go now. Do you want to come?"

First, I look over at Papang in the sala, at Ináy's silhouette lying on the sofa. "o.k.," I whisper, slipping into a pair of tsinelas from the pile beside the door. The flip-flops—too big for my feet—are blue, rubbery, and worn. I kiss Lola Ani good morning, and hold onto her arm as we walk out the door.

The moon is still out and by her light we follow the muddy road, through thickets and down paths where overgrown trees seem to slip in our way. The kuliglíg are louder than the roosters now, chirping wildly. Underneath our feet we hear the squish of red mud, the crack of a stick, the rustle of trees. We travel without speaking. The too-large flip-flops clip at my heels. We are so quiet I think I hear the moon breathing as we walk. I lean over and kiss Lola again. Her bony fingers run through my hair. Pulling me close, she sniffs the fat flesh of my face for a long breath and bestows upon me a lola kiss.

As we come to the edge of the church cemetery, the moon makes the marble caskets, rising from the earth, luminescent. These above-ground coffins climb the path on either side of us, fitting together like puzzles in the earth. As we get closer to my grandfather, we pass neighbors, Lola's girlhood friends, and nobyos who lost to Lolo Ninoy. Lola Ani pauses when we come to our family tombs, brushes her hand on their cool stones. We greet my great-grandparents, my titas, my titos, and cousins who died in the middle of their birth. The coffins are stacked upon a hill, a little village of white buildings. There is an open cement tomb the size of Papang's casket, waiting for him, adjacent to my lolo's crypt. I run my hands along the dark stone, wondering how this capsule will contain my papang. Can it?

When we come to Lolo Ninoy's tomb, I feel my lola's body shiver. Branches have fallen on the marble. Someone has dropped a paper cup and a crumpled bag of french fries from Jollibee. She hisses when she sees this, grabs the garbage off the tomb. From her basket, she takes a rag and begins dusting. I help by clearing off the branches, pulling off the weeds that have begun to climb the walls of the stone that surround his casket.

I know I would have loved my Lolo Ninoy, had I met him. Had I known his voice and his corny jokes. When we are in Manila, Lola Ani talks about him as if he is still alive, off on an errand, or vending fish at the market, not dead and lying in a faraway tomb. Her face gets soft and the wrinkles disappear when she tells of his antics. "He makes me crazy, sometimes," Lola Ani would say, "He's always flirting with me, still, after all these years." And when she talks like that, I see him dancing with her late at night. Not like the young couple in the photographs, but as two old people with white hair, small bones, and skin as brown as sweet tamarindo. I see their arms wrapped around each other and I hear them whispering words I cannot understand.

Lolo Ninoy was an ambitious man too restless for the province. After World War II devastated the town, left all the nipa huts burned to the ground and the bodies of men and women scarred in places too deep to see, he thought it best to find a new place, a clean place, a place without memories of war. So they left for the city shortly after my father was born, only to find a difficult life, vending fish in the palengke. I once asked Lola why they left so many people who loved them to live in spaces built of concrete walls and floors and ceilings and so tiny you could hardly move. At first she got mad at me and told me I was being disrespectful, but later she said, "He's always thinking about the future, about the city and how the family has better opportunities."

"But we have such a big family," I said, "We have so much when we are all together. We have everything!"

And she smiled, her eyes squinting and tearing up. "But Ninoy believed that starting fresh would be good for us." She kissed me quickly. "And it was."

She's crying now, scrubbing the dirt off the tomb, polishing the plaque that bears his name and hers. "When I die," she asks me in her dialect, "will you visit us and take care of us, Angel?"

"Lola," I say, tugging at her duster, "don't talk like that."

"I'm old," she answers. "It's going to happen. You better start getting used to it. Halimbawa, I never thought I'd live to bury my own son. You just never know, anak."

Sometimes I think she cannot wait to leave this earth, to slip into this concrete coffin and let her bones mingle with his, let their spirits merge, finally.

"Besides," I say, "even if we place your body here, you won't really be here." And then I glance over my shoulder at the new tomb where later today they will place my papang.

"Oo ngâ," she tells me in Tagalog. "We'll be with all of you. Together."

She places a candle on the center of the tomb and a fresh vase of plastic carnations. She lights the candle, then she pulls me to the side. "Don't be sad, Lola," I whisper. "They have each other now."

We make the sign of the cross and pray the Our Father, a Hail Mary and Glory be to the Father and the Son and the Holy Ghost, as it was, in the beginning is now and ever shall be, world without end.

SIX

At the house, there are so many people waiting to see my father off that I can't make my way through the crowd without pushing an arm aside, without stepping on toes, or feeling an elbow in my torso. I have to fight to see my mother sitting just where I had left her this morning. I see them looking down at him, at his hands and his torso, but not his face. The people turn to my mother, but she doesn't notice them, she doesn't take their hands. They lean down to hold her and her body remains stiff. Lola asks me if I have said good-bye to him. She knows I have not. "Ayaw ko," I tell her.

Why not, she wants to know. "He is your father."

I shake my head and try to speak, but nothing comes to me. Instead I leave the room. I walk down the stairs and out the door. I bang the gate. The roosters crow. The carabao's hooves pound the earth. My feet flip-flop up the street. His drumsticks poke out my back pocket and I hear my breath magnified in the sky. My chest thumps, pintig. Pintig. Pintig. Pintig.

There are birds in the church rafters. I hear them taking flight, but I cannot see them. It is a black cave here. There is one little light, a small red candle burning at the altar. Of course there are the other candles too, the ones that burn all day and night for the sick, for the poor, for the loss of family, of friends, of self. They line the walls of the church. But this is all the light, flames the size of thumbs, barely breathing.

I walk right up to God. I sit right on His altar. There is no sound. There is the echo of nothing. I look God in the face, his head bent down and full of sorrow. I wait for Him to say something, to look at me, to make me move.

My eyes close and I let out a long breath.

"It's not fair. Bring them back. Bring my parents back."

He doesn't answer me. He hangs on that cross, looking down at me as if I am the one that should help Him. Has He forgotten how old I am? I need them.

And that is when I hear the beating of wings. That is when I hear the bells. My whole body vibrates with the sound. I close my eyes. A light full as the moon shoots across a black sky. A bright star chases that moon with a tail fat as an alley cat in heat. The vibrations shift and push through my skin, tingle. It is as if God is the sound of tom-toms, of bass and snare and little toy drums. God is the cowbell, the triangle. God is the timpani. I stay quiet and I listen for a long, long time. He is saying no. He is saying Papang has gone home. He isn't coming back. He is saying I am on my own. Your mother will never be the same. I listen to that sound, loud and rhythmic in surprising and irreverent ways. I am mad at God. I am done with praying. Pintig, I shout. Pintig. Pintig. Pintig. I grab the sticks and beat the marble steps, fast and so loud I am sure that God must hear me. God and Papang and all the angels.

At the house Papang does not cooperate. When my uncles lift his casket, he squirms, he struggles, and they cannot get him out the door. The front entrance is wider than the coffin. The men are young and strong and used to doing hard labor, and yet they cannot seem to fit him through the door. They turn him on the side, they pull him from the front. They push. But as they move, the casket grows in weight, widens at each turn. It is as if Papang has placed his hands and feet along the doorjamb and will not let go. Will not go. I know it because the white light is there, shining bright and steady, hovering just under that doorway.

By the time they ease the casket out of the house, the sun is slipping behind green mountains, washing our barrio in oranges, yellows, and brilliant reds. Everybody has come out, the barangay captain, the mayor, the farmers, and all the little children. The whole town weeps with us, walks with us, some hundred people from the village and the houses on the outskirts of town. The men raise Papang up on their shoulders and he is like a boat drifting aimlessly in a sea of mourners. Behind Papang and all his barakada, Ináy glides along the paved streets like a supermodel in her big black shades, her wide-brimmed hat, and her skinny little black shift. With one hand she carries a Spanish fan and waves it at her chest, and every time Lila or I try to take her free hand she pushes us away. On our heels, the sister grandmothers, Lola Kula, Lola Ani, and Mother Mary walk arm in arm, holding each other up, reaching deep inside for strength to walk the village, but I can feel them wavering, because the crying is steady and low and every now and then a howl comes from one of them. Mother Mary, the Mother Superior at my school, has come from the city to usher her older sister through the town. She is the one that says, "Sige, let it out, tell God how you feel." She is the one that tells her older sisters, "Ernesto is not far from here, he knows, he knows." And then our lolas wail, "Bakit? Why? Bakit?"

The mourners surround the casket like ants on a sugar cube. We take Papang for a walk, to the school where he played hooky, to the cantina where he first learned how to bang his drums. We take him by the houses of all his friends, and when we pass the children and the old people come to the doors and wave at us, hankies in the air. Some make the sign of the cross. The church bells ring louder than the roosters who crow from dawn to dusk from various mountaintops.

We walk until the sun goes down. We pray out loud. Long black veils cover the heads of all the church ladies who slowly parade the streets, carrying white candles in one hand and black rosaries in the other. They call out, *Hail Mary full of Grace the Lord is with you. Blessed are you among women and blessed is the fruit of your womb, Jesus* and the people answer them, *Holy Mary, Mother of God, pray for us sinners, now and at the hour of our death, at the hour of our death.* And every time we get to the last line, I choke a little thinking about Papang in that van with those loud Americans and the heavy rains pushing them over the crevice of the mountain to their hour of death. Poor Papang, I think, he was alone. When all the stars are out and the kuliglíg are chirping in the trees, we come to God's house. We throw open the doors and the men bring Papang to the very steps where I had been just earlier that day. I toss God a dirty look, I sneer at his bowed head. Coward, I think. I asked you to bring my parents back and you wouldn't even look at me.

The people file into the church and all their whispers rise like birds fluttering up into the rafters. When everyone has crowded in, the children march up to my papang with their plastic buckets and their hand-whittled drumsticks. A dozen children bang the drums, play from the inside out. Pintig, they bang. Pintig, they bang, pintig, pintig, pintig. Their music is like fireworks, bursting into the air, exploding in hot flashes of color, fading when you least expect it and then clashing bright as the sun. Suddenly, the church lights surge, and for a moment the votive candles flicker in the dark. The cathedral, rumbles as the band of drummers stomp their feet. And then there is silence for one beat—pintig. And another. Pintig. And then the sound of rain hitting tin roofs like a thousand drumsticks—clack, clack, clack. And the lights flash. This is the only time I see my mother react behind those dark green glasses. She doesn't cry. She doesn't wail. But when the children finish, a smile slowly blossoms, as if she heard Papang playing with them, thumping on his chest

45

with the palm of his hand, shifting his head to the beat, his heart going loud like it will never quit. A heart that won't quit, I hear her saying, that's what drew me to your Papang, a heart that won't quit.

SEVEN

For one long month we remain in Papang's barrio and Mother Mary returns to the city and tells us to take as long as we like. "The school understands," she tells us. "Your mother needs to heal."

Lila and I do not know how to bring Ináy back. For weeks our mother's body continues to sit before us, unmoving. We recognize her calloused hands and her scrawny feet. We know the soft curves of her belly and her breasts. We sniff her skin and know her by her scent, a soft jasmine and baby powder odor. My mother puts her arms around us and we melt into her and breathe with her—but she does not know us. Her eyes remain open but she does not see us. She only calls his name. The only reason Ináy gets out of bed is to wander the house and constantly search for my father. She opens all the doors, calling his name, rummaging through closets. "Mahal," she says, "Mahal, where are you?" And when she can't find him and desperation takes hold of her, she flings the windows open and her feet stretch and her toes push her up into the humid sky. Her body goes light and she floats away, far away and out of sight.

The first time it happens we understand. We know she cannot handle the shock of losing Papang. We cry for her. Lola Ani tells us to be patient. "Just sit with her, Angel," she says. "Just love her." She brushes Ináy's black hair back and tells me, "If you want to, you can use your hands. You can make her feel better." But I tell her I can't. "I don't really heal," I say. "I only pretend."

"Then pretend, anak. She will remember your touch. You can do this."

I want to at first, but every time I get close, I look into her eyes or I hear her talking to Papang as if he is in the room and I run away. Instead I watch Lola Ani bathe my mother as if she is her own anak. I watch Lola Ani dry her body with baby powder and dress her, sing to her, tell her stories about her life with Papang like telling bedtime stories to a child.

And Lila! Whatever Lola asks Lila to do, Lila obeys. She'll run to get a wet rag, she'll boil ginger in a pot of water, she'll climb the roof to pull santol off the branches of the tree and feed the white seed to my mother. Lila takes to rubbing Ináy's feet and hands with tiger balm, pretending she's a hilot, all the while tears streaming down her face. "Please Ate," she begs me. "You do it. If you do it, she'll come back." Maybe I let her down, but there's no way I can pretend. Lola Ani says touching Ináy will bring her back, ground her to the earth. "Hold onto her," she says. "Hold on so she will not float away."

It's not fair, I think, pulling out my Papang's drumsticks, hammering at pots and pans and anything I can get a hold of.

It's not right. I see my mother in the sky, airy and angel-like and beautiful in a sad way and I hate her. Come down, already, I think. Let's go back to Manila. Enough.

One day I can't take it anymore. "Lola," I ask, "why aren't you mad?"

"Bakit?" she wants to know. "When Lila falls down and skins her knees, do you get mad? Pasensya lang, anak."

These days I look for Papang too. Sometimes I sit in the middle of rice fields, soaked to my waist in water and listen to the crickets, I sing with frogs. Are you there, I ask, looking up at the hot blue sky. I count to eight over and over again and mix a beat in my head, one that he might dance to if he were here. The carabao swishes his tail, a living metronome, breaking down the hour. "You would not believe Ináy," I tell him. "She's scaring me," I whisper. "Is there anything you can do?" And then I hear the squish of my feet as I tap into that wet earth, mud seeping between my toes, drenched with rainwater and all my tears.

One day I am sitting in a tree at the edge of town, banging on branches with Papang's old sticks when I see Ate Rosalie and Charing riding in the back of an NPA truck. There are four, maybe five of them, no soldiers. And they talk at once, so fast and so loud over each other's words. I can hear them, but it's hard to understand what they are saying. I see something in her, something dark and angry. Something strong. And I wish for a moment that I was Ate Rosalie, riding off with my friends down the road like they owned the world.

When I see her later, I ask and she says nothing back. Her red face twists up all tight. There is nothing but silence between us. She's changing her boy's diaper, sitting on the floor with her legs spread wide and the baby between them, rolling side to side, attempting to escape. Her hair is a curtain that slides across her face and hides what she is feeling. Her hands move fast. The sun blasts into the room through an open window. I sit next to her, watching.

I ask again, "Why were you riding with the People's Army?"

"You're dreaming," she answers. "You're seeing things."

And when I insist she says, "Someone has to do something about it."

"About what?"

"Cousin, don't you see? Our country's in suicide."

The baby's strong and he squirms out of her grasp. A spray of urine, sparkling and light casts an arc into the air. "Toby," she says. "Huwág." She spanks his thigh, but he giggles at her.

Then she runs her hands through her hair, pulling the long strands into a ponytail. "Sometimes," she says, "it's too much to take. So you gotta do the right thing. You got to take matters into your own hands."

"What things?"

"Everything. The government. The power. Change everything."

When Ate Rosalie speaks her eyes are so clear and her voice is strong. Toby's face goes blank at the fire in her voice. Startled, he opens his mouth. His eyes go wide. He begins to wail and scream.

*

When Mother Mary returns the following month, she brings a letter in a long white envelope. We are all sitting at the kitchen table, drinking cool pitchers of calamansi juice and nibbling at Lola Ani's pan de coco.

"Here, Milagros," she says, sliding the envelope to Ináy. "It's the news you've been waiting for."

My mother gazes at the kitchen window, at the soft morning light that streams in past the curtains, at the breeze that blows like a kiss.

"Good news," Lola Ani says. "We need some good news. Open it na, anak." She picks up the envelope and waves it before my mother. When Ináy pushes her chair out from the table and begins getting up, my grandmother digs her finger into the edges and rips open the paper. "O.K.," she says, "Angel, you be the one to read it." She shakes the paper open and handing it to me, I say, "She passed. You passed, Ináy."

The old women clap and Lila hugs our mother, but Ináy just closes her eyes like she is exhausted and this is too much. I see her that morning Papang left, and she is lying in her bed worn out from being ill and I hear Papang saying, "You will know what to do." I take my hands and grab hold of her shoulders and I plead, "Wake up, Ináy. Tama na."

"Good," Mother Mary tells her. "You're a certified nurse, ha? When you are ready, you come back to Manila with the girls. They can go to school half the day and if you want them to work at the convent, they can earn money too. Work half the day. Angel can work in my office and help me with campaigns. Right, Ani?"

"Sige na nga," my grandmother says. "I'll go back and cook for the sisters. We can live at the house and ride the train to work. Pwede na ba iyon?"

Ináy opens her eyes and I am sitting before her. "Please," I whisper again. "Tama na po."

"At di ba—you and Ernesto have a savings? Weren't you saving for your ticket to the States? If you want to go, you can. We'll get your papers ready."

The old women talk so fast, like they have been practicing this, like this is the answer they've been waiting for. They watch my mother, looking for some sign—a smile or a light in the eye, but even I am lost in their words, in their plan to ship my ináy away.

"No," I say, not waiting for my mother's response. "She doesn't want to go anymore, don't make her. No America. No States. No!"

I have fallen into a dream where everyone is wearing new shoes. We eat lots of mocha cake with butter icing. Everybody is dancing to my daddy's drums. We laugh so hard we nearly pee in our pants. My papang is dressed in white and he is happy where he is. Ináy grabs us all together into a giant embrace. Lila laughs and cries and then I realize she is next to me, screaming, and I am suddenly awake, shaking her by the shoulders.

"What's the matter?" I say. "Wake up." I nudge her with my eyes shut, trying to keep my dream state alive.

Lila says she's having a nightmare about that little sister, the one who cursed the foreign soldiers, the one who got lanced by the sword. "Why did they do that, Ate Angel?" she cries. "Where was their ináy?"

"What kind of nightmare is that," I whisper. "Stop that." I put my arms around her and squeeze her tight. She is small, but sturdy.

Lola Ani rolls over in her bed, snorting in her sleep.

"The Lolas," Lila says. "Sa Gera."

"I don't know anything about that," I say. "You sure that's all?" And then she asks me. "Is Ináy leaving us?"

"No," I tell her, "they were only talking."

"But if she wants to, she can go?"

I tell her only for a little while, only long enough to earn our airfare. "She'll send for each of us, one by one—me then you then Lola Ani."

"And why you first?"

"Because I'm older." She looks at me and I see confusion.

"What are you talking about," she asks.

"This was the plan," I tell her. "Before. This is what they've been working on."

"Girls," Lola Ani hisses. "Sleep now or tomorrow you'll be tired."

Lila looks like she's going to start crying again, and I start singing a song and tapping at her belly like it is a drum. I smile at her until her eyes light up and we break into a giggle.

"Girls," Lola Ani whispers, "If you don't go to sleep right now the angels will rob you of your dreams."

"Who ever heard of such nonsense, Lola," I say.

"Last night you said they would rob us of our beauty," Lila says.

I hear Lola Ani smile when she says, "I know I did and see what happened. You think I want to talk to you with my eyes closed? Hay naku! I can't look at you two, you're so ugly."

We're quiet for a long moment and then Lola Ani asks, "What was your bad dream about, Lila?"

I tell Lola Ani that Lila dreamed of the girls kidnapped by the Japanese soldiers.

"Did I ask you, Angel?" Lola says, reaching her arm for Lila. My sister slides into bed next to our grandmother. "She can talk. Let her tell me."

And so Lila describes the dream, the way we are all walking through the mall and one by one, an army of little yellow men race past us, swiftly slicing throats, wrists, hearts with thin bayonets. "Just like the soldiers that the Lolas talk about."

"The Lolas?" I ask.

"The Comfort Women."

"Naku," Lola says. "what a horrible dream naman." She strokes Lila's hair.

In this way, the three of us stay awake, invoking mini spirits in white robes and breakable wings of glass. We see God's messengers confiscating our new shoes, eating our mocha cakes, and stealing Daddy's drums and all those syncopated beats, leaving such silence nobody can dance. Giggling, we refuse to sleep, and the little spirit thieves return, running off with Lila's fat cheeks, my dark eyes, and Lola Ani's perfectly shaped legs. All our beauty gone, just like that.

Soon after Mother Mary leaves, Ináy gets up like it is any other day. I hear her singing in the kitchen, making breakfast. I peek around the door and I watch her spinning rice and garlic in a giant frying pan. "Do you want fried bangus or egg or what?" she asks me. "Ano gusto mo?"

I walk over to her and put my head on her shoulder. "Are you o.k., Ináy?"

"We don't have time to dillydally," she says. "I want to be there before dark. Move, anak."

"We're going home?" I ask.

I wrap my arms around her as if it is the first time since Papang has died. I hold onto her tight even as she struggles to be out of my arms. Though it's early, her body's already warm with perspiration. "Anak, we have to get going. Call your sister. We don't have time for this," she scolds me. But I am crying now, my heart beating all syncopated and out of whack. I can feel it growing so big and then closing up fast like a fan then ballooning open again. I hold her, but she pries my fingers off and pushes me gently away as she holds me by my shoulders. "Angel," she says, looking deep into my eyes. "This is hard for all of us, but we have to keep going, ha? No more crying from now on."

I don't understand, but I nod. I'm just happy that she's back. I climb to the top of the house and text Karina: *Uuwi na kami. My mother is O.K. na. Be back Monday.*

Finally. You are missing everything.

We spend an hour tossing our clothes into maletas, counting the cash for the journey. I dig into my purse and find the thousand pesos.

"Here," I say to her holding out the pera.

"Where did you get this?" she says. "Did you take it from someone, anak?"

I tell her no, I tell her Papang gave it to me and she says again, "Your papang's gone. Tell me where you got it. Don't lie."

"Before he left for Bagiuo," I tell her. "When you were sick." The words pour out of me like tears. "Sabi niya, uuwi siya. I'll be home in a few days, sabi niya. Just in case. Tapos, yun na." I reach to hug her, but she just grabs the money.

"Sige. We have to take the bus," she tells us. "No other way. No more Papang. No more driver."

She is moving around the house so fast, passing Lola Ani and Lola Kula and all the chickens in the kitchen that I cannot find a moment's peace. I cannot stop. I cannot hear a thing. She pulls me through the house by the arm, tossing plastic bags at me, filling them up and saying, "Who knows when we can come back. Make sure wala ka nang gamit dito. Take all your stuff, anak." It's too noisy and there is no beat at all, no rhythm or flow to what we do. When I ask Lola Ani what has happened she shrugs. "Baka she needed to rest," Lola said. "You know, become strong again." But Ináy isn't just strong now; my mother is hard. Everything about her is so hard—her skin is like bark and her bones seem to jut out of everywhere—her hips, her elbows, her hands, her face, her voice.

She moves so fast she is difficult to hold, to nestle into. She says there's too much to do.

And that is how my mother comes back to us. She swirls through the house like a provincial bagyo during rainy season, casting water everywhere, the wind from her movement toppling everything, leaving us weak and broken in her wake.

EIGHT

It is some other Manila, not my Manila. When I first wake to the rumble of jackhammers and the call of morning roosters, when in the distance a band of mixed-up car horns ring and when old Mang Pepito climbs up the hill with his squeaky corn cart and his eternal serenade, I think, I'm home. I'm here. But when I look out my window at the cranes scratching at the sky, and city traffic tossed about like a child's open toy chest, somehow it doesn't feel like home.

I run into the kitchen where the morning song is playing—the frying of eggs and the banging of pans, the boiling water, and the sizzling milkfish. And I think, yes, this is what the morning is. My lola hums to herself as she moves in the dark making breakfast for Lila and me. Even the smell of the street garbage that wafts from the alleys is a familiar nuisance that I welcome. It means I'm home. But when I close my eyes, I know I'm still sitting in that same movie house watching me on the big screen.

Four months ago, we'd sleep another two hours before rising. My mother's and father's voices would wake us with their teasing and singing. The whole family would board the van and we'd get a ride to school. But since we've come back from the province, Lola Ani and Lila and I rise at 4 a.m. and we're out the door. We walk three city blocks to wait for a jeepney to pick us up. We take two jeepneys and ride three stops on the LRT train before we get to St. Magdalena's. Then Lila and I follow Lola Ani into the convent kitchen and help her cook another breakfast. We wait for the nuns to arrive, to sit at a big round table and bow their heads in prayer. We pour calamansi juice in their glasses. Fill their plates with rice and eggs and fried milkfish. Sometimes I run to the palengke and bring the sisters jackfruit or lychees or santol, round as softballs. "Sarap!" they say. "Ambrosia," they say, "truly the food of the gods."

After we do the dishes and Lila sweeps the dining room floor, it's time to go to mass and there we are in our school uniforms, dressed like all the other rich girls, walking among them like we are one of them. But I have lost my energy for school. Nawala na ang gana ako. It seems so different now. When we first started, I loved it. The private school for girls was so big and clean and freshly painted, so wide with its stone floors, marble columns, and elegant statues of great saints. I thought I was in heaven. The nuns were wise old ladies, and I would sit in my classes, absorb every single lesson, and make it my own. So different than our filthy open-air classrooms where there wasn't even room for a real desk, and every book was shared. At St. M's we had everything.

Church bells marked every hour and during the day there was always someone reciting the mysteries of the cross. Certain hours of the day, you could be anywhere in the compound and a bell would sound and a voice from the speakers would recite a Hail Mary, a Glory Be, an Our Father, and the students would stop in their tracks, go silent or they would recite the prayer too. Every hour was filled with God and I loved it. But that was when I thought God was on my side. That was before.

These days, I walk the halls of St. Magdalena's weeping. I cry all through my classes, including grammar drills in English, even while conjugating verbs, looking for metaphors, and identifying modifiers. My face is always wet. Every time I appear in class or in the cafeteria, or in a bathroom, the voices go silent. Even the rich girls—Yoli, Marite and Patricia—don't say anything. They just stare.

In God's house, the wind circulates freely throughout, sweeping the sound of traffic, of jackhammers, of Manila life up to the rafters and back. The pews are orderly in front, but on the sides and in the back of the cathedral, benches skewed as vehicles on Manila's superhighways sprawl in all directions. People come and go, speaking in regular voices and all their movement echoes. I used to hide in this house, to find some kind of regularity, to understand my place. I used to be friends with God. Now I come because the nuns make me, because it is a part of my education. Like healing my mother, I come and I pretend to pray.

Today, I file into mass with my classmates, head bowed as if in deep prayer, but all I'm doing is this, listening. Waiting. All

I'm doing is counting the ticking clock, feeling its steady beat, waiting for the end of mass. God can be so mean, I think. I choose to ignore Him.

The ceiling rests on large pillars. There are no walls. Birds fly in and out, chase one another into heavenly blue windows. I imagine Ináy floating right into a stained-glass window and shattering the brilliant sky.

I hear movement behind me. Text messages beep intermittently into the air. I pull my rosary closer to my heart. I pound a fist into my chest. Before me, white sampaguita blossoms drape the hands and hearts of the saints. Flowers assault the feet of Mama Mary, hang like ornaments around her porcelain neck. I used to think the church was the perfect place to tune the world out, to go deep into your own thoughts and think about the things you could never share.

"Not so high and mighty anymore," says a voice.

"Just a driver's daughter."

"I hear her mother has gone mad."

I bow. I use my hands to mask my face. I close my eyes and push away the footsteps, the whispers, the pews squeaking and the kneelers banging down on marble floors. I focus on my heart and its steady beat—pintig, pintig, pintig. It seems that this is all I do. Shut out noise. Focus on the heartbeat. Ignore the banging of doors and the slamming of windows. At night, when the house is finally silent, I close my eyes. But then I hear my father's drums rattling in the upstairs closet, like an earthquake shifting side to side. I'm sure it's just my imagination, but I cannot help but hear those drums, the boom and the swish and the bang of those drums.

Mother Mary stands at the podium. She leans into the microphone and her white habit blows off the collar of her garments and reveals a long brown neck. Her words come out in English, big words, clean and sharp. She's praying for the poor. And we respond, "Lord, hear our prayer." She is praying for our families. Lord, leave me alone.

When the choir sings, their voices are lost in the calamity. I stay silent. I close my eyes. I dream about a quiet place. I feel like swooning.

And then the giggling. I glance behind me at a row of girls sitting one identical to the other, each of them beautiful, flawless, and fair. The girls sit with their legs crossed, and their hands pressed on the benches, leaning forward. I shake my head, pushing my hair, wild, curly, and out of control, out of my eyes.

Turning away from them, I look at my hands, how brown they are, how dirty. More whispers. "I suppose being related to the Mother Superior is of no use now."

"Don't listen to them," whispers Karina. "They are so plastic." Karina has light skin with freckles and hair that is almost too light to be Filipina. I gaze at the pale spots sprinkled on her cheeks like angel dust. Her new-moon eyes squeeze shut when she smiles. Karina wraps her arms around me and holds me. In that moment I close my eyes and let a shiver run through me. I am silent, waiting, and for a few seconds I hear him, the soft beating of that pintig, pintig, pintig, the hush hush hush of the breath, the music that comes without singing. Papang. Karina's crying too and only then she whispers, "Sorry, Angel. Peace be with you." Another shiver.

"Ignore them," she whispers. Then turning to the girls she hisses, "Mind your business. God is watching."

"God is watching you too, Karina Lopez."

One of the sisters has snuck up behind us and is waving her hanky at all of us. The girls put their hands to their mouths and all around me there is the commotion of garments rustling and rosary beads knocking one into the other. I pretend I'm praying the Fifth Glorious Mystery. Mary is crowned Queen of Heaven. I place an imaginary tiara on the statue before us, and then I picture my mother and place a ruby crown on her head, and one of sapphire atop my Lola Ani's mane of white, and on my head, I wear a crown of white sampaguita blossoms.

NINE

Lila and I attend four hours of class a day. We get half of the learning we're supposed to receive. At lunchtime, we move back to the convent where Lila spends the rest of the day sweeping the halls, the bedrooms, and the front porch and steps. My ten-year-old sister, who should be reading books, dividing numbers, or charting maps, fills buckets with soapy water and after she sweeps through the entire building she begins scrubbing the floors. If the bells ring up front, she is the one who stops her work and runs to the gate to ask, "Sino sila?" And if it's an appointment, a delivery person, another worker, she opens the door and welcomes them. Then she goes back to the business of the floors.

I work in Mother Mary's office. I run errands. I pick up files and deliver them to the school. I wait. I bring back other files. Sometimes I go to the sari sari store to pick up small cakes and puto and sodas for merienda. Sometimes I take the jeepney or LRT to the city to retrieve a letter or deliver a package.

Today, I accompany Mother Mary in the white school bus to a small house in Quezon City. The bus pulls up to a tall green gate with a hand painted sign on the door—LOLAS' HOUSE—and I assume that we are at a senior citizen's center. When Mother Mary slides the green gate open and we crawl through its little door, we are greeted by dozens of little lolas, white haired, smiling, and planted in plastic chairs that are scattered throughout the patio. I am right, I think. So many grannies, I walk up to each one of them, and I take their hand and pull it to my forehead. "Bless, bless, bless," they say, but the third old lady pulls me to her, pinching my cheeks and kissing me, squeezing me tight. Before I know it all the old lolas are standing and as I walk through they are kissing and hugging me too. They swarm about Mother Mary and rub her back, greeting her with loud hellos.

I wander around the room, reading the articles on the walls, gazing at black-and-white photos of the ladies standing on the streets in front of the Japanese embassy and Malacañang Palace, holding up picket signs. It's hard to imagine the faces on the walls are the same ones here, greeting us with such joy.

The organizers introduce Mother Mary to them in a formal way. Mother Mary, Mother Superior of St. Magdalena's is a long time aktibista. A friend of the lolas. She fights for justice. For the people. I nod as if I have heard this all before, but I have no idea what will come next.

When Mother Mary gets up, her body seems to grow taller and her skin brighter. Her voice is so strong and her words slip into the air like music. From her talk I come to see that these old ladies are not just grannies either. "Ang hirap naman," she says. "First you are a biktima of the Japanese Imperial Army, di ba? So-called 'Comfort Women.' Then you are silent for fifty years! Now you come forward and the world thinks you are liars, or your families are ashamed. No! You are right to speak up. You are right, mga Lola, to seek your justice. You are not tira ng hapones. You are heroines." And then she tells them what my parents have always told me—When you don't know what to do, you must listen to your heart. Follow your intuition. I look around the cement patio, at the faces of the women, brown and wrinkled and tearful, but smiling. And I think back to the day when my cousins and I floated in the dagat under the bright sun and the little ones whispered the story of the two girls taken by Japanese soldiers. You are the ones, I think. Which one are you?

After the talk the women break into song, dancing to a karaoke machine. In the kitchen, I help organizers fill up plates of noodles, rice and fish. Then I walk around the little center with other volunteers and offer the food to each lola. As I do, I look into each woman's soft wrinkled face and I search for the sorrow, the pain. I look at them to see if I can see my own self, that feeling of belonging and not belonging at once, but instead what I see are smiles without teeth, black eyes gone blue-gray with a glimmer in them. Instead what I get are old ladies sniffing at my skin. And then an old hand pulls me from the corner and swivels me into the crowded patio where everyone has their hands up in the air, faces pointed to the sun, and mouths spitting lyrics to popular dance songs from the seventies.

In that moment something inside me wakes up, a tiny seed, smaller than a match flame, but hot, really hot, and it is burning. I think about Ate Rosalie running about the countryside with her band of activists, charging into farms and turning life upside down with their People Power ideas. Taking control. This is it, I think as this burning flickers just below the surface of my skin, threatening to spread and wake my whole body up, my whole spirit up and up and up!

I close my eyes, and I am inside Ináy's womb, swimming in a sea of love, and from inside her belly I can hear the rhythm of the march, the people calling out, MAKIBAKA! I answer with a fist, raised, HUWÁG MATAKOT! This memory comes to me, I think, or what I imagine it must have been like. It doesn't matter, I feel it now and I'm not so sure why. My arms lift to the patio ceiling and the waves of music wash over me. The old lola looks up and poking her painted face at me she twirls me around the room, rolling me into a sea of dancing queens seventy-years-old and up. I cannot wait to go home to talk to Ináy about this, to get her to bless this idea and help make it real.

TEN

I know how Ináy must have felt when she woke up out of that floating dream. It is hard when your feet cannot find the ground. When it seems that every time you try to place your foot on the earth you are slipping, falling, bumping into the whole wild world. She was like a cat that was lost, calling and calling in the middle of the night, walking the house and finding no rest, no Papang. But that morning when I woke and she was all business, she must have had the plan all laid out for she wasted no time at all.

Ever since we've come back the house is always full of people. She starts just as the sun comes up and heals them all the way to midnight. When I get to the house, the sala is full of clients, waiting patiently. Ináy has set a changing screen made of rice paper near the window, with two chairs behind it, one for herself, and one for her patient. During the day the light from the window throws their shadows on the screen, big and exaggerated like spirits moving right before our eyes. At night she places candles in the windows of the house and lets the flames cast their bodies on the walls. She talks loud enough for everyone to hear, but whispers as if their business is a secret.

I sit in the room, waiting, my hands in my lap, my eyes cast to the floor, looking at my dusty toes. The sounds of the room bump and cough, swish and laugh, melt into walls. I can feel the people. I glance up and they all smile at me like I should say something so I look back down again and drum on my legs. Pada pada boom. Pada pada boom. Two, two, two. Pada pada boom. I shake my head.

There is nothing fancy about the way she heals them. She can look at someone and know where the pain is. She can place her hands near the body part—the leg, the arm, the heart—and be done with it. But people come for the drama. They love that she lost her mind after Papang's tragic death, that she came back from that dark place somehow holier than before she went insane.

"Milagros de la Luna is an angel," says an old manang as she moves her arthritic knee back and forth on its hinge. "Bilib ako!"

"A gift from God!" says a mother whose child burns with five-day fever.

On the mantel of her altar are statues of Mama Mary and Jesus. Papang's photo is framed in gold so he looks like San Ernesto de la Luna. There are saucers and buckets that people stuff with pesos. They thank her for healing them, they thank her for giving them hope, for putting on a show better than the theater down the street.

"She has suffered tremendously and this is her reward," says a husband. His wife has been going blind for weeks, and he is hoping my mother will place her palms over her lids and make his wife see the votive candles.

When it's my turn, I rise from the sala chair and I slip behind the screen.

"Angel, anak, busy ako," she says. "Call the next one."

"I'm the next one."

"Stop playing around," she says, combing her hands through her hair and taking a sip from her soda bottle. "Go now."

"But I waited to see you," I say, tears rising from my belly. "It's my turn."

"Naku, how am I ever going to finish. Did you see all these people waiting?"

I want to tell her about the house of old women, how there was something so wonderful about the way they lived, the way they danced even though they were burdened with war. But I can see how impatient she is. I can see how in a hurry. So I say, "Maskit ang tiyan ko."

"Talaga?" she says, finally placing her hands on my belly. "Where does it hurt?" Her hands are warm and firm. I can feel the heat right away. I can feel the love. She looks up to the ceiling, searching my stomach for something strange, anything. "Wala, anak. There's nothing wrong with you."

"But there is. Ang sakit. It hurts so so bad." I want to fall into her arms.

She places her hands on my face and looks into my eyes. She sees something, but she says nothing. I can tell. "We don't have time for this, anak."

70

"Can I bring out Papang's drums?" She closes her eyes like she is trying to remember what are Papang's drums? "Can I play them?"

"No."

"Bakit?"

"Leave them, anak."

"But Ináy—"

"We have to move on. Someday you'll understand." And then she stands and ushers me out of her way.

In Sister Bernadette's classroom we practice English grammar, conjugating verbs like prayers. The English is heavy on my tongue and the letters crowd up against my teeth and make it hard for me to swallow. The words taste bitter. The words are greasy. The letters are too bulky, too sharp, too abrasive. I cannot hold phrases in my mouth—they slip out like slippery wet fish. Sister Bernadette is telling us we must go past feeling uncomfortable. We must learn to use English like a tool, like a weapon. "This is how you can change the world," she says, holding up Webster's dictionary. "Use your words, my dear girls. Use your words. And use them well."

I eat, you eat, he, she, or it eats. We eat, you eat, they eat.

I have eaten. You have eaten. He, she, or it has eaten.

I look at the clock. I'm hungry. I know Mother Mary is making rounds, going from classroom to classroom with a special lecture on organizing protests. I think about Ate Rosalie running about the countryside with her band of activist friends, all dark and brooding over the state of the nation. When the door to our classroom pops open, everyone stands up.

"Magandang umaga sa inyo," Mother Mary greets us.

We wish her a good morning too. She tells us that we can speak to her in Tagalog, and we look at Sister Bernadette, waiting for her to give us permission.

"We were just practicing our English," Sister Bernadette says. Her English is syncopated with sudden starts and stops. She has not given us permission to speak in Tagalog.

Mother Mary hops up on Sister Bernadette's desk. "You need your English to be world citizens," she says, "but do not forget how to speak Filipino. And do not forget the dialects you have grown up speaking." Her legs swing back and forth as her words begin to fill the air, and I think this not the behavior of a Mother Superior. "We can't let foreign imperialists brainwash us. Ours is a beautiful, literate language." Sister Bernadette looks at the floor, shaking her head.

"We're going to send you girls on an excursion outside this ivory tower," she says. "You are going to research and define social justice for the Pilipino."

Mother Mary points to herself. "It was 1986, the year many of you were born. Everybody was fed up with Marcos and his martial law. Everybody was tired of serving the Americans," she tells us. Her voice is so big right now and full of so many colors. I can practically hear the marching on the streets. "And you know, suddenly it's like the Philippines was no longer the Philippines—no justice. Puro corruption. So, what else can you do? Fight!" That's when she got thrown in jail. I close my eyes and see her on the streets, running from tear gas, breaking down pulis barricades. I feel the energy of the crowd marching and drumming and chanting and then I remember that I know this march. It is my birth march. It is my moment when I toppled Ináy to the streets with my resistance.

Mother Mary waves her fingers like protest banners. "So on Thursday," she says, "Angel de la Luna is going to organize you and your batch will paint your own flags and hang them from the windows so everyone will see our jeepneys charge the streets of Manila. Oh," she sighs, "it will be beautiful. You'll never forget it."

Yoli, Patricia, and Marite turn to me and hiss something I cannot quite make out. "They're jealous," Karina hisses back.

"I know," I answer loud enough for them to hear. I don't know what excursions are, but the word sounds powerful. I roll my eyes at the girls, and after class I walk up to Yoli, Patricia, and Marite and I say, "My papang was a driver. He was taking his clients to Bagiuo when a storm washed his van off the side of the road. Is that what you want to know? Or do you want to know what it feels like to have your father die? Masakit. Everywhere it hurts." I point to my chest and my head and my belly. I rub my legs and my arms. "Napakasakit. Every night I think he is in our house, I think he's talking to me or playing his drums on the roof because I can hear him but then I wake up and I remember, he's dead." They don't answer. I can't believe I said it. Then Patricia puts her hand on my back. Yoli has tears in her eyes, and Marite takes my hand and holds it.

73

On those rare occasions when I am home early, I join Ináy in the sala. She thinks it's because I am learning the art of healing, but I do it to be with her, to sit nearby, and get the scent of her. Like everyone else in this crazy movie, she is my mother without being my mother. I watch her not to learn how to be a hilot, not to refine my own powers—because I have none—but to see if I might catch a glimpse of her, if I might recognize the tone of her voice or the smile on her face. But she is always all business.

Bring my parents back, I hiss at God, but nothing.

Ináy mixes a jug of lotions full of herbs from Lola's garden with tubs of baby oil. "Halika," she tells me as she lifts the vat and pours it into bottles. "Help me, anak." I run after her, capping each bottle and putting it on a shelf. She motions me to follow her behind the screen and I watch her rub the potion on the sore knees and backs of her patients. "Ganito," she tells me, glancing up. Her hands move over the leg, kneading the calf like bread dough. "And then ask them how it feels." She smiles at the young vendor and whispers to him, "о.к., ba?"

He nods and says, "Sarap."

This is how she heals them. She sends them home feeling soft and fragrant. She breathes heavy and says her prayers like witches' chants, but really she's just reciting the Glory Be in Tagalog or the Hail Mary in Spanish, the very same prayers the sick say every day. For very sick foreigners she recites the Apostle's Creed.

"Get the next one," she tells me.

I call the next one, a young woman planning to go abroad. She is engaged to one of the foreign men, but has been diagnosed with some rare form of cancer. Her mother, Manang Grace, is a manicurist in a salon in Ermita. Every week she waits for her daughter in the sala and picks at her fingernails, watching Ináy and her daughter's shadows on the rice paper screen. She drinks glasses of ice tea from a pitcher we leave in the sala for the clients. They come every week because they swear the lump is shrinking.

The old manong from the States, a widower with grown sons and daughters, enters the house and greets everyone like he is the mayor of Quezon City. He is dying from a bad heart. The doctors in the States said that if he wanted to go home to say good-bye this would be the time. They didn't think he had very long at all. So his son went to the States and brought him home. The old man smiles a charming grin, wide and dimpled with a whole set of white teeth. "I came all the way from Chicago to see you, Milagros!" he tells her winking. "I'm taking you with me and that's that."

"Well, Manong Jack, let's see what we can do," she flirts back. She told me that if she could keep his pain away, that might be enough. He was dying, she told me.

She sings to that old man, holding one hand over his heart and the other on his back and the heat from her hands travel back and forth, crossing his tired and crumpled chest. Breathing, she sends fresh air into all the chambers of his heart.

Old Manong Jack comes to our house every night for two weeks. When he arrives he's shuffling his feet, but when Ináy is done, he leaps out from behind the screen and dances her across the room. We all love him for the way he flirts with us. He brings a little happiness where normally there is none. Joking with this old man, her voice goes soft and her eyes go light and it is almost as if Papang is here with us again.

"I may not remember your name," he tells me, "But I'll never forget your face."

I can smell Lola Ani's baking bibingka rice cakes with shredded coconut on top and condensed milk. The house is warm with that sweet scent.

"Stay," Lola Ani tells Manong Jack and his son. "Have some merienda with us."

Later, we all sit around the kitchen table, laughing. "After all those years," Manong tells us, "I saved my money and I even became a U.S. citizen, but do you think I will enjoy all my hard work, now in my old age?"

"You are not enjoying my rice cake?" Lola Ani asks him, smiling and nodding at him and they all break out in loud laughter.

Manong Jack wipes tears from his eyes, still smiling and placing his hand on my mother's he tells her, "Milagros, don't stop singing. You know it is your voice that unburdens this old heart."

That night she is so happy that I cannot wait to talk to her. It is like my mother is really back. While Manong Jack and his son say their good-byes, I decide to wait for her. Instead of getting ready for bed, I creep up the stairs past our bedrooms where Lola Ani and Lila are cuddled up before another great telenovela. I pull open the closet door where my father's drums are kept and I pull each one out into the room. I have not seen or touched these pieces since the last time we played together, though I have heard them rattling in the middle of the night, bumping heads and cracking beats like a heart that's breaking. I gather the pieces around me on the floor and I close my eyes and walk my fingers around the rim of each drum, brush the palm of my hand against the skins, feel the smoothness there, the awkward shape of a cowbell, the grooves on cool thin sheets of metal. With my fingers I lightly tap on the snare's skin—rattle, tattle, tat, tat. I tick at the rims on downbeats and boom beats as if they were congas, but I do it all in a whisper, so quiet, so hushed that I could not disturb anyone, not the sick in Ináy's waiting room, not my sister or lola gazing at the television. I play for Papang. I play for me. I close my eyes and for just one second, I am in my own skin. I am here, living in this house.

"What do you think you're doing?"

I jump before I open my eyes. I bang the tom-tom.

"What are you doing?" she asks again. Ináy looms before me, her shadow reaching over me, her darkness big as night. "These are your papang's drums. You do not touch them."

"But Ináy . . ."

"Wala ka ng galang! He's not dead three months and you are banging on his drums!" She is waving her hands at me, running at the drums like she is going to kick them, and I jump up, stand before the set and place my body like a shield.

"Stop, Ináy, stop!" I yell. Lola Ani and Lila run up the stairs calling out our names. Noise everywhere. It's so loud in here. There is nowhere to place my feet, nowhere to ground myself. This is not my house. You are not my mother. But all I can do in this moment is hold my hands and wait.

TWELVE

Go! It's not like you were here anyway. And if you get sick? Well, then you'll know what it's like, what it's been like. Who needs you anyway? Take Papang with you for all I care. Go!

I'm not sure how she does it so quickly. Not only does she pass her nursing boards, but she also earns the rest of her passage and gets her papers from a hospital in Chicago. They tell her, come, we need nurses. Come. So in less than a month, she buys socks and sweaters and long-sleeved shirts and loads all her things in a big carton. She wraps up her life with a sturdy hemp rope. And then she's standing in my room, begging me to see her off at the airport.

I refuse to get into the white school bus. I say, I'm busy studying for my social justice class. We have just begun to study the Philippine Revolution. I'm busy. I say, what do you care if I say good-bye? Since when do you hear me anyway? She says I am disrespectful. Wala akong galang. She says I am going to make her cry. Her? Cry? Since she came back from the dead she feels nothing. Go, go, go, that's what she does.

We stand a room apart and we talk with our bodies, flinging our arms and kicking our legs, turning counterclockwise like two monsoon storms clashing. We haven't talked this much since my papang died. Lola Ani sits just outside the room on a footstool, listening. Lila dances around us, trying to grab our hands, trying to get us to move closer together. She is wet with tears. She cries for both of us. I can feel my jaw tighten up, the bones in my face hardening. My eyes refuse to blink.

Stop it, I tell my sister. Stop your whining. From now on, no more whining. No more crying. That's what she wants us to learn from her. No more heart. And then I block everybody out. Boom boom boom. And then I rap at the desk. Bang bang bang. I turn my back on all three of them. I try not to notice the white light flitting back and forth. Shush shush shush, hiss the pages of my book. My palms are hot. Woo blows the wind. Woo blows the wind. I don't have time for these interruptions.

We are a nation of poor. Wait. Three hundred years in the convent, God pushing us around and making us speak Spanish. I read about the Philippine Revolution, but Ináy's voice is so loud, hurling words at me like bricks. I push my hands against my head, but I can still feel the vibration of her tirade zinging through my body like electricity. I focus on the words, big words, words I am going to have to look up—*feudalism, proletarian internationalism, imperialism, bourgeois populism*. I look at the back of my text. Are these real words?

She is so loud now that even though I am not listening, she blocks the words on these pages, shifting the blood flow from my brain to my heart to the bottom of my feet. For months she has not had time for me, she has not had the heart for me, has been mourning the loss of her husband without me and now, because she's ready and packed and walking out the door, she wants me to listen?

I read the words again—*feudalism, proletarian internationalism, imperialism, bourgeois populism*—and I am so frustrated that I don't feel the hot tears exploding from my face and running all over the page, blurring the text.

I turn around once and for all, "No, I will not say good-bye to you. I will not go with you. I do not approve."

And then I turn my back on her and I flip to the glossary and read the definitions, little cyclones leaving me dizzy and confused.

Outside I hear the engine of the bus rumbling and I lean over, shifting the curtains so she won't see me. I see three small figures climbing the steps of the white bus, my grandmother, my sister, and the woman who was mother.

After Ináy leaves for Manila International Airport, I double over in pain. My insides burn. My stomach bloats. Every hour I run to the bathroom and I roll on the floor, cramped and angry.

When Lola Ani returns, she strokes my hair, rubs my back, but the pain persists. "It's for the best, anak," my lola says. "She'll send for you soon."

"It's not about her," I say, "I'm just sick."

Lola Ani sits by my bed and wipes my brow with a cool towel and Lila lies next to me, stroking my hair.

"Use your hands," Lila whispers. "Use your hands."

I'm so scared. What is happening? Half the time I'm throwing up or ridding myself of watery wastes. Nothing makes sense to me. Not even my father's death made me this ill. I place my hands on my stomach and leave them there until the heat begins, and I feel my insides slipping about, my stomach breathing right into the palms of my hands, the tension swimming left and right. The heat calms the knots in my belly. The weight of my hands stops the movement. After three days of lying in bed, my mother calls from America to say that she has arrived. "Angel," she yells across the seas, "what's the matter?"

"Nothing," I answer. "O.K. ako."

She says, "Remember the dream?"

But Papang is gone. How can we live the dream? I tell her there is no more dream. She insists. I tell her about my stomach, I tell her about the illness, but she only laughs and said, "Good, use your hands, anak. Take care of your sister and your lola for me, until I can bring you all over here. You be the ináy."

After she hangs up, after I cry myself to sleep another night, I feel a warmth running through my body, the heat leaving my hands and a liquid flowing out of me. The cramps are gone, the throwing up gone, the diarrhea all gone. I have become a woman.

Tonight, after we kneel before Mama Mary and pray the Sorrowful Mysteries—one hundred and three Hail Marys, seven Our Fathers, seven Glory Bes, and one Creed—Lola crawls into the bed in our room and she begins her stories.

If she wanted to, Lola Ani could move into Papang and Ináy's room. But she insists she wants to be with us, lying in the same

82

bed, watching the moon from the same window. "It's important, ha?" she tells me, brushing the hair from my eyes, "That we stay together and that we take care of each other." I explore her face, small like a seashell. I examine the fine grooves that line her brown skin and run my hands through her silver hair full as the fullest moon. "O.K., La," I say.

I roll to the edge of the bed, gazing through the curtains. Her voice is hoarse and she speaks as if she is telling us a great secret. "That is our way. One woman helps her sister. Many women help many sisters. Even though we disagree with each other, maybe we don't even like each other, we help anyway."

"What about Ináy," I say. "She only helps herself."

Lola Ani pinches me. "You don't know, anak. You don't know what she's going through—what she's doing for all of us. Look beyond yourself."

I don't answer her. I don't apologize. Instead I close my eyes and try not to listen. I try not to hear the music coming from the walls, the voices of my parents teasing one another and laughing in the middle of the night. I try not to hear them moving through the house as if they are still living here. Feet walking across floors, doors shifting, fans turning off and on, dishes moving in the night. Maybe they don't understand this, what I am going through, what I am letting go. I try my best to shut my heart down, to stop this beating sound, but I cannot and so I let it rock me, send me to another world, someplace quiet and new and not so full of memory.

THIRTEEN

I throw myself into my studies like a good student, knowing now that our country has been under siege for so long we can't figure out how to rule ourselves. *Feudalism* sounds like *futilism* which sounds like *fatalism*.

I press my ink pen hard into a notebook, etching definitions onto the blue lines. The kitchen table shakes with each stroke and the single bulb hanging swings to the rhythm of my words:

Revolution Notes

BASIC ALLIANCE. The alliance of the working class and peasantry serving as the foundation of the Philippine revolution or specifically that of the national united front.

BASIC FORCES OF THE REVOLUTION. The working class, the peasantry and the urban petty bourgeoisie in the Philippines.

BOURGEOIS POPULISM. Rhetorical partisanship for the poor against the rich, but without class analysis and for the purpose of advancing the class interests of the bourgeois.

BUREAUCRAT CAPITALISM. The use of public office in the Philippines to accumulate private assets in capital and land.

CAPITULATIONISM. The tendency to surrender to the class enemy.

CAREERISM. Participating in the revolutionary movement not to serve the people and the cause but advance one's personal career, chasing after position or fame to satisfy one's self.

None of it makes sense to me and that is why I love it. I go through my text, *Philippine Society and Revolution*, as if it is a map to some better place. I start at the beginning and I get so lost, that I have started following the definitions by tracing my fingers along the lines of the complex sentences. My brain works so hard that sometimes I fall asleep at the kitchen table, head to the text, words swimming into me, rearranging themselves like a beautiful dream.

Then I start to meet some of the people from the book in real life. I accompany Mother Mary to the provinces and visit the Aetas. I see them toiling in rice fields, a carabao dragging farmers by the shoulders—the yoke on the man not the animal—and the hot sun scorching his skin. The wages he earns go into an envelope and are sent to someone far far away. He earns nothing. Now I picture the word feudalism etched in my notebook in my heavy blue ink. The word has no shoes and wears clothing that is so tattered that brown skin peeks from its holes like a secret waiting to be told.

Some days Karina and I study for long hours at the library, going over our books and searching through scrolls of film strips, watching historical protests and rallies unfold on scratchy black-and-white screens. When Ferdinand Marcos declared martial law, the young people revolted and many were thrown into jail. We page through scrapbooks with yellowing articles, newsprint fragile as dried flower petals.

In one clipping a skinny girl's body stretches across the front page, her bell-bottom legs kicking dust in the pulismen's faces, her T-shirt tight with protest. A pair of too-big sunglasses masks her petite face and hair flies in all directions like a scream. I run my fingers on the photo to flatten it out, to see if I can make it any clearer, but this action makes the wrinkles pop and all I see is the girl's mouth, wide and distorted and somehow beautiful. The pulis armed with face gear and bulletproof vests struggle to drag her away, but they cannot hold her. She is slipping from their grasp as she raises her placard, blood-red and hand-drawn to the sky like a shout. And in her other hand? There, shooting out from her hip, laced in her slender fingers is a clove cigarette, skinny and dark, its ashes scattering everywhere, its ribbon of smoke sailing up to God.

"Do you know who that is?" Karina says. "Can you tell? It's her. It's Mother Mary."

And then I look at the caption, at Mother Mary's name typed in bold letters: *Ana Maria de la Luna.* "This is before she was a madre," I say, ripping the article out of the binding.

"Ana Maria?" Karina asks. "Isn't that your Lola Ani's name?"

"She's Maria Angelina," I tell her. "Like me."

I hold it up to the light and stare at the tiny dots that make up her face. I place the newsprint carefully between two sheets of paper and bury it in my *Philippine Society and Revolution* textbook. And in that moment, Karina and I decide to take up smoking.

The next time we drive into the community, Mother Mary and I meet activists looking for my Ate Rosalie and J.R. Outside the bus, a guy and girl stand with Mother Mary, their hands in their pockets and their faces squinting in the sun. From the bus, I can hear everything they are saying.

"It was hard," Mother Mary says, "Kasi, I warned her to be careful."

The young woman lights a cigarette and shaking out the match she says, "She thought he'd stick by her."

"Bakit," asks the guy, "Why did he take off like that? We need the both of them. We can't do this alone." He takes a cigarette from the girl and hands one to Mother Mary and the two of them light up.

I look away, at a nearby rice field and the green stalks pushing through the water, but then I glance at them and find myself just staring. She stands there, as if she is one of them, puffing on a cigarette, tossing her head back and blowing smoke to the sun, her habit falling off her shoulders. Ana Maria de la Luna. And then she turns to the bus and yells, "Write down 'sex education.'"

"Opo," I yell from the window, pulling out my notebook. I scribble the words down fast, peeking up at her, her mouth skewed to the side, smoke trailing out of it.

"Remind me," she continues. "I want to try and push that program." And to the two she tells them, "I wanted to teach sex education years ago, and I told Rosalie to be careful, huh? But too late. I hope you're being safe."

The young woman pulls her hair off her neck, wraps it into a bun and ties it there. "And what about Billy? When is he coming back?"

"Oo ngâ," Mother Mary says, "I almost forgot." She points at the bus and adds, "Also write down, 'Billy Morgan,' he's coming back next week to finish his film."

Imagine, Ate Rosalie leading all her warriors down city streets with their arms up and their faces squished up tight, fighting for justice, a cloud of smoke rising from the streets while they move as one body. He must have seen that same fight in her, the way it made her so strong and beautiful. He must have feared her as much as he loved her.

On the ride home, Mother Mary asks me how I'm doing, if I miss my mother. I don't answer her. I don't hear her. She asks me three times all together and finally I answer without turning my gaze from the window. "I'm o.k. po. I've been so busy, I haven't even missed her."

"Sige," Mother Mary tells me, placing her hand on my shoulder. "If you need anything, huh? You're like my own granddaughter, so ask me anything."

At the prison, I think we are going to meet hard-core convicts, the kind that scare you at night—killers, thieves, and dangerous drug dealers—but when we get to the room where all the prisoners are gathered, I meet fathers and their sons, farmers and workers. They are the ones who have been protesting the government, trying to bring justice to the poor. I think that maybe Mother Mary is going to bless them, give them words to think about to make them better men, but when she walks in they greet her as if she is their Mother Mary, smiling at her, bowing slightly at the sight of her. She tells me wala silang hanap buhay, no jobs, no support from the government. "Some of them are bad, sure," she tells me, "but some are just frustrated that they cannot make ends meet."

The prisoners sit on chairs that have been arranged in a circle. They plant their feet on the floor and rest their hands on their knees while Mother Mary reads them a poem by St. Teresa of Avila, talks about the house of light and the quiet space of God. She tells them to close their eyes and I cannot believe it—they do it. They close their eyes and they breathe with her. The breath is low and gathers like wind, pushing through the room, buzzing lightly. I'm not sure where they go, but it doesn't look like they're in the room. Their heads fall to their chests and their shoulders slump. A roomful of prisoners, sleeping like babies. I don't know how she does it, but Mother Mary calms them. They look so small and helpless like that. I think of my own papang, how lucky he was to have a good job that kept us clothed and fed. I try to close my eyes too, to breathe like the men, but something is keeping me from it. I peek every chance I get, I hold my breath, I glance at Mother Mary who has also gone into some altered state. Unlike the men, she sits cross-legged with a blanket on her lap right in the middle of the circle. As we leave she whispers that if only President Estrada cared for the people the way he cared for his own interests, if only the Philippines was more important than the u.s. government, then maybe our men would be working in the fields, not hiding in some dark cell.

FOURTEEN

Our life blows through the house like wind. The air smells like Saturday night dinners and Sunday morning breakfasts, like late-night jam sessions with Papang and his musician friends, like a circle of women waiting for my mother to rub homemade lotions into their skin to heal them from their pains, their fevers, their bad marriages, or ungrateful children. Our home still has the faintest scent of jasmine from our mother's late-night baths. Papang's cigarettes have stained the walls with cinnamon, clove, and some memory I cannot name. When this life taps me on the shoulder, when it sneaks into my day, I turn my back on it. I say, "Go away."

Lila loves when the letters from Ináy arrive. She flies off the ground with her arms in the air and the envelopes sailing from her fingers. There are always three and she delivers them to each of us with a kiss.

"Open it, open it," she tells me, but I have already stuffed the thing in my pocket or shoved it to the back of my book.

"Later," I say so she'll leave me alone.

She and Lola Ani make such a fuss and they sit there reading Ináy's letters like news anchors while I bury my head in my books:

OLD DEMOCRATIC REVOLUTION (in the Philippines). The 1896 anticolonial revolution led by the newly risen Filipino bourgeoisie and inspired by liberal bourgeois ideology.

And I say the definitions over and over again, holding my hands to my ears, feeling the words vibrate in my skin. But sometimes I hear Lola Ani and Lila anyway. I stop what I'm doing and then I read the lines again.

OLD DEMOCRATIC REVOLUTION (in the Philippines). The 1896 anticolonial revolution led by the newly risen Filipino bourgeoisie and inspired by liberal bourgeois ideology.

I say them out loud. And Lila and I compete until I cannot take it anymore and I slam my books shut, pull my papers to my chest and storm away. I leave the letters in my satchel, thinking I will burn them one day, or drown them in the dagat when no one's looking. Let go, I think. Let go.

On Monday, Mother Mary sends me to Dagat-dagatan to bring Lola Carmencita Jimenez to our Holy Feast of Saints celebration. I take a motor tricycle to her, riding low to the ground, so close I can smell the garbage piled up on either side of the streets. We pass children bathing in tires and old labanderas scrubbing other people's dirty panties in plastic tubs on major streets. To get to her house we zip down a narrow esquinita and roll to a stop.

When I knock on the door, a little boy in diapers and a white camiseta answers and I can hear pop music streaming from the television. As I walk in, a chicken runs past my feet. The cement floors stretch throughout the concrete house. The ceiling is only half-made and the sky falls through the darkness and spreads in pockets. Lola Carmencita's grandchildren fill the dark sala and sit before the little television, watching noonday game shows, nibbling on crackers and bits of pan de sal. The house smells of things that rot and I have to hold my breath when I greet them.

"Nasaan ang magulang ninyo?" I ask, "Working?"

"Tulog pa po," answers the oldest girl.

I think, why are they still sleeping when the children are awake? A basin of peppercorns and bundles of bay leaf balance on her lap, as she stuffs little plastic envelopes with two leaves and two peppercorns. She staples the plastic bags onto a cardboard for the local store. "Our parents lost their work."

"How much do you get for that?" I ask, pointing at the pepper and bay leaf stacks.

"Ten centavos for every ten packs po."

Then Lola Carmencita comes out from behind a wall, calling out tasks that are to be covered while she's away. When she sees me, her face lights up.

"Oh, beautiful," she says. "Nandito ka na? I was waiting for you already!"

93

I approach her with my arm extended, pulling her hand to my forehead, whispering greetings as she blesses me.

Her face is painted with soft rouge and blue eye shadow. Her lips have been drawn in with pink lipstick. "You look beautiful po," I say. "But maybe you should take off your jewelry." I'm thinking about the streets and our trip through the city on a flimsy motor trike. "Baka mawala po ang hikaw ninyo," I say, even though I know there's a greater chance of having the earrings stolen than lost. She pulls them off her ears and slips them into her pocket.

"Sige," she says. "Don't let me forget."

We don't talk too much on our way back to the school, though she smiles at me quite a bit and sometimes holds onto my shoulder or squeezes my arm as if I am her granddaughter too. If this tricycle topples over, her frail and wrinkly body will break in half.

"Kamusta si Lola Ani?" she asks me.

"My lola?"

"She is the one who feeds us at the rallies. She is the one who keeps us strong. Mabait siya at masarap magluto."

Ah, I nod my head smiling, and I tell her Lola Ani's cooking is like magic.

"And your mom?" she asks me. "Kamusta siya?"

"o.k. lang po," I tell her, even though I don't know and really I don't care.

FIFTEEN

I scan the schoolyard, searching for my little sister, squinting at the sea of black-haired girls in white sailor shirts and pleated skirts trimmed in sky blue. Girls shift in their seats, the youngest ones closest to the front and the secondary girls in the back. At the walls and hedges bleachers are full of college-aged women. The student body flutters every now and then as pamaypay open and close, fanning the still air. I spy Lila under a magnolia tree, whispering into another girl's ear. The other girl nods and giggles and reaching up, snatches a leaf from the tree. I stare at Lila, hoping she will feel me looking at her, hoping she will find me too. Another little girl with braids tugs on Lila's shirt and she turns her back to me.

Up front, Lola Carmencita's skirt blossoms around her skinny legs and her body is lost in the fabric's folds. She stands at a podium, barely reaching the microphone.

"Listen to me," she says in Tagalog. "Are you listening?"

Lola Carmencita paints a picture of herself as a girl—skinny like me, disobedient like me, a dreamer like me. She makes the day beautiful with a blue sky and a soft breeze. And she brings us to the ocean where she is bathing herself and her younger sister. As she closes her eyes, we feel our bodies floating on the wave of the bay, our feet lifting up off the sandy bottom, our heads resting on the cool waters, our arms drifting with the current. As she falls into a lazy sleep, she forgets the day, the time, the need to get back to her family. She has forgotten all the warnings, the reasons to be home before the sun goes down. Her little sister gathers shells, walking in and out of the cool tide, when suddenly a jeep carrying foreign little men storms the beach. The men hold up bayonets sharp as razors, pointy as sharks' teeth, hold guns on the sisters.

"Kura! Kura!" the little yellow men yell. "Kura! Kura!"

The angry little sister curses the foreign men. She throws a fistful of sand in their faces and makes the slits of their eyes disappear. The ate, the older sister, sees the bayonet falling into the little one, sees the blood surface along the line of her jaw. Another soldier lances the side of the little sister and now the surviving sister is an old woman, standing before us, lifting the hem of her cotton dress to her eyes and wiping the tears dry.

"I was powerless to stop them," she says. "I saw what they did and I understood, so I lay down in the water and I was very quiet and I let them use me. Ginamit nila ako."

Karina has tears in her eyes and her mouth quivers.

I don't cry. I say, "Come on." There is a wind inside me blowing, a kind of rage that starts small and spinning it fattens up, nearly exploding in my belly.

"If this happens to you," Lola Carmencita tells us, "You won't know how to forget."

I look around at the students, how silent everyone has grown. Lola Carmencita's voice falls like rain.

The sun is so hot that my face and hands are moist, and I feel like I am soaking through my uniform. I am melting. I think about how she never saw it coming. What was she thinking as she floated back and forth, her body spinning gently in circles and laps. What was she searching for in the sand, the moment the jeep charged out of nowhere and changed her life forever?

We bring Lola Carmencita to the convent for a feast. Dignitaries and high-powered nuns fill the house. While the guests devour the rice cakes, Karina and I sneak up to the roof to grab a smoke. Giggling, we walk along a balcony that runs around the convent building and climb a ledge to reach the flat-topped roof. From here we can see most of Manila, miles and miles of roofs, alleys, and in the distance, the rise of half-made skyscrapers, their concrete skeletons poking holes into the night sky. I take a deep breath, close my eyes and listen to the roar of diesel trucks and busses idling for miles across Manila. Horns impatiently sound. The noise is familiar, comforting. I am breathing in the city as everyone makes their way home, and just as I am relaxing I see Lola Carmencita, standing before the girls in the courtyard, wiping the tears from her face with the hem of her skirt.

"How old do you think they were?" I ask Karina.

"I don't know. Our age?"

"Why do you think she tells us like that?"

"What?"

"I'd keep it to myself. I'd act like it never happened," I say.

LRT railways rattle in the distance. The sun has almost gone away and streaks of red and purple stain the sky. I see the red blurry taillights winding up the streets, headlights flowing in the opposite direction against a dark road, streaming down the hill like lava from a volcano.

"That's not what activists do," Karina says. "We never forget."

The buildings light up one at a time, like stars set on fire. Below the convent courtyard, a garden of palm trees, bamboo groves, and mango trees floats like a little island in all this city.

"Can you imagine anything more beautiful than this?" I ask Karina, stretching my arms and leaning back against a wall.

She has been searching her pockets, unable to sit still. "What about a smoke?"

"Give me one," I say.

"No, what's more beautiful than this is a smoke. I can't find my sigarilyos or my lighter. Do you have them?"

"Do you suppose that the basic forces of the revolution to oust the Erap government will really change things?"

"What?" She tosses items out of her bag, searches for the smokes. "What are you talking about?"

"You know, the basic forces of the revolution—the farmers, the workers—the people!"

"You need a smoke."

We love the way the slender stick feels, the delicate way we balance the lighted end slightly up and away from us. We love the smell of nicotine on our fingertips, the fragrance that fills our lungs and makes us whole, the way the smoke moves through our bodies, filling up our emptiness, escaping from our mouths like a beautiful promise. Karina smokes like a man. She holds the cigarette with two fingers, likes to inhale fast and pull it away from her mouth, tilt her head and blow. The whole act makes us feel like we are twenty. Like we have already changed the world. At first we smoked because all the other activists did. We studied the way the women lit their smokes, the way they spoke with cigarettes perched between their lips. We did it for the movement. And then we started yearning for the taste. When things got heated. When we were mad. When we felt small. "I need a smoke," Karina would say.

"Yeah," I'd agree, "I need to breathe." Smoking bonded us.

"Where did you leave them?" I ask her now.

"I don't know. If I knew I wouldn't have asked you, di ba? Look in your satchel," she tells me, grabbing at my bag. Everything falls out—pens, a brush, my wallet, and the letters. "Ano yon?" she asks me, picking up the bundle.

"Give it back," I say, reaching for them.

There are maybe five letters stacked together and bound with a string. They are thin like onionskin and they are covered in stamps, ink smudges, and lipstick blur. Karina holds them in the air, "Teka muna," she says reading them in the light. "You haven't opened them?"

"Give it to me," I say again, getting angry now.

"Why don't you open them?" she asks. "They're from your ináy. Open them."

"Sige," I tell her. "Take them. I don't want them anyway. Throw them off the side of the building. Sige na. Do it."

Karina scrambles to her feet and swinging her arms in wide circles she makes her way to the edge of the roof, the bundle of letters held lightly between her fingers. "Fine," she says. She peers over the edge, at the street below, at the cars stuck in long lines and the people moving about like grains of sand. She looks over at me and winks, "Are you sure?" She holds her arm up, the letters wafting in the breeze. I look away.

Karina hangs over the ledge, waving the airmail letters in the air. Do it, I think. Toss them. And then I don't know why, I push off the side of the building and reaching out to her I pull the bundle from her, the string sailing open and flying out into the blue. The papers crumple up in my fist and snarling at her I shove them back into my satchel.

SIXTEEN

One morning, Lila wakes me with her wild sleep. She knees me in the back and slings a warm hand onto my face. She moans soft like a kitten looking for its mother.

"What's the matter," I ask, pushing her away from me. "Be still," I hiss. The air smells like fever, my body sticky with her sweat. She's too drowsy to tell me what's wrong, so I get up to find Lola Ani.

When I get to the kitchen, Lola has already squeezed the calamansi into a pitcher of ice and sugar. "Take care of your sister," she says. "I'm going to work."

The silence makes the house feel so empty. Of course, outside, in the distance, the traffic moans and horns chirp sporadically like birds. Outside the kitchen window I watch how green the leaves are, how massive, how graceful. Beyond the trees a cement building crawls up the sky, ceilingless, exposed and gray. A large crane swoops back and forth, its arm extending into the interior of the building like a child placing toys in the middle of a dollhouse. Jackhammers make the building feel closer than it is.

The water in the sink is cold and the soap is hardly bubbling. I wash a few dishes and turn my back to the window, to a radio singing pop forty from a house down the block. I make my little sister lugaw out of leftover rice and the bones from last night's chicken. I boil a piece of ginger in the soup and squeeze the juice of calamansi into the pot. This is the same lugaw Ináy made for us when we could not hold anything in our belly. It is the same soupy rice that we have come to expect. It is the one thing I know will make her feel better.

When I enter the room, the air conditioner kicks in. "Lila," I whisper. Blankets cover her small form. Her hair sprawls out around her and she looks like a younger version of our mother. "Are you hungry?"

When Ináy was sick, I'd go to her dark room and when she held her hand out, I would knead her palms, putting pressure on the flesh between her thumb and pointer fingers. Her skin was so taut, the flesh hard as frozen meat.

The day Papang disappeared, I worked my fingers into her skin, pulled the tiger balm from my pocket, and worked the ointment into each cell.

"Angel," she said. I didn't reply as I worked her wrist with my thumbs, pulled on her forearms like I was making them longer. "Thank you, anak."

She held out her other arm and I took it. My palms itched from the heat. I looked for cool places to lay my hands. I felt something pulsing under her skin, a movement, a thought. "What is wrong?" she asked me.

I said, "Nothing." Wala.

"No," she said, "meron."

She looked like a glass doll with real hair and long dark lashes. She was too weak to lift herself out of bed. I wanted to talk about moving to America. I wanted to say, take me with you. Or let's wait and all go together. I wanted to say, maybe this is not such a good plan. But I said nothing. I leaned over and kissed her on the cheek.

And then my mother pulled me to her. Her skin was damp and her hands cool. I felt like I was three years old. "You worry too much."

"Only about you."

"I can take care of myself."

"No, you can't."

I looked into my mother's eyes and swam in their black pools. She didn't answer me. Instead she leaned back into her pillows and asked me to open the curtains, to let the light filter into the room. "I'm feeling better, anak," she said. "The headache is leaving."

In her dark room, the television barked prices and the audience applauded. "Game ka na ba?" shouted the former president's game-show daughter.

"Game na!" shouted back the audience.

Ináy sighed like a wind sailing through the room. "Angel, anak, halika," she said, drawing me close to her. "Everything is as it should be. Why must you torture yourself?"

That memory feels so long ago, that mother and daughter strange and far away. I shudder. Why should I care about Ináy? She can heal her own self.

I feed Lila the soup. I give her aspirin. I bathe her body with a cool towel.

"Ate," she whispers.

"Ano?" I ask her. What more can I do for her?

"Pwede ba, can you use your hands?"

"Naku," I whisper brushing the hair from her sweaty face. "That won't do anything."

"Please, Ate," she says, turning her body toward me. "I'm so sick. Won't you heal me the way Ináy taught you?"

"That was a game."

"But what about all the people who came to our house?"

"That was in their head. If you want to feel better, just tell yourself you'll feel better and before you know it, that's it." I pull a blanket over her shoulders and she pushes it away.

"Ang init," she complains. "I want ice and air con, not blankets."

"You have to let the fever burn away."

"It will go faster if you lay your hands on me."

I won't do that for her. I won't perpetuate that silly game. I tell her I'll stay with her all day. I'll cook for her. I'll change the towels for her. I'll read to her if she wants. But no nonsense. No healing with hands.

"Ináy says you were born with your hands stretched out. It was the first thing that Papang and Lola saw when you were born. Your two beautiful hands."

"Ikaw naman," I say, kissing her forehead. "That's just an old wives' tale. How can a baby come out of its mother's womb hands up in the air like it's being arrested? It's impossible. It's the head or the puwet that comes out first. Maybe the feet. But not the hands."

I pull the hair out of her face; I wipe muta from her eyes.

"What do you want?" I ask her. "I'll get it for you."

She asks for Ináy and I tell her not to be a baby. That's when she starts crying. "No really, Ate. I miss her so much. Ikaw? You don't miss her?"

I tell her that our mother has been gone a long time. "Get used to it."

From under her pillow, Lila pulls her own stack of letters from America. They have been ripped open and are soft with Lila's perspiration and sweet with our mother's perfume. "Ate, will you read them to me?" Her eyes are so brown.

"That makes it worse."

But she insists that it makes her feel better, that seeing Ináy's perfectly drawn penmanship scrawled in blue ink across the page somehow takes the pain away. "You're wasting your time," I tell her. "Do what I do."

Now I feel my own skin getting hot and clammy too. The flush starts at the temples and in my ears. I tell her that if I feel something at all—or even start to—and even that I don't do anymore—but if I do, I simply think of something else. I feel something else. I focus on what is right here, what I can see and what I know won't let me down.

"Like what?" she wants to know. And then I start to tell her of my adventures with Mother Mary. I describe the prisoners at the jail, how they look like they could be any of our uncles or cousins, not dangerous men at all, but small, sad, and worried about their families. "And what about those lolas?" I say. "Helping them is like a full-time job." And when her lips crumple up like Kleenex, I say, "Oh, I know." Then I pull out my textbook and ease the fragile article from the sleeves of the book. "Look," I whisper, showing her the photograph of the young aktibista being dragged away.

"Do you know who that is?" I ask.

"She looks like you," Lila says.

I squeeze her hand and I say, "Really?" And then I share with her my own dreams, that sometimes, I imagine I am her and that I am marching the streets with thousands of other protesters, my fists raised and my voice crying out. And I imagine bringing relief to the farmers and the fishermen and the workers in the streets because I care about them and I care about the Philippines.

"So who is that? Ináy?"

And I say, "No way. It's Mother Mary. See the mouth?"

"Oo ngâ," she says. "I see it."

"Someday," I tell her, "only thieves and murderers will be in jail."

"But how does that make you stop missing Ináy? Sometimes, Ate, sobra akong malungkot. Parang may buto sa dibdib ko, tapos, it makes it hard for me to breathe. Ang sakit."

The heat's rising from my belly, and just as I am about to lecture her, I see those young girls floating in the sea and the soldiers running out to them with their bayonets held up. But the girls are not Lola Carmencita and her sister, they are Lila and me, swimming like fish. The sun slips into the darkest rain clouds and hovers over the ocean, cooling the waters around them. Lila means that stone is stuck right in the middle of her heart, blocking the flow of everything. "I know it hurts, pero nandito ako," I tell her. "I'm not going anywhere."

"At si Papang? Don't you miss him?"

"Si Papang?" And then I tell her he is always here. He has never left. I put my arms around her and hold her tight. And together we breathe just like Papang. Pintig, pintig, pintig. Her small heart pulses just underneath her nightshirt and I feel the push and pull of her belly as it fills with air and then releases. The clock in the room ticks and then the birds outside chirp and the window rattles with the air conditioning and before you know it, there is a groove in the room, a dance of sound so soft it lulls my sister to sleep.

SEVENTEEN

Papang once took me to *Tondo Boy* starring President Estrada before he was president. His clients were at an all-day conference and so he dropped them off at their convention and snuck me into a theater where they only showed Tagalog films. It was a scratchy old black-and-white movie with missing frames that made the scenes jump from one image to another and everyone shouted their lines like they wanted to make sure the audience would hear.

In the movie, Estrada greased back his hair and ran through the streets of Tondo saving the poor from each other, picking fights with the upper class and flirting with the sampaguita flower girls. Tondo Boy was a crime fighter. My mother got so mad at my dad for taking me to that corny movie, but it was the first time I had been to the movies and the pictures made me think of comic book superheroes with square jaws and over-drawn muscles. I still think about the exaggerated way Tondo Boy would leap into a scene and yank the crooks by the collar, his too-large fist rising up in the air and then POW and BAM! Since he has won the popular vote, we have been hoping he really is Tondo Boy, a figure who will fight the corruption of foreign governments and help the people rise above poverty. But he is not Tondo Boy, though he does grease his hair back. And he does not save the people. Instead, Estrada fools them like a cheap imitation of the U.S. president who was also once a movie star, a Hollywood good guy gone bad, a man with thick wavy hair combed back away from his face and greased down with expensive perfumes.

Today we have come to Malacañang to remind Estrada what it means to be president, what it means to be Tondo Boy. I'm in charge of pairing up my batchmates with a lola. Karina and some of the other girls in school stand at the foot of the white school bus, helping the ladies climb down, placing them on their skinny arms. The bus engine idles as they escort the old ladies across to the gates of Malacañang where they plan to make their demands known. Lola Carmencita and her friends cloak themselves in purple scarves and they carry poster boards calling out for "Justice" and "Apology Now." One of the women calls out "Laban!"

"Laban!" we respond.

"Fight until we have justice!" calls another lola. "Lumalaban kami!" The traffic is impatient, inching their wheels forward, but we make them stop. The jeepneys overheat. Steam rises from the engines. Our words scatter across the skies while an orchestra of vehicles clamors against our chants.

A line of pulis stand guard, still as toy soldiers, little plastic men with little plastic hearts. I charge the line. Climb a curb. Glare into the eyes of one pulis. The young man winks and reveals beautiful brown eyes. We gaze at one another intensely and then he whispers, "Dahan dahan, anak." When I don't answer him his mouth breaks into a smile. "Dahan dahan, ha?" I spit words back at him. LUMALABAN KAMI! And just as suddenly as I am on him, I leap away.

The lolas stop at the intersection and enact a drama, a kidnapping of their bodies, a raping of their lives. While the old women pantomime the atrocities they endured, a long black limousine turns the corner and drives right through their drama. The wheel of the limo turns and the car's bumper shoves Lola Carmencita ever so slightly and she begins to fall. Karina and I reach for her, we try to pull her away from the road and we nearly fall to the ground. "Take her," I shout to Karina. I pound on the hood of the car and leaping up from the ground, I jump on the windshield.

A camera pops out of the passenger's window. Shoots. A white face floats out of the window, squinting into the long lens of the camera. The door eases open and the man steps out, still shooting frame after frame.

I hear the shutter rolling film. I shift. Stall. Stop. The fair skinned Kano with salt-and-pepper hair has skin so smooth and lashes so black they rest like wings on his squinting face. His long body snakes its way through the traffic. He wears jeans and work boots and a black T-shirt. I smell his cologne from here.

What is he doing? I wonder. What does he want? "Can't you see what you've done?" I yell as I run toward him. "Can't you see what you've done?"

And I cannot help myself. Fists fly like sticks on drums. Feet kick. Feet kick. Pintig. Words rain from my mouth. Hit like bullets. Pintig. Pintig. Pintig. Everything appears extreme close-up, out of focus—so I hit. Pintig. I push. Pintig. I hit. Make out images with my hands: hair, skin, lens, sleeve, boot, battery pack. Pintig. I hit. Pintig.

Pulis leap from the side of the road, come down on me like hornets. Arms slip out of meaty palms. Feet hop through arms long as bamboo sticks. They go for the legs. They go for the spaces just under the arms. The body writhes like a firecracker about to explode. Pulis pry me off the American filmmaker. The heat from the pavement makes everything seem hazy.

Strands of black curls fly in every direction. Heat flushes my face red. Their laughter corrupts the air. Mother Mary grabs my wrists. My heart pounds. Pintig. I kick at him. Pintig. I twist. I slip out of her grasp.

"What do you think this is," Mother Mary says laughing, "A boxing match?" She turns to the pulis and tells them, "Let that one go. She's with me."

"But Mother Mary," I say.

"Angel meet Billy Morgan."

And then I remember writing it all down in my notebook—first "sex education" then "Billy Morgan." My eyes go wide and I can feel tears swelling up my insides. I throw him the dirtiest look I have. My body wants to respond like drum sticks against the world. I hold back. I hold back. I want to hit. I want to spit. I hold back. And then I ask her, "Couldn't you get a Pilipino filmmaker?"

The St. Magdalena school bus waits for us—door open and engine growling. We climb on. The lolas and the girls are all seated. It seems I have missed the entire protest.

"Ano," Jun-jun the driver asks. "Did you change the world na?"

"Almost," I answer.

"What's the first rule of protest and resistance?" Mother Mary says. Her voice looms up over the engine.

"No violence," yell the girls.

"Di ba nonviolent tayo? That means we don't hit, we don't carry weapons, we don't jump on people. What came over you?"

I don't listen. Instead I whisper to myself, "PROLETARIAN REVOLUTION: A revolution led by the working-class party and involving the overthrow of the bourgeoisie by the working class."

I get up and move to the center of the bus, a world away from them. I surround myself with the noise of their voices, the old lolas laughing, my classmates singing, and the rattle of a diesel engine. Outside the bus, pulis trucks are pulling away from Malacañang. And then I see the long limo crawling next to us, the snout of the camera sticking out of the window, the shadow of the cameraman hovering in the dark.

EIGHTEEN

I fling the door open and drag the heavy, cold pieces out one at a time. I fit them together, arrange them just the way Papang did. I'm moving so fast I nearly drop one, trip over the bass drum, and fall to the ground.

"Angel," Lola Ani says as she climbs the stairs, holding the rail with two hands. "Diyos ko! What are you doing? Parang earthquake dito." When she hears the drums she calls out, "Not that noise."

"Please, Lola. I need to."

"Did your mother give you permission, anak?"

"Ináy's not here."

"But you remember what happened last time?"

I sigh and bring out another snare drum.

She stands on the step with one hand on her hip and the other wiping a hanky across her brow. "Anong nangyari?" she wants to know. And I would tell her what happened, if I understood. But I don't. I just know that all this energy inside me is itchy and it makes me want to hit. I just know that I don't know.

"Wala," I say. "Nothing unusual."

"Today was your rally, di ba? How did you do?"

I don't tell her. I don't say that I was so busy getting mad that I attacked a foreigner and that all the pulis were on me. I don't say that the Lolas and my classmates were so surprised when I leapt onto Billy Morgan with both fists that they dropped their placards and their voices went silent. That instead of protesting President Estrada's apathetic ear, they stood around me and watched in disbelief. Anyway, I figure, Mother Mary has told her.

I pretend I don't hear her. I bang the drum. I imagine Papang jamming with me—beating tom-toms, smashing cymbals, flipping our sticks high into the air, the beat surrounding us. We play loud. Our sound takes up the whole world and the rhythm is so divine that everyone moves to our beat. The whole world struts to our four/four, six/eight syncopated beat, stirring pots to this jam, washing clothes, tapping pencils. When I play, I bang so loud and clear even the heart cannot keep still. Pintig, it says, pintig, it goes. Pintig, pintig, pintig. I clutch my sticks and see my hands go red. I hold my breath and then let it all burst out of me, counting, beating, hitting. The tears are falling now, the breath is moving. I fill the whole room with sound. I send it to the heavens. I make the moon hold her ears. It is that loud.

I don't notice Lola climb the last step onto the landing. I don't see her coming up from behind or wrapping her small arms about me. As I continue to play, she holds me tight and I cry like a baby. The sticks drop. The room reverberates with the beats. We breathe together and she says, "O.K. na, mahal."

And then she leans down to pick up my sticks and hands them to me. "Sige, anak. Play." Lola Ani closes her eyes, she waits for me to begin, to summon her son. To bang on these drums. To make music sound like love.

NINETEEN

We make supper for the sisters. A hard rain falls and though I stand at the sink running water over milkfish, I'm lost in the green leaves swaying with the wind. Children stand on balconies, naked and laughing, soaping their brown bodies clean. Water pounds the streets, and currents of energy sail over us, brushing the downfall east and west. We move through our days in slow motion, cycling through the water, soaked in its love. We are months from monsoon season, but this rain insists. The storm rushes onto the tin roof and every drop makes itself known, rattling like a series of drum rolls, spilling into the gutter and falling several floors to the ground level. Outside, a stray cat searches for shelter, its skinny body soaked and sorry looking. Lola Ani chops onions fast and loud against the cutting board. She snivels and sniffs at the onions, fragrant and raw. She cracks garlic open with the butt of her cleaver. Her cooking and chopping competes with the radio program.

"Your mommy says she's been filing for your visa papers, anak."

I watch the rain hitting the neighboring roofs, bouncing off the corrugated tin. I hear cymbals crashing.

"I know it's hard," she continues, "but you have to see that we are all going over one by one. First your mother, then you, and then Lila, and I will follow."

The announcer on the radio squeaks, cutting in and out of the intermittent frequency. His words sound like rain too. I lean over the sink and look for the calico cat. I think I can hear her mewing out there.

"I don't want to leave either," Lola Ani says. "This is my whole life. But what can you do?"

"You can say something," I finally speak.

"But your mother is the head of this family now, she's the one making the decisions."

And of course what I want to say is too disrespectful to utter. What I want to do is remind Lola of those months after Papang's death. Nawala siya sa sarili niya. A crazy woman. That's what she was.

"And this is what your papang would have wanted you to do. To obey your mother. To go to America. Can't you be grateful, anak?"

Lila enters the room with an empty tray and searching through a cabinet, she pulls tall glasses from the shelf.

"Shhh," Lila says, "Listen."

Through the static a woman's voice emerges, small, nervous, faint like a ghost's. We all stop moving. We listen. "Ako si Marisa

Romero. I was born in the mountains near Benguet in 1933."
Lightning brightens the sky like a photo flash. Thunder cracks.
The three of us huddle close to the radio, straining to hear the
woman, Marisa Romero. Her voice is so wobbly. Hard to tell if
she is crying or just very very old. Lola Ani places her ear right
next to the radio. "Naku," she whispers. "Si Marisa."

"Sino siya?" Lila asks, leaning her chin onto Lola's shoulder.

"My friend from grade school. Akala ko she was dead, but
here she is alive and old pa rin, naku!"

The three of us pile one on top of the other like pillows
stacked and leaning on the kitchen counter. I reach over and
fiddle with the reception. Static crackles like shards of thunder
shooting out the old speaker. Marisa was captured along with
her three sisters during the war and brought to a fishing village.
"They tied us at the waist with a rope, like this. And they
dragged us for I don't know how long. When we slept we were
like that. Even to relieve ourselves, we were like that. At night
they throw us down. Ginagamit nila kami. Sometimes four soldiers at one time. If they rape one of us, they rape all of us, still
tied up like that. Here are my scars where the ropes used to be.
Give me your hand so you can feel it."

The announcer sighs. Says nothing back. It is enough for us
to imagine the scars.

Lola Ani closes her eyes and places her head down, breathing
heavily.

"When we got to the fishing town, they tossed us in the cages
where they put the fish. Made of wires. And the ground was just
mud."

"How many were you in the fish cage?" the announcer asks.

"Marami. Maybe thirty girls? When the soldiers wanted something, they just reach inside and they pull out a girl by the arm. They do it right there, under the palm trees or in front of everyone. Walang hiya. They use us every day like that."

"More than once a day?"

"Always."

Lola Ani sits up and she pushes the two of us away, and we see the tears there, the anger. I rub her arm. I kiss her wrinkled shoulder.

We ask her what she remembers about her youth. "Where were you?" we ask. She thinks about it like she's trying to remember. "I don't know anymore. I'm old you know. So much craziness back then—ang gulo. Who can remember anymore?" She smiles and tells us her cooking is going to burn. "Hala! Let's move. The sisters are waiting and hungry." She snaps off the radio and pats us both on the back. "Lila, is the table set na?"

Lila and I walk through the dining room doors bearing plates of rice and milkfish with eggplant and sweet tomatoes. The nuns chatter as always and it takes a moment before we notice the sisters' guests.

"Good evening, Angel!" Billy Morgan sings. "Good evening, Miss Lila!"

"Good evening po," Lila answers and the whole table greets us.

I feel my jaw locking. I look at their pale faces mewing over the plates like stray kittens. I turn to leave the room and in my head, I am reciting: "PEOPLE'S DEMOCRATIC STATE. The type of state that the Philippine revolutionary movement strives to set up—encompassing all patriotic and progressive classes under the leadership of the working class."

And before I can make it out of the room, Mother Mary says. "Angel, can you bring out the Nescafe, anak?"

"Opo," I answer and then I lean over her and I whisper, "Bakit po? Ano po ba ito?"

Instead of whispering back in Tagalog, the only language she ever uses, she says in a loud American way, "Billy will be with us for the next month working on the documentary about the movement. Remember, Angel, I told you about that at the protest."

"Opo," I say.

To him she says, "The girls are Rosalie's cousins."

"I love Ate Rosalie!" Billy says. "How's my girl doing? How about J.R.?" He shakes his head like he is remembering and says, "They're out of control. Talk about nationalists."

"She moved back to the province," Mother Mary says.

"With J.R.?"

"Do you know, Angel?" Mother Mary asks, even though we all know that J.R. has been gone for months.

I say, "She has a baby." And his eyes go wide. "And rides with the NPA."

"The New People's Army? For real?" He looks at Mother Mary and says, "We should interview her, don't you think?"

My heart pumps double-time. Thumps in my ear. To keep from falling I define 'the people's democratic state' like a prayer, like a mantra that will get me through.

*

We get back to the house that night and the three of us are lying in our bed, watching the moon rise, pretending to sleep. But Lola Ani's thoughts toss her about. Since Papang's death, her body has shrunk. Her skin is even browner now because it is no longer stretched taut against her flesh. She has no flesh, just soft skin that falls like lace about her beautiful bones. I love to run my hands along Lola's arms and smooth her skin flat, stretch its millions of wrinkles open. I can see her youth that way. I can imagine her fair and plump and curvy that way. Her hair has grown silver, all shiny and wild and luminous against her dark skin.

"Bakit po, La?" I ask her. "You can't sleep either?"

"Si Marisa," she says. "Kawawa naman. I feel so bad. I can't stop hearing her voice."

Lila rubs our grandmother's back. "You should be happy for her, Lola. She made it fine."

"When I was a girl, so many say, 'War is coming, war is coming,' but no one understood what is this war. So we wash the clothes, and we cook the rice, and before you know it smoke swallows us up and banging comes from the heavens and metal stones rain from big black clouds. Naku! And in the sky, mosquitoes the size of elephants buzz. Now we know what war is. You can be walking down a road and suddenly feel a knife go through your heart and you know that someone you love has died. Or maybe you have died. It is so hard to say. But there was a band of women who used to hideaway in banyan trees, who sat among the aswáng."

"So were the women evil too?" Lila asks. She leans on her elbow, the palm of her hand framing her round face.

"Oh no," Lola says. "Naku, these sisters were so good that even the aswáng leave them alone. The aswáng understood that if all the Filipinos died, especially the women, there would be no one to feed them the unborn children. So when the women escaped the Japanese camps, when they survived the torture of being used like that—you know what I mean by being used?" She waited for us to respond yes and then she said, "When the survivors were strong enough to climb the trees, to near the moon, then, oh then even the aswáng said—o.k. na, save the women if you can."

The kuliglíg are so loud tonight; their chirping fills the room, competes with Lola's story. When she talks, my spirit leaves, goes into the provinces and sees the women, big and small and perched on branches. She tells us the women developed new ways of talking. "They spoke to each other like animals in the night—owls and frogs and wild crickets."

"Did you see them?" Lila asks.

"Everybody knows about them," Lola says.

But I say, "That is just a legend, Lola. Hindi po totoo."

"Tunay iyon," Lola says. "Everything I tell you is true. You must understand we do whatever we have to do to watch out for each other, to take care of each other. That is our way."

The image of Lola Marisa and her sisters strung together like paper dolls and dragged through the mud keeps me awake. Sometimes, instead of Lola Marisa and her teenage sisters, it is my lola and my sister and me, tied at the waist, unable to run, unable to turn left or right without the other. The soldiers are dark monsters, shadows, and I cannot imagine the rest, it is so horrible. I cry instead, I dream. I say to myself, better to fight this now, to hold my fist up in the air, to cry the lolas' battle cry. Laban! Laban! Laban!

TWENTY

Karina carries a stack of flyers in her hand and we wander SM Mall, hanging onto each other's shirts, weaving our way through the crowds. Her flyers are poems about the revolution, national love poems with ink drawings. At night, when her parents are tossing objects on the other side of their Makati condo, their voices traveling through cold empty halls on into her room, she sits at her desk with her speakers blaring dance music and she scratches poems onto scraps of paper. Then she decorates each poem with little ink drawings. She says it's the only thing that keeps her from going crazy.

"What do you mean?" I ask her.

"When I start writing down how I feel about the movement, I stop hearing them."

"I know," I answer. "Revolutions keep you from feeling sorry for yourself."

Karina thinks her poems are going to start a revolution. She leaves them scattered all over the place, on buses and jeepneys, on the LRT and on counters at Jollibee. She stuffs her poems in church pews or tapes them on bathroom walls.

"That is such a waste of time," I tell her, grabbing a poem from her and reading it. "You don't even have any keywords here."

"Keywords?" She smiles at an old lola and her grandchild. "Kamusta po?" She hands the old lady a poem.

"Ano ba ito?" says the old woman, waving the poem in the air like a fan.

"A love poem," Karina says.

"Walang revolution or propaganda," I say. "It's just love love love. Walang Pilipinas!"

"Open your mind, Angel, there are a thousand ways to start a revolution!" Karina marches off and, standing over the railing, looks down at the first floor, at all the people wandering about, malling.

"Fine, huh? You think the only way to reach the masses is through protest? Then here." She takes her stacks of poems and flings them in the air. They fall like a flutter of hot pink petals down three mall levels.

"Sira!" I say and we both laugh as we watch the people below. Some hands reach up and catch the poems, some swat them away, others dodge them as if the poems are boulders hurtling down upon them. "You're so crazy, naman!"

"If one person reads my poem and shows up, then it was all worth it. That, sister, is how to start a revolution."

When I ask her if she knows my Ate Rosalie, she says, "Who doesn't?" She says that all you have to do is look into the crowd

125

and see the woman marching two steps ahead of everybody. She is long and lean and full of fire. There's a darkness about her, a kind of beauty that makes everyone scared to disappoint her. "If people were late, she'd do their work swiftly and when they arrived, she ignored them. She never yelled, but you knew that you had messed up pretty badly."

"And people put up with that?"

"Because she's right. And everyone wants her fire. Everyone. Especially J.R. Too bad she quit the movement."

"Maybe she didn't quit," I say, "Maybe she just had a baby."

We spend the rest of the afternoon at Icebergs, spooning cold mouthfuls of sweet halo halo from tall glasses, gossiping about the movement. I wish that I was fire, that I could get lost in the crackle of that heat.

Between tsismis, we write new poems for Karina's revolution on a fistful of napkins we've stolen from the counter. She tells me what to write and I carve the letters out, careful to leave room for Karina's ink drawings, images she will create later tonight when her father comes home drunk and smelling of other women's perfumes and her mother will scream at him.

Waiting for the LRT, we sit on a bench and pull out cigarettes. Below us, the setting sun bathes the city in orange. I squint as I search my pouch for a light.

"Wala," I say, "Do you have one?"

"Wala rin," Karina says.

"Why don't you ever have a light?" I say.

An incoming train zips onto the platform, bringing with it a wind tunnel of sound and dust. My body shakes, rattles, vibrates. The doors open and people pour out of several doors, their voices humming above the hiss of the LRT.

"Hello, ladies." It's Billy Morgan shaking a match and tossing it over the edge of the platform. "Wanna light?"

Karina looks at me and smiles. I shake my head, no way. "Sure I'd love it," she says getting up to walk toward him.

"Karina."

She pops her cigarette into her mouth. Then shielding the light with his hand, Billy leans his head toward her, cups his free hand over hers. What are you doing, I think. Stop!

"Angel?" he asks.

I shake my head and put my hand out like a traffic cop. "No, thanks."

"Come on," Karina says. " You know you want to." I stare at her, standing next to him like they are boyfriend and girlfriend. The last of the sun is now sinking behind them and the shadows of their bodies fuse together into a figure with four legs, four arms, two heads. Inhaling she cocks her head back and blows the white smoke into the air, smoke that's so light it glows. She says, "Mmmm, that hits the spot all right. Can't you taste that? Sarap!"

"Fine," I say smiling. "Just one."

He saunters over to me, and bends his long neck low to light the tip. I can smell his thick cologne, a sweet scent of musk. I pull away, take a drag, and look him in the eye.

"So I think I've met your mom," he says.

"When you were here last year," I say.

He looks at me and waiting, blows smoke out of the side of his mouth. "Naw, in Chicago before I left. At least I think it was your mom—Milagros?"

"Wow," says Karina. "How'd you manage that? Isn't Chicago a big place?"

He shrugs and says the Fil-Am community is not so big.

"Oh yeah," Karina says, nodding. "I think I heard you were part—can't tell. You look so American."

"I'm a quarter," he says.

He looks nothing like us. His face is too light. His eyes too round and too close to the color blue. Even his hair is wrong. He is not one of us. Not even one quarter's worth.

I feel my whole body growing small and hard. I take a long slow drag, close my eyes, hold my breath. I am still just long enough to center myself. I exhale. "No," I say and I elbow Karina before she can contradict me. "You must be thinking of someone else."

What I know is that I cannot handle this stranger who seems to be connected to everyone in my family in ways I will never be. First Mother Mary, and then the way he talks about Ate Rosalie and J.R. like they were barkada running all over Manila in protest. And now this? My mother? I am done. I am done with God, my mother, and this American freak. From this moment on, I focus all my energy on the campaign to bring Estrada down, to help the lolas get their justice, and to use my voice to change the world.

TWENTY-ONE

At dawn, we hold a prayer vigil at the gates of Malacanañg Palace. St. Magdalena's a cappella choir stands on the curb in messy rows, their hair falling out of ponytail holders, their T-shirts rippling in the wind like pink flags. The girls crane their necks, searching for the sister's magical baton. If we were in church, their voices would sound like angels, bouncing off marble ceilings, echoing and ringing like Christmas bells. Here, the crowd drowns them with their rebel cries. Here they sound like lost cats.

I'm waving at the sky, my clipboard fanning the already hot air. Where are the farmers? They are next. Where are the extra bullhorns? I text Karina and then I search the crowd, gently pushing shoulders and torsos out of my way. There is a long line of rebels queued up and winding along the road leading up to the platform, waiting to receive the Eucharist. Above the choir, the priest holds up a host without looking at the wafer, the person, or the sky, and he mutters, "Buddy of Christ, buddy of Christ, buddy of Christ." The crowd crawls past me, climbing the stairs to meet the priest. They stick their tongues out, eyes closed, fingers running sloppy signs of the cross over their hot bodies. I move through them, shouting into the bullhorn, "The farmers are next—after the Eucharist the farmers are next!" No one hears me. Then I see Karina herding the farmers with their steel-string guitars up to the stage. I breathe a sigh of relief.

Lola Ani and Lila arrive with plastic bags of rice, hard-boiled eggs, tomatoes, and fish. They hand the lunches to the old women, to the mothers on the streets who untie the bags and dip their fingers into the food and eat. "Ang sarap!" coos an old lola. "Salamat, mare," says another. Yoli, Marite, and Patricia sit on folding stools with their legs crossed. They make faces at the plastic bags of food, like they are too good for Lola's offering, but they reach their hands out anyway and snatch their bags. "May kutchara at tinidor kayo?" one of them asks.

"Use your hands," Lila tells them. "The old-fashioned way."

Lola Ani and Lila hand out bottles of cold orange soda and cola. My grandmother has grown too old to march, too frail to stand in this heat, and too small to be seen in a crowd this size, so she and my sister work at the convent, behind the scenes, making meals and handing them out. Lola Ani hands me a supot with special treats, bunches of sweet lychee.

"Anak," she says, pulling wild hair out of my face. She looks into my eyes, wiping the sweat from my brow. "Parang galit na galit ka."

"I am angry, Lola. Kita niyo po? This government is so corrupt. I can't stand it."

Her wrinkled face is soft, her brown eyes teary. "To fight, you have to be calm, ha? Don't just react, ha? Observe. Think. Tapos, act. Huwág ka magalit."

"Opo," I answer, looking away. She's old, I think, she thinks this is a phase.

"If you are always so mad you might not see what is really happening and you might lose your fight, anak."

I kiss her, not because she's right, not because I will listen to her, play it cool and all ladylike, but because she says everything with such love. She's too old to know what we are doing here, to understand this passion I have for justice. When she was young, World War II broke out of nowhere and into everywhere, they didn't see it coming, there was no time to prepare, to understand, to plan your battle. I wish I could explain it to her, but she's my lola and I know better than to argue with her.

I sit under a tree and unwrap the plastic supot. The fish is crispy and salty. I dip my fingers into the bag and taste a mouthful of garlic-fried rice. Fresh tomatoes, red and juicy, balance the salty fish, the heavy rice. The food grounds me, reminds me how hungry I am, how long the day has been. Lila walks over to me and hands me an orange soda. Leaning over she gives me a red, white, and blue airmail envelope.

"You should read it, Ate."

I fold the letter and slip it into my back pocket. "What for?" I say, grabbing another handful of food and stuffing it into my mouth.

"Just open it. Every week she writes and sends us money."

"I don't need her money."

"But we do."

I yank the letter from my pocket and toss it at her. "Then you open it."

"You break her heart, Ate."

Lila storms off, stomping her feet and kicking up dust. "Thanks for the drink!" I yell out to her. She waves at me without turning around.

After the protest, we have to paint new placards for the next day's campaign. Instead of waiting, Lola Ani and Lila make the trip back to the house on their own, because what happens is this— I get so lost in the details—the words from my text have taken on legs and arms and a pulse that beats almost as steady as my own heart. And I cannot stop myself. I think I am painting one more placard, but really I am creating a dozen more. I think I am texting one organizer, but in the end, I am texting everyone on the list and looking for drivers, for actors, for musicians. The country is so fed up with Estrada, we are going to overturn him, bring the people on the streets. We are going to end this madness. All night long, Karina scribbles line after line, long after the moon has risen through the window. The wind sings through the bamboo grove, quiets the night. I close my eyes and I listen. We are all working in silence. There is nothing to say. Preparing for the revolution lifts me out of my body and I watch myself from above, moving through my list of things to do, organizing.

And then my cell phone beeps and I get a text from Lila.

"May aksidente. Nandito kami sa ospital."

Karina's driver guns the Mercedes through Metro Manila and I watch the full moon. I cannot tell if we are following its path or if the moon is coming after us. It is big and bright and low on the horizon. I'm wondering why it was not more watchful of my family. "You should've been with them," I say. "You should have protected them."

Karina lights a cigarette and hands it to me. She slides open an ashtray. "He won't say anything," she says, pointing to the driver. She hands me a fistful of poems and I stuff them in my pouch.

"Salamat," I say. "Thanks for everything."

We roll down the windows of her father's car and we blow smoke to the sky, puffing fiercely one stick at a time.

"Did she say how?" Karina asks.

"Going home." There were three boys riding with Lola Ani and Lila in the jeepney. "I should have been with them," I tell her.

"You can't always be with them," Karina says.

"I should have protected them."

"But how?"

From the hospital, Lila described the boys like thugs in an old-time movie. They were silent and mean looking, staring them down. "Masungit sila!" Lila said. They sat on the bench across from Lola Ani and Lila, three in a row, just watching them and when they got out to catch the second jeepney, the boys got off too.

I close my eyes and imagine the route the jeepney must have taken. The streetlights barely glow, flickering and dimming as if too tired to shine. In the business district, there are no people, just dark streets and more dark streets. The sidewalks are broken and usually, when we walk, Lila and I take Lola Ani by the arm and we navigate her small body around the dips in the walkway, around the rubble jutting up from the ground. They walked the block and a half to get to the next jeepney stop, and the thugs must have been close behind them, whispering softly to each other. Was a stray dog running past, maybe a skinny rat? No pulis. No stores open for business. No people on their way home. Nothing. They must have thought Lola and Lila had money.

"What did you have with you?" I asked my sister.

"They took her wedding ring," Lila had whispered. "They took her coppice purse."

"What was in it?"

"Wala."

After all that, the boys took everything, but got nothing. All she had was her wedding ring, all she had was her beautiful purse full of nothing. They got mad, Lila said, they were put out. The big one struck Lila. Defending her apo, Lola Ani attacked him.

"How did she do that?" I asked her. "She's so small."

"Hindi ko alam. I was on the ground."

Lola Ani must have thrown her whole body at the boy. She must have hit him with her fists, pinched him with her scrawny fingers. And that is when he struck her back, kicked her down. Kicked and kicked. Kicked until my Lola stopped yelling. I imagine

Lila crying out, filling the air with her small voice. No one came running.

"Don't worry na," I said. "Karina and I will be there soon." I could hear her breathing on the hospital phone. "Huwág ka umiyak," I told her. "Crying is for babies."

Karina puts her hand on my shoulder and rubs, but I push her away.

Now and then the moon throws shadows and I see a ghost of a man running between alleys, crossing the street. One, two, three shadows. Who could beat an old woman like that? Who could strike my dalagita sister? Why?

Karina and I light up over and over, send our smoke up to God like prayer.

"Where were you?" I say to the angels, "What happened to you?" I ask the women of the night. You are like my ináy, I think. Always say you're here. Always far away.

TWENTY-TWO

Lola Ani is the color of eggplant. She lies so still in her hospital bed I must press my ear to her chest and listen for a long time before I hear her heart. It is a faint and subtle thumping. And her breathing. Breathing so low I must hold my own breath still to feel the air moving through her frail body. When I place my hand on hers, she does not hold on, she does not move. She is so blue I think maybe it is the dim light of the room that colors her skin this way. The blue and purple bruises tumble across her arms, her chest, her forehead, and legs.

At first Lola Ani is all I see. It takes me a moment to hear Lila weeping in the corner of the room. Her cry is soft and low and constant like one of the machines that Lola Ani is hooked up to.

I whisper in Lola's ear. I sing a little song to her, the one she used to sing to me when I was little and too makulit to settle down and rest. It is a song about rice paddies and little girls and birds. Does she remember, I ask her. Does she hear me? I don't tell her what I'm really thinking: I should have been with them tonight, making my way to the house too. Friday night. I should have been with her and my little sister. Maybe then the boys wouldn't have bothered her. Maybe I could have fought back.

I won't leave you again, I tell her. I won't do that. I don't care what Ináy says. I don't care how disrespectful people think I am. I will not leave you again. I whisper so many prayers in Lola Ani's ear, I say them so fast, that I am sure she will think back on this night and swear to me that angels had come to her, had sung to her, had brought her to the very breath of God. And I will say, "It was me, Lola Ani, your apo. It was an angel, yes, but it was me, Angel de la Luna." I can already hear her laughing and telling me to be quiet, to take her seriously. "Totoó iyon," she'll say. "Maraming angels with beautiful voices and soft faces."

The tears are falling fast and they wet everything, make all the visions so blurry, make the blue and purple swirls on Lola Ani's skin shift and turn and seep into my own brown body. I don't notice that at some point, Lila has come to the bedside and collapsed right on top of me, holding me, weeping too, wetting my hair and shirt with her tears. We stay like that for a long time, the three of us lying one on top of the other, with Karina sitting in one of those hospital chairs, scribbling more revolutionary love poems onto paper towels.

Lila and I take turns giving Lola Ani baths, running cool washcloths over her face and her arms, washing her torso and her legs. We alternate bathing her and rubbing lotion into her skin—a fragrant mix of petals and oils from her garden. We have to be careful to work around the tubes they have placed in her nostrils, in the veins of her arms. We have to be careful to keep the needles in place, feeding her liquids, supporting her breath.

In the days to come, the room fills fast with garlands of sampaguita flowers. The sisters bring her fresh ones every day and hang the fragrant white blossoms on her bedposts and on her mirror; they string flowers from the ceilings and by the window. They bring a small statue of Mama Mary and adorn her holy hands with them.

At first, I refuse to look at Her, at her glass eyes and long lashes, at her hands folded neatly in prayer position. Because of You and Your God, I have lost everyone, I think. But as the days go by, and the sisters return hour after hour, I begin to wonder if maybe I made a mistake. If maybe I should have focused less on the movement and more on my family.

Each night a few of the nuns come by and together they pray the rosary. On Monday it is the Glorious Mysteries. During the Holy Marys I imagine Lola Ani opening her eyes and rising up out of her bed all fiery and full of commands. On Tuesday it is the Sorrowful Mysteries and I weep, thinking of the very worst thing that can happen to my family, to my beautiful Lola Ani. I decide to pray with them anyway. Just in case.

Sometimes I put my hands on either side of her face and hold them there as I gaze and I wish her eyes open. I treat her like she is already well. The doctors say that her body is strong, that her heart is beating steady, that all the tests say she is just fine. She just won't wake up.

"Maybe she needs to rest," Mother Mary told Lila and me on one of her daily visits. "We work her too hard."

Mother Mary is brilliant. She knows my lola so well, she knows what she has done every single day for the past twenty years. Yes, a sleeping vacation. A week of rest.

Billy Morgan comes to Lola Ani with a giant bouquet of red roses, with wild stems of grass poking between red petals. He sits in a corner of the room and he hardly speaks at all. He watches Lola Ani for hours, waiting for her to wake, to open her eyes, to speak. Once I glance over and find him making the sign of the cross, bowing his head and looking at his feet. When he leaves he tells Lila and me how much he respects our lola. "It's amazing how much she does for everyone," he says. "Don't worry, she'll come out of it." Lila tells him not to worry either, not to be sad. She reminds him how strong Lola Ani is and clever too. This is the first time I see Billy Morgan and I don't hate him, I don't think of imperial capitalist pigs, I don't see his three-quarter-white self or that browner version of him either. I just see Billy. When he leaves I let him embrace me and I thank him.

One night Lila and I stay awake, lying in Lola Ani's hospital bed, curling our arms and legs around her old bones, stroking her hair, whispering stories into the fine folds of her skin. It is the night we name the Mahalaya Sisters.

"They are freedom lovers," Lila says.

I brush the white strands of hair off of Lola Ani's forehead and I begin to recite the story she's told us so many times: The first Mahalaya was a fourteen-year-old held captive by the Japanese in a schoolhouse in Quezon. Japanese soldiers took her when she was walking home from school. Mahalaya's lola warned her to watch where she was going, to watch the trees around her, the sky and the road before her. "Dahan-dahan," her lola said. "The gera is near na. Watch where you are going."

But she was only fourteen and "gera" was just a word. So Mahalaya went paikot-ikot down the roads, following beautiful dragonflies into the fields, lying down under mango trees, and peeling the juicy fruit with her fingers. One day just as she was reaching for another mango, gunfire rained from the sky and a jeep of yellow men captured Mahalaya and took her to their camp. From then on, her days and nights were filled with terrible sounds—thunder so loud the earth shook and the skies filled with fire, bullets shooting into trees, and rocks falling like monsoon rain. And the worst of all was the constant scream of girls.

Every morning soldiers forced her to cook rice and fish and in the afternoon, they tossed her into one of the classrooms with several other young girls. Soldiers would enter the room and rape the girls. Ginagamit nila. Over and over they used them, until one day, Mahalaya could not take it anymore.

I stop speaking long enough to check Lola Ani's breathing. Long enough to put my hand over her chest and let it rest there to feel the subtle movement of her heart.

"What happens next?" Lila wants to know.

"You know what happens next."

"Of course I do, but you have to say it to Lola. Let her hear your voice so she can come back."

My hand feels hot and the palms tickle under Lola Ani's skin. I let my hands move and rest on her tummy, and I wait. I tell her that every day Mahalaya greeted the soldiers at the gate when they returned from a skirmish, and every day the last soldier would lock the doors and march ahead, but one day the last soldier was hurt and many others carried him in. Mahalaya held the door open for the soldiers and when they were not looking she snuck around the door and closed it quietly behind her. Then she ran to the mountains to find the Hukbalahap guerilla soldiers.

When she found them, she told them about her horrible experiences, how there were other girls locked in the schoolhouse. Ginagamit nila araw-araw. Every day, the soldiers used the girls like bathrooms, relieving themselves whenever they felt like it. The guerillas were so angry they nearly stormed the camp. But Mahalaya told them to wait, to be watchful and to attack only when the Japanese guard was down.

"Paano iyon?" demanded a guerilla fighter. "How are we going to know when their guard is down?"

"Ako na," Mahalaya said. "I can wait in the trees by the schoolyard gates. I know those trees. I can watch for you and when it's safe, I'll whistle for you, I'll call you."

They thought she was too young, too small, too much. But she gave them a look that scared them and they knew she too was a guerilla, a fighter.

As I talk, my hands get so hot on Lola Ani's belly that I almost pull them away, but I wait until the heat subsides. I get up from the bed and I stand over her pelvis, placing my palms on her hipbones, bones that jut from her frame and are hot to the touch. I let my hands rest there and soon they guide me to her legs, her knees, to the bottoms of her feet.

"Her face too," Lila says. "Put your hands on the bruises here, on her eyes." I move to the top of my lola's head, and I cup my hands and curl my fingers as I place them gently on her. There is such a buzz vibrating in my own skin, I nearly jump. It feels as though her eyes are breathing.

When I'm done, I run my hands along her body and push away all sickness, all the bad dreams. I chant the Hail Mary, the Glory Be, the Our Father. I make the sign of the cross and I remove my hands.

"You see," I say as we watch her sleeping figure. "Nothing. I told you it was just a silly game."

TWENTY-THREE

I am surrounded by Papang's drums, all of them stacked and spread about me like a silver cityscape. I light a cigarette and hang it from the corner of my mouth. I think of my mother and I want to explode. I see Lola Ani lying in her hospital bed and I want to hit someone. If only I truly was a hilot. If only I could do it. I would. I open my mouth and hot flames of wind shoot out of me. No words. I puff on the cigarette and trails of smoke float to the rising half-moon.

Words, like little grains of uncooked rice rattling in a tin can, tumble inside me. Through the sticks, I tell myself, through the sticks. Let the words vibrate through the skins, I say, through the skins. Syllables escape. Words release themselves in hiccups, in beats—staccato, syncopated, long and short, quarter, half, sixteenth beats with spaces in between for silence. With silence. It is in the beat. Silence. It is in the knock knock knock at the center of my chest.

I roll my sticks across the skins of all the drums. I bang the drum. I bang the drum. My words fall out of me loud and clear in Tagalog. In Ilokano. And if you've forgotten the mother tongue then hear the words in your precious English, Ináy! I kick the bass drum. I kick the bass drum.

Ináy shows up even with my eyes closed, staring at me with those big brown eyes, smiling like she thinks my anger is funny. Says she loves me. I bang the tom-tom. Says everything she does is because she loves me. Boom bang pop. Where is she now? Lola Ani's dying.

Where are you now?

Boom bang pop. Ano ba iyon, anyhow? I kick the bass and it booms louder than my heart. I pound on one drum with two sticks. Bang, bang, bang. I pound with two sticks on two drums.

I kick the bass drum. I kick the bass drum. Now my eyes pop. Now my tears fall. I kick the bass drum. Bam, bam, bam! MAKIBAKA! I hit the drums. MAKIBAKA! I clash the cymbals. HUWÁG MATAKOT! HUWÁG MATAKOT!

For a second I let the light from the sky in, I open my eyes, but only for a flash, and I see my mother standing right in front of me, weeping, watching, reaching out her hands to me, and I hold the sticks up like she's the biggest drum of all, like rolling sticks on her skin would somehow make her understand.

But then I remember who I am and I smash the cymbal instead, I pound the tom-tom, I kick the bass drum. I kick the bass drum.

TWENTY-FOUR

Lila and I have fallen asleep, tucked like two little eggs in the nest of Lola Ani's body. We have grown used to the smell of her perspiration, faint and milky like old people, to the flow of her breath and the soft way her small body moves. We don't hear her stir. We don't feel her hands on us, rubbing our backs, pushing the hair out of our faces. We are too tired to open our eyes. We assume we are taking care of each other, Lila and I. We assume that the other has gotten up out of bed to use the comfort room or to pour a glass of water for herself.

I dream about women perched on branches, their hair growing long and free like banyan trees, their eyes big and white like pearls in the dark. They sit without speaking. They hum soft like wind. On a branch, Lola, Lila, and I watch our mother in a house of red, white, and blue. Lila climbs down from the tree, reaches out to my mother who is bent over a desk and writing a long letter, but Lola Ani snatches her back by unraveling a tongue, long and skinny and sticky. A tongue that snaps from her mouth and wraps around my sister's waist, reeling her back to the tree. When Lila tries again, long black strands of hair bind her ankles, her wrists, her waist, hold her down. Meanwhile, Ináy moves about free and unencumbered.

When I finally wake, Lola Ani is sitting up, hair combed, face slightly swollen from two weeks' sleep.

"How long have we been sleeping?" she wants to know.

"Not we, Lola Ani," I say. "You."

Lila stirs, mewing when she realizes, weeping openly as she wraps her arms about Lola Ani. The two are nearly the same size now. Little people with years between them. "Akala ko tapos na," she says. I pinch her underneath her skirt.

"She doesn't mean that," I say. "She's so stupid sometimes."

And here Lila and I work our way into a fight, a meaningless exchange that has us so lost we don't see Lola slip back into a deep sleep and when we finally do, we scream.

"Please girls," she tells us. "Wag kayo mga ingay, ha? It hurts to hear you fight."

So I pinch Lila and she flies right out of the room.

We have to sell the house to pay the hospital. Mother Mary takes care of it. We sell other things too—the pots and pans, plates and saucers, the statues of Mama Mary and Joseph and Baby Jesus. We sell our ináy's rice paper screen and her two stools for healing and all the sala furniture. We sell our papang's clothing, his shoes, and all my mother's silverware. The drum set we keep.

We take the cash and hand the pera to Mother Mary, who gives it to the hospital.

"You girls can move in with me," she says. "After all, we are family. Ani is my ate and it's no problem."

Something is wrong, because Lola Ani is here, and her body is getting stronger, but her mind is weaker than before. Her memory scatters everywhere like ashes from fire and her conversations are often incomplete. I try talking to her, holding her hand and singing to her, but sometimes it's like she doesn't hear me.

The next time my mother calls I tell her to come home. "Hindî ko na po kaya," I tell her. It's too hard. Even I can no longer deny it—I need my mother.

She tells me she can't. "Who knows what might happen if I go back there? Maybe I'll lose my job. So you be the one, anak. Since I cannot be there, you be the one to take care of Lola."

Take a deep breath. Hold it. Let it go. Pintig. Has she no memory? Pintig. Who does she think pulled her down from the sky when she was hovering over us? I tell myself, Close your eyes. Forget her. Pintig. Listen to your own heart, small and wrinkled like old ginger. It beats quick and shallow, fast like a drumroll. Breathe deeply. Hear the song. Pintig. Pintig. Pintig. You set the beat. Slow down.

I can feel my papang's hand on my back and his love filling up the room. Woosh go the monitors in her room. Buzz buzz hum, spit the lights up above. Honk the horns out the window. Zoom the trucks down below. It is that music again, it is that love. Finally I can see myself nursing Lola back to health, my heart blowing up big, the light growing brighter, the beating steady and hip and now. I see Lola Ani's beautiful brown skin breathing and I am fine.

At Mother Mary's, Lola Ani, Lila, and I share one room like we always have. Lila continues to go to school in the mornings and to come home to wash floors and linens and holy undergarments in the afternoons. I have stopped going to school because Lola Ani cannot take care of herself.

In the mornings I am the one who rises before the light to fry eggs, garlic rice, and milkfish. I slice mangoes and papaya, break open atis palms and lay them on the table. I squeeze the juice of a dozen little green calamansi over a fork, catching the seeds to make a cool lemonade for the Sisters' breakfast. And when Lola Ani rings the tiny bell at her bedside, I am the one to run up the stairs and pull my grandmother's white diapers off of her, replacing them with something dry and clean. I lift her from the bed and help her to the comfort room, where I take a wet sponge to bathe the night sweat from her skin. I powder her. I comb her hair. I lay my hands on her every day and I ask God to make it true, to let my palms heat her skin and move the energy throughout her body. Sometimes I crawl into her bed with her and run my hands through her hair, away from her face, the way she does for me when I am feverish. I sing her songs. When she's hungry, I spoon lugaw into her mouth, cut bananas into small pieces, and feed her the way I'm sure she once fed me.

By the time her breakfast is over, it is time for me to cook the Sisters' lunch. Here is where I learn to be creative, stewing chicken adobo and sautéing eggplant and okra, kangkong leaves and kamatis. If Lola Ani naps all afternoon, I steam a leche flan or grate cassava and coconut to stir into my bibingka batter and I bake sweet cassava cakes for the house.

I grow quiet. I do not think of the movement. I do not think of Estrada or Karina or Mother Mary. I forget about my mother in America and my father, who I am sure is still with me, just a little more preoccupied than when he first crossed over. I slowly forget the definitions in my textbooks, letting them go, thinking that protests and marches and changing the world is a luxury meant for the rich. When Mother Mary urges me to leave the house, to visit the activists even for just a little while, I tell her I cannot. "Lola Ani needs me," I say.

"But this is the most exciting time," Mother Mary says. "We are planning to oust Estrada and the senators are talking impeachment! Go. I will watch her for awhile." But I know Mother Mary cannot lift my lola, cannot even understand her, for her words have collapsed one on top of the other, and sometimes she swallows her vowels or chokes on her consonants and this, I know, embarrasses her. I even refuse to shop for Christmas gifts. "I don't need to buy gifts," I tell her. "Is it not enough that I am here? That's my regalo, huh? Merry Christmas!"

Instead, I wait for Lola Ani to wake from her nap and then I help her stretch her arms and move her legs. I lift each limb and rotate it left and right. Together she and I bend her legs and arms. I bring her oranges to squeeze. We scrunch up our faces tight then open our eyes wide, letting our jaws expand big as the room.

Sometimes we just breathe and let the air travel in and out of us. That's an exercise to get her to sigh, to get her to let go.

Between the chores, I sit with my lola and I watch noonday game shows and telenovelas, and when she asks me to, I pray with her. I pull out our rosaries and I kneel. The Resurrection, the Ascension, the Descent of the Holy Spirit, the Assumption, and my personal favorite, the Fifth Glorious Mystery, Women Crowned Queen of Heaven. I like the idea of all that glory filling up our room.

Lila is such a good girl and I never have to tell her anything. She does everything without question. Sometimes when I am in a nasty mood, I snap at her and all she does is say "Opo" as if I am the adult. As if I have any answers at all. I watch her grow and think that it is my mother's loss not to see Lila's body changing, her baby fat disappearing, revealing her true face. When she gets her period, I am the one who shows her the napkins and how to wear them. I warn her about cramps and mood swings. I tell her hot water bottles are just as good as a hilot's hot hands. And boys are delikado. I say, "Pay attention to Mother Mary's Sex Ed class, huh? We cannot afford another de la Luna."

One day I am running to the kitchen to get some water, and in the dark hallway, I see Lila bent over a pail, with her two arms stretched onto the cement floor, hair falling in disarray. She breathes with each stroke, grunting ever so slightly. It is the hush hush hush of the scrubbing that makes me stop. Her silhouette is so small and dark at the end of that long corridor.

We live like this for a few months. Lola Ani recuperates, and soon she ambles about, pushing her walker, clutching the metal frame, her feet lifting as her arms pull her forward. Her words come together now and her voice sings, but her spirit worries me. Those thieves stole all her energy. And one day, she pulls on my sleeve and reminds me tomorrow is the day we commemorate the anniversary of Papang's death.

TWENTY-FIVE

Lola Ani and I sit in front of the small black-and-white television and watch her favorite game show. The contestants are given a choice—the money or the prize? A housewife from Pampanga has just picked a small parcel of cash over a new house.

"What do you think of that, La?"

Lola stares at the moving images on the screen and then says, "Anak, these are just distractions. So we don't have to think."

She's holding a picture of herself and Lolo. It's a candid photo of them dancing at a barrio fiesta. He is young, with wavy black hair and dimples deep and devastating. "The only thing worth getting crazy over is something you cannot buy," she says, putting the photo into her duster pocket. "Learn to be patient with your ináy," she tells me. "You are the reason she works so hard."

I take hold of Lola's hands and I look right into her eyes. They have lost their dark brown and have faded into rings of light blue and gray. We breathe. We smile at one another and I know she is the only one who really understands. I rub her hands. They are soft. They are cloaked in wrinkles. I give her a kiss.

The audience on television cheers the next contestant onto the stage and we turn our heads and watch a little while. Everyone on the game show is so happy they cannot sit still: their arms flop around loose and wild.

If everything is perfect, then why is Lola Ani sitting in this room all day? Why have I stopped going to school? Why is my little sister afraid to ride the trains and jeepneys? Where is my mother? There is so much noise coming from the television, competing with the traffic outside our window.

"La," I say, "aren't you mad at those boys? Look what they did to you."

"Everybody's life is hard. Pray for their souls, anak. Sana you learn compassion."

"What good is prayer?"

Her face changes. Her eyes shut. She takes a breath and I can feel the sadness. I wait for her to reprimand me. I wait for her to tell me what she is really thinking. To lose her self-control. Finally. But instead she leans into my ear and sniffs my skin and says, "Naku, what trouble lives inside this angel of mine."

As she speaks, the game show fades away and images of the protests down Commonwealth Avenue flash before us. I see the placards rising high above the masses. I hear voices singing in the wind. My heart jumpstarts just a little.

"Look at that," my lola says. "Sana nandoon ka. Why aren't you with them? Look! There are girls from St. M's!" She points

153

her crooked finger at the screen, her whole hand shaking, the blue veins popping out. "That is your life now. You should be there."

But I tell her no, my life is here, with her. I change the channel only to see senators impeaching President Estrada. I lean over to make the sound louder. Then several senators walk out of the chambers—like a protest! The cameras flash as they walk down the corridor and everyone seems to be shouting at them. It's hard to make out what is going on. Then the camera cuts back to the streets, to the masses gathering and waiting to march. My phone beeps. The light flashes.

"Sino ba yan?" Lola asks.

"Karina."

"She's texting you, ha? Go!"

Lola Ani doesn't understand that when Lila texted me the night of the robbery, I made a promise to myself. I swore I would not be my mother, that I would not leave my family anymore. What was I doing out so late, anyway? Why couldn't I take them home before doing my work? But right now Lola Ani grabs my hand and squeezes it hard. And when I don't respond, she pinches me as if I have been a bad girl.

There is so much fire in her eyes, such anger in her voice, that I have no choice but to let her words in, to hear them once and for all. It is only the second time she has been this mad with me in my whole life, only the second time I fear her.

"When this Mahalaya of yours escapes the garrison, what does she do?"

"Finds the Hukbalahap," I answer. And then I say, "You heard us talking in your sleep?"

"I heard everything, anak." Then she waves her hand and says, "And then she let the guerillas take care of the rest and went home?"

"You know she didn't, La. You said you heard everything."

"Oo ngâ," she says nodding, "She didn't go home to her mommy and daddy, she stayed and helped the community. She risked her life to save the other women. Delikado iyon. Siguro, her family wanted her home."

We watch one another, examining each other's faces, the changes and the things that remain. I am a mirror of Lola Ani's younger self—the same heart-shaped face, the wide eyes and the flat little nose. The same unruly head of curls. But she is old and everything about her face shows it now. This is me, I think. She is me.

"A person has to be true to her nature," she says. "And we do what we can, but we do not give up our nature. Otherwise, why are we here?"

The crowd on the television is shouting now, moving like a wave in the ocean. I see the colors of the Philippine flag, flecks of red and yellow and blue shimmering in the masses. Even in the distance, the chant syncs with the beating of my heart. Lola Ani bangs her walking cane to the beat of the chant. I tap my fingers to its rhythm, I move my foot to that beat. I feel my insides opening up and melting. What is my true nature?

TWENTY-SIX

On the anniversary of my papang's death, I revolt.

We march through the streets of Metro Manila, fighting the globalization of the Philippines. I wrap a scarf around my head and twist its cotton strands around my neck like a third-world Muslim princess. I dance among the people, waving my arms as I call to them, spitting rebel chants into a bullhorn. Karina directs the traffic of resisters with her whole body. Her arms wave in two directions, her head tilts left and right. She calls the people to chant with a voice hoarse from two days of marching.

NASAAN ANG MGA BATA?

THE CHILDREN ARE IN THE STREETS!

The sun is not even an hour old and still she blasts us with unbearable heat. We squint, see the world through pinhole eyes, a view focused so far into the future we welcome the heat like a fever that burns the illness away. The protesters line up for miles, one hundred in a row.

Karina rears her whole body back, her chest opening up to the sky, her head falling backwards. She closes her eyes, holds her hands to her mouth, and sings out with all her heart.

ANONG GINAGAWA?

Overhead, the helicopters hover like dragonflies, their engines drone in and out of range, nearly drown our voices out.

My father would have wanted me in school today. He would have wanted me sitting in the benches of the cool marble house of God, dispatching prayers, not protest songs. But I cannot sit still. I raise my fist to God and yell, MAKIBAKA! Fearless, the crowd rallies and shouts back, HUWÁG MATAKOT! I sway my hips to the beat of the march. I throw my hands up in the air like I am dancing, the bullhorn dangling around my torso like a purse. We are going to oust Estrada's corrupt soul!

A band of farmers gather round a steel-string guitar, a set of bongos, and a bullhorn. They sing a folk song into the bullhorn. Out-of-tune strings vibrate awkwardly. The farmers sing about the crops they used to plant, the land that used to feed them, the military settling down among them. Where are you, Erap, they want to know. Where are you now? The crowd cheers, and their applause resounds like a herd of carabao marching down Epifanio de los Santos Avenue.

ANONG GINAGAWA?

LUMALABAN!

The pulis line the boulevard on either side of us. They stand at attention with their shields held up across their chests, protecting them from our words. They shield themselves with face guards and helmets, staring down at us as if they are somehow superior. But I think they're scared. I think they're ashamed. From the streets I can see billy clubs hanging from their belts. Bullies. Mama's boys.

Each time I call and the people shout back, my heart surges with their energy. I fly. I respond even louder, "ANONG GINAGAWA?"

FIGHTING! FIGHTING!

The revolution explodes from the fifth chamber of my heart. Vibrates out of me. Fills sky with hope. We shout. People look out their windows. Climb down their steps. Join us. Resisters carry hand-painted banners the length of four car lanes, wave flags with eight sunbeams and a ball of fire bursting from its stitches. Last night, the cardinal told the people, "Go to EDSA. Stay at EDSA. Keep watch and pray. God is in this place. This is a holy place." And so the sun has come out to guide the masses.

On this day, the anniversary of my papang's death, I march. I think about the way his van was drenched in rain, racing up the mountainside. I see it shifting, sliding, diving to the earth like a little boy's toy. Today, I let the voices of the people rise and I hear foreign noise, the loud Americans, calling out perverse jokes to my Papang who was only minding his own business. Today the sun is so bright, the sky so clear. No rain in sight. No rain.

NASAN ANG MGA BATA?

That night, the rain, the wipers, the roll of thunder blurred the road, made everything dark, save for the shooting lights from an oncoming truck. Who could see in that night? Who would know? I no longer fight the visions of that night—do not resist the Hollywood director calling out, "Watch out, man!" while his arm reaches for Papang's sleeve, yanks the wheel from his hand. I surrender to the tires swerving left instead of right, the van shooting down the ravine as lightning dashes across the mountain peaks. Where are the children, my father cries, wanting to see us one last time. Where are the children? Sparks blow into flames, explodes in the van, and that nightmare that I have every day is an image I am finally going to confront. I am in the streets. I am fighting. What if foreigners stayed away? What if we did not need them to make ends meet? What if the answer to poverty was not to run away, but to stay? Where are you, Papang? Where is my mother now? A thick leather skin stretches across the landscape of my heart. What if the president did not sell our treasures to the world and pocket all the profit?

WHERE ARE THE CHILDREN?

I release the noise inside me. I hear Papang calling from the other side, naming each of us—Ináy and Lila and Lola Ani and me. Today I march among the workers, the farmers, and the teachers, and I revolt against corruption, I cast spells against the whole world stealing all our treasures.

ANONG GINAGAWA?

The crowd's energy swells. We get closer to the EDSA Shrine. If the people had the power from the start, we might not be here today. My fist rises up over and over. The tendons of my arms ache. My feet swell with each mile. My voice weakens but the words burst forth nonetheless. Our voices rise in unison, in solidarity, rise from the earth, so loud, so strong, not even God ignores us.

And that's when we hear the marching from both ends of the street. That's when the helicopters appear in the sky, so low to the ground that they make the wind blow above us. The flags whip with the wind. Our clothing lifts. Our hair flies everywhere. Pintig. Pintig. It is as if we are trying to fly. As if wings on our backs are flapping madly. I bang the drum. Pintig. I bang the drum. Pintig. The people spit words at the sky. I bang the drum.

In this moment, there is no time to think. Only to act. I bang the drum.

Everybody scrambles to their posts, holds up their signs. I grab my drums and Papang's two sticks and I begin to call out our hearts' desires with each strike to the drum skin. "HUWÁG MATAKOT!"

It's like the skies have filled with dark clouds and a storm erupts in the streets, in the skies, in all of Manila as the people call and respond to one another.

Cell phones buzz with text messages like bees charging from their nest. More people come to the streets. We swarm around the palace and I feel the crowd growing, standing at attention, drawing a collective breath. And just when we raise our fists to charge and my drums go boom and boom and pa pa pa boom, I realize that we are shouting together, "MAKIBAKA!"

"HUWÁG MATAKOT!"

The pulis infiltrate the lines. I soar through the crowds like a seven-winged angel. I buzz. I push my body between them. Interfere. Red. Orange. Yellow flames. The pulis lift their masks. Reveal wide smiles and handsome jaws. Billy clubs drop. Wrap free arms around workers, farmers, comfort women. Fists fly in the air, but not to attack.

The pulis grab our hands and our banners and they lift our arms up and push the banners higher to the sky. They are not arresting us. They are not taking us down. Oh, my God, they are joining us!

CHICAGO, 2002

TWENTY-SEVEN

I am rising off the ground, watching Las Islas Pilipinas dissolve into the sea. We fly so high we tunnel through clouds and burst into the infinite blue. I have never left the island of Luzon, much less the country. Papang's drumsticks, worn and scarred, rattle in my hands, roll with the motion of the flight taking off. My heart beats irregularly, stops and starts and shoots right down to the bottom of my seat. I throw up three times. I curl into a little ball, sweat matting my hair, blankets covering my body. What kind of hell is this? There is no air here. There is only the stench of someone else's breath. Like an old man's belch. Like a toddler's wet diaper. No air for breathing.

I am surrounded by so many other Pinoy. It is the one thing that comforts me, the sound of their voices, the soft cadence of their banter.

I finger the wood of the drum sticks, feel the imprint of each mark. I close my eyes so I can hear better. I breathe to relax. But my stomach swirls, wants to spill all over the small space at my feet. The plane travels twenty hours and in my ear drones a swarm of mosquitoes hungry for blood.

When my sister and I said good-bye at Manila International Airport, we embraced for almost ten minutes. The scent of Lila's fruity shampoo and the dusting of baby powder rubbed onto my clothing. I felt her breathing. We fit together like that for so long, Lola Ani had to pull us apart.

"You don't worry about us," Lila said. "I'm not a baby. I can take care of Lola Ani. She can take care of me."

But all I did was weep and think that every night since her birth she and I and Lola Ani have slept in the same room, sometimes in the same bed. "This is not my choice," I said.

And I can't believe what she said next. "I know. Just like it was not Ináy's choice to leave us. You have to."

When the plane gets to America, it hovers over the city of Chicago for almost an hour. Below us the storm swirls, but up here, all I see are light and blue sky. When the plane descends through streaks of sunlight, this plane shakes like it's going to explode. The sky goes black. It feels like we are tumbling to the ground. The engines grind like teeth chattering. Strange sounds knock at my feet, pound on the sides of the plane, and I imagine angels are trying to get in from the storm. I ask God why I have been stolen away like this. Why didn't he leave me in the Philippines?

The plane hits the ground wheels first, and in the windows I see streaks of water freezing in midair. I see nothing but white wind, white skies, white land. White dust covers the trees and all the buildings. Winds howl and compete with the engines.

"Ladies and gentlemen," says the flight attendant over the speakers, "welcome to America."

TWENTY-EIGHT

Inside O'Hare Airport I wait for hours. The officials examine every single object, rummaging through my clothes and tossing everything out of place. Nobody smiles. Nobody apologizes for the mess they make. This is it? I think. This is the way people are welcomed to America? To hell with America.

When my things are finally released, I do my best to repack the balikbayan boxes, stacking them onto a huge cart and wheeling them down long corridors. As I push through glass doors, I scan the crowd, looking for my mother in a sea of foreigners. Everyone is so much taller than me, hidden underneath heavy sweaters and thick jackets—I cannot make out the shapes of faces or bodies. A harsh, cold air whips throughout the area. I bump into several Americans who toss me dirty looks. My boxes are toppling over when I hear my name rising from the blur of voices. In the distance a tiny but loud group of people move toward me. I can tell from the voices they are Pinoy. A woman just younger than my mother walks toward me with one arm out and the other holding a boy on her hip. Behind her, Ináy looks so small and fat in her winter clothes. She is crying.

"Is that her, Tita?" says the woman with the baby. The boy leaps into my mother's arms. She lets go of the boy, who chases after her. Ináy embraces me, whispering so many things in my ear, but she is too close and the tears are so wet. I don't understand anything but my name. Suddenly, I'm reciting definitions in my head again, trying hard not to fall under her spell. I am still mad at her. I hate her. I think, *feudalism, proletarian internationalism, imperialism, bourgeois populism.* I let their meanings reverberate inside me: *feudalism, proletarian internationalism, imperialism, bourgeois populism.* But it's no use, her tears wash me. Her skin has been bathed in jasmine. And though her hands are cold, they are still my mother's hands. She runs them across my face and through my hair, threading each loose strand behind my ears, and the definitions disintegrate from words to letters, into black spots, into nothing and before I know it, I am crying too.

The other woman says, "Naku, dalaga na!" She gives me a kiss and says, "Angel? I'm your Ate Gina."

Her hair falls to her shoulders in large curls, tinted light brown and shiny. When she talks her red lips overtake her whole face. They're all I see.

An old man comes up from behind Ate Gina, lugging a giant plastic supot in his hand. Like Santa Claus he says, "Welcome to America!" Opening the bag, he pulls out a navy-blue-and-orange jacket—thick like a blanket, with a hood and fur around the edges. "You'll want to wear this, Angel. It's cold outside."

I look at my mother as she says, "You remember Manong Jack Montenegro?"

From inside his bag, he pulls thick socks, a scarf, and gloves without fingers. He also gives me a pair of rubber snow boots. "Bundle up, Angel," he says.

Ináy says, "Thank you, mahal." Naku, I think, ang friendly naman.

"Angel," my mother says. "This is Gina, Manong Jack's youngest daughter." She lifts the boy. "And this is Danny."

The baby smiles wide and kisses my mother all over her face with an open mouth. "Naku!" she says, "Ang sarap naman." She hands the boy to me and says, "Say 'hi' Danny. This is your Ate Angel."

Hmm, I think, so in America everyone is your sister, an ate, a cousin. Everyone is your tita, your ináy. Every old woman your lola. Is that how it is?

Everything is happening so fast. Before I know it, we are carting boxes outside and lifting them into the trunk of Manong Jack's Buick Electra. The wind fights us, hurling snow and ice into our faces, pushing our small bodies back as we struggle with the packages. My cheeks go numb with cold. I watch snowflakes, soft and delicate and too numerous to dismiss, traveling down from the sky, melting on my face and blurring everything. When I look at Ináy, I see her body has been dusted in snow like the trees and the buildings and the cars. Gina straps Danny into the car, where it is warm and the heater blasts so loud we have to shout to be heard.

I had forgotten that Manong Jack lived in Chicago too. I was surprised to see him, but happy to see a familiar face. Sitting in the backseat watching the world go white, I think about the weeks when he would come to our home in Manila, full of stories of America. He immigrated years ago, when Filipinas were not allowed to migrate, only men. Like Ináy, he left his family in Manila while he worked as a doorman at a fancy hotel. He worked years before he could bring his first son over, then his daughter, then another child, and finally, his wife. He left two more sons back home with his mother and father. Thirty years later, he went back to the Philippines, a widower with a weak heart. That's when his son brought him by and Ináy would hold up her hands like human stethoscopes, warming up his heart, healing every weak vein and artery.

"This is a special day for Milagros," Manong Jack says. "I won't ever forget when Gina arrived. I was so excited to see my blood, to show her everything, I didn't sleep for weeks."

"Oo ngâ," says Gina. "But I was lucky kasi I was the youngest, so my elder brother was here na. My kuya paved the way for me, helping Daddy work and save money for the rest of us. You're the one going to help your ináy."

And what have I been doing in the Philippines, I think. Wasn't that helping my ináy? What's so great about imperialist America?

"It's a special day," Ináy says. "Finally we're together again. Di ba, anak?"

When I don't respond she says, "Angel, o.k. ka ba diyan?"

I sniffle, wiping the tears away with the back of my sleeve. I push my hair into my face and I ask how far we have to go.

There is traffic here too, I think, wrapping the scarf tight around my neck. I stretch my fingers, feel them snug in the knitted glove. The roads are slippery and the Buick crawls, sometimes sliding a little left, a little right.

"Ano iyon?" I ask. "Why are we sliding?" The movement makes me think of my papang's van losing control and slipping down the mountain.

"Yelo," Ináy says.

"You have to be careful when you drive in blizzards," Manong Jack says. "The ice is so dangerous. But there's nothing I wouldn't do for your mother. After all she's done for me. Naku! It's the least I can do."

I see other cars stuck in little mountains of snow along the road. A giant truck swerves close to us and then slips the other way. I look out the front windshield and I cannot see the road, only the white. I look behind us. It is the same white fog in a white sky with a white flurry falling down on us. Danger everywhere.

"You know, Angel," Ináy says. "Nandito ang pamilya ni Billy Morgan nasa Riverdale sila. He's going to have his family invite us over."

"Oh, I know Billy Morgan," Gina says. "He's a good kid. He dated my daughter, Chelsea. You remember him, Daddy?"

"He's making a movie sa Pilipinas and Angel was his helper," my mother says. "Di ba, anak?"

I close my eyes and try to settle back into my seat. I dream of home. I think of riding in Billy's fifteen-passenger van, some pop station announcer shouting songs at us, the air conditioning blowing cold air onto our faces, the traffic crawling, and all the cars honking at once. There was always heat surrounding us. When I rolled my window down, Manila noise sailed into our van. I imagine the palengke on the side of the road. All its baskets of brightly colored fruit, of fish packed in ice, of green leaves of gulay displayed for shoppers.

I want to be home. I want to be in the sun. I want to be out of this car.

It takes me a long time to figure it out, nearly the whole ride, really. At first when they say that they all live in the same house, I think nothing of it. I think they mean Ate Gina, Danny, Manong Jack, and my mother, the boarder. I mean, this is bourgeois, capitalist America, di ba? How can she afford her own apartment? But as I listen to them talk, I watch the way Manong Jack glances at my mother, and the way Danny calls out to her. A slow burn makes my stomach rumble. Heat begins to flow in my veins. I am meeting my mother's American family.

I hear the drums inside me, the way it beats, pintig, pintig, pintig. When we pull up a driveway, and Ate Gina jumps out of the car, the heat in my belly is pushing so hard at my insides that I am ready to burst. She does not unbuckle the boy in the seat. She does not take him with her. "Give Ate a kiss," she says to him and he does. Oh, my God, I think. Who is he? Am I really his ate?

I pound on my knees, a rhythm that's fast and syncopated, one that has lots of rolls and beats that fly offbeat. Pintig. Pintig. Pintig. And when I can't take it anymore, I say, "What shall I call you po?" I watch Manong Jack's eyes in the rearview mirror. They light up and he says, "So you told her, mahal?"

I can see the profile of my mother's face and I watch the color drain. "Hindî pa," she says. "I haven't had a chance."

"Do you want me to call you Papang Jack or Daddy? Ano?" I ask. I hate my mother. My fingers tap lightly, close together and soft inside the mittens.

"Kahit ano," Manong Jack says. "We are all family. After I met your mother in the Philippines and she cured me, parang it was love that healed me. I couldn't believe it when she agreed to marry me. What does this beautiful lady see in an old man like me?"

"You're not so old," Ináy says. "He is only twelve years my senior. And still very gwapo."

Mostly I want to light up and smoke my way out of the car. How could she do this to me? How could she keep this from us?

"And Danny," I ask, "how old is my little brother?"

"Almost two na," says the old manong.

What? I focus on the windshield wipers, how they flip-flop across the window, softly beating pintig, pintig, pintig. How they thump on the downbeat like a breath, like a sigh. Pintig. Pintig. Pintig. I focus on the sound of the tires rolling on the icy road, the uneven flow of the wheels, the bumps on the road, how sometimes the rhythm skips and slides like a needle on a long-playing album. Pintig, pintig. I listen, and that is what I focus on. I lift the hood of my coat up over my ears, create a cave for myself, and I fall into the rhythm of my own breath, of my heart as it beats despite the howling of unnatural winds wailing under brilliant white skies.

TWENTY-NINE

In their house, she brings me to a room on the second floor with a giant bed the size of four of our cots back home. Manong Jack tosses my bags in a corner and, clapping, he says, "Welcome home, anak! Hope you don't mind sharing the room with Danny boy." He checks the windows and pulls the curtains shut. Then he says, "This way you keep the cold air out, huh? Tapos kung giginaw ka, may blanket dito." He points to a pile of quilts the color of sand.

Ináy hovers about me like a gnat circling sweet mangoes. She brings her hand up like she wants to touch me, but I scoot away from her. I sit at the edge of the bed and I drum on the tops of my legs, looking for a beat, a rhythm that Papang once taught me. I can hear it in my head, but I cannot seem to play it. I start, I stop, I tilt my head like all my thoughts will shift and make room for this beat. We sit like that for a long moment, the three of us. We listen to the wind whipping trees around, snapping branches and twigs. When I glance up, Manong Jack winks at me. "Bet you two have some catching up to do, huh?" He leaves us, closing the door behind him.

After he's gone, Ináy draws the drapes open and a hazy sun shatters the darkness in the room. A sharp whistle blows through barren tree branches, surging through a crack on the sill. There's a mirror the size of a large painting facing the bed. All this time without a mother and suddenly, she is everywhere—reflected in the mirror, in the windows, in the photos on the dresser. I take a breath, but cannot breathe.

"Alam ko na, anak," Ináy says.

I look at my feet. I drum on my thighs. When she moves to run her fingers through my hair, I go to the luggage on the floor and I wrestle with the zippers. The heaters rising from the floorboards hiss.

"I tried to tell you and your lola. I tried to write it," she says. Then she sniffs like she's feeling emotional. So plastic, I think. "Nakakahiya naman," she whispers and I almost want to believe her.

If you're so ashamed, I think, why did you do it? Why didn't you tell us? I peel the suitcase open, thumbing through T-shirts—purple and pink, yellow and red and bright orange bearing letters of resistance—*Makibaka* or *U.S. OUT!* or *Never Again*—each one scrawled wildly across the chest. I count three pairs of jeans. Panties. There's really nothing in here, but I continue to rummage. My stack of unopened letters nearly falls out of a pile of clothes. It's thick and bundled together with hemp.

"At first, I couldn't do it," Ináy says. "But then, what? Walang jobs. Walang trabaho. Even if I'm a nurse, they don't pay nurses sa Manila. We couldn't afford to keep you girls in school. And you and Lila working as maids—ang hirap naman iyon. What kind of life is that?"

She moves closer to me and I lean farther into the suitcase. "Jack's so nice naman. Mabuting tao talaga. He really does love me."

I don't look, but I can hear her crying. Why is she crying? She crouches down to the floor and places a hand on my shoulder, but of course, I pull away. Her touch feels like ice on my already cold skin. "So I married. Ito na. He's helping our family."

I count the T-shirts over and over, remember the different rallies—the ones before the U.S. Embassy, the Japanese Embassy, Malacañang Palace. So many memories. I finger the stack of letters, her words all gathered up and saved like money in a bank.

Her hair is short and wavy, with fine streaks of white. Her skin is soft around her eyes, soft around her mouth. Her body is fuller than the last time I saw her. The American Dream has made her fat. She is not as tall as I remember. She is still pretty. I pretend to focus on my hands, but I watch her anyway.

"Anak," she says, taking a step to me. "I hardly recognized you."

I say, "You got fat from the baby, older too." She stands there and she takes it, like she knows she deserves it. I think, Good.

"What was I going to do, anak? Tell me."

177

A respectful daughter would have answered her. A respectful daughter would have kissed her and said, "It's O.K., Ináy." A respectful daughter would have been grateful. And that is exactly what I would have done if I respected her. Instead, I pull the T-shirts from the suitcase and hold them to my face. They smell like Manila sun, like the wind in the courtyard where I hung them to dry. They feel hot like a good fight, like a march down EDSA Boulevard.

I fall asleep that night in the new bed, the boy nuzzling at my ear. We are under several layers of quilts and all night long the sound of the lake reaches me, knocks at our window, howls in winds so strong I fear the house may collapse. I try to stay awake, but my body feels heavy. Each finger weighs my arms down, each toe sinks into the bedding, my legs, my back, the crown of my head just melting into nothing until I am lost for days. The boy comes and goes, the sun shifts in and out of the windows. The song of the wind is constant. My mother comes to me, bringing me soup and rice, but I cannot shake the sleep long enough to eat. The old man sits at the end of the bed and watches me, but I am feeling so drugged I cannot tell him to go away. My body insists I sleep for three days.

The only spaces I move through are in my dreams. I feel like I have walked across Luzon and swum the distance between my seven thousand islands and the West Coast of the United States, and then walked the rest of the way to this little shaky house in the middle of America. I am in no shape to fight it. I sleep.

THIRTY

Sometimes snow finds its way into the house through cracks in the door. The floors are worn soft with footsteps. The heaters hiss steam into rooms, smell like water burning. It never gets hot enough for me. I feel ghosts among us. And I am one of them. I'm awake when the whole house sleeps. I have no words for these days. No words. I am here and not here.

If I am not at home, watching the boy, or doing laundry or cleaning the kitchen for my-mother-the-nurse, I am expected to attend class. Every day I walk to school in the rubber boots the old man gave me when I arrived. I wrap myself up and I listen to the weight of my body push against the snow, packing down the white powder.

In Chicago, the sky is a brittle sheet of ice floating to earth in shattered pieces. Unlike Manila, where the skies are moody with the hot and changing colors of the sun, and heavy soot and fog, Chicago skies are white on white. The streets are wide and orderly, but cold. The air, the people, the earth. Everything is so cold.

The rhythm of my footsteps echoes on sidewalks where ice cracks, on banks of crunchy snow, on rough cement. My breath escapes me, a spirit breaking free. The cold keeps me numb. Fat clouds sail above and I know they are messages from the other side of the world. I walk to school, a big four-story building with large gates and barbed-wire fences, with metal detectors that monitor students for firearms and knives.

This morning I listen to the traffic, feel the rhythm of the lights going yellow and red and green. I count the cars driving past. Wait for the lights to make everyone pause.

My body is not used to being packed like longganiza sausage, stuffed into tights, long underwear, and pants. Isang kamiseta, a shirt, a sweater, and then on top of that a sweatshirt and then a coat. Two pairs of socks. Gloves, then mittens. Ear muffs under knit caps and scarves. My arms cannot bend. My knees are stiff. I feel fat and immobile.

I wait for the lights to change and I watch the cars roll past me. Traffic always moves here, trucks and buses respectfully taking turns. So different than the chaos of home. I take a deep breath and the sharp pain of this below-zero-degree air pierces my nose, stabs the heart. This is the American Dream?

In school, I peel layers and stuff them into a metal locker with my textbooks. Here, we don't wear uniforms. Students dress for the mall, for the dance club, for Saturday night out. They walk around the halls like window-shoppers.

We don't go to mass every single day, or recite prayers as we walk from class to class. Instead they have bells that tell the students when to rise and when to sit. They have buzzers. Here, between classes there is joyous chaos.

And here, the boys. It is so strange being around boys all day. They are loud and talk without listening. They smell like old clothes ready for the wash. And what I can't get over is the way they are always holding onto girls, arms draped around their shoulders, fingers wrapped in the belt loops of their jeans or holding onto their painted hands. Walking down certain corridors, all you see are girls leaning on boys, nestling like bugs in dark cocoons, kissing boys two heads taller than them.

The first time, I refused to look and I focused on the red exit sign at the end of the tunnel of boys. But I could hear them pushing one another into lockers, joking around like they were at a ball game. At one point, I walked past a crowd so large I had to walk right through them. That's when I heard them whispering.

"Ah so, pretty girl, where you from?"

"She's a black China doll, man."

"No speak English?"

I couldn't get past their bodies, around their smell. I started to get dizzy looking for that red exit sign.

"Shut up, man. You guys are whacked," said a boy. An arm came down before me and shoved the bodies away, and when I looked up from my books, the boy was smiling, saying, "They're fools. Ignore them." The boy had the most beautiful face—round like a moon, and hairless. His dimples were deep and to look at him embarrassed me. Past his shoulder I could see the red light. I darted through the crowd and pushed through the heavy metal doors.

My teacher, Ms. Anderson, wears jeans and big sweaters and boots that make her six feet tall. Today she saunters into the classroom singing. Her earrings and heavy bracelets chime softly under her voice.

"How you all doin' today?" she asks, and everyone groans, something we'd never do back home.

Words travel fast here—so fast I cannot catch them. Not the sound of them and certainly not the meaning of them. Americans distort letters, drop consonants, add vowels, sometimes mix non-words in their sentences. Sometimes I recognize a sound, and I translate it in my head—English to Tagalog—and then I translate it back, but by the time I do, Ms. Anderson has moved on to ten thousand other words I cannot decipher. Isn't this English? Isn't this something I have been studying all my life? Why doesn't it sound like English?

Ms. Anderson spreads her long arms out and her sweater falls open like wings. "So, it's February. What do we celebrate in February?"

"Valentine's Day."

"Presidents' Day."

People Power One, I want to say, but I know that can't be right.

For every answer the students give, there is more whispering and joking that happens under each breath. I strain to hear, but not much makes sense to me. There is too much noise. Too much altering of words by the mouth.

The kids are even harder to understand than the adults. They speak under their breath. They slur words together like they are under some spell. They shorten them. But I know more or less what they speak of, because I can see it in the body. I can tell by the way their arms are moving, by the way a head sways, the way they saunter down the halls—who's friends with whom, who's cool and who's not. I can tell who is the one they hate, the one they wish they could be.

"Very funny," Ms. Anderson says, "You know what I mean." She puts her hands on her hips. She's so pretty, I think, not any older than Ate Rosalie. She doesn't look like a teacher.

"If you know we know what you mean, why ask?" says a boy sitting next to me. He is the boy from the halls, the one with dimples that crease when he smiles, the one with an easy walk.

"Oh, come on, Jordan," Ms. Anderson says, laughing. "Stop playing."

Jordan smiles like we've got a secret. He's too big for the desk, and his legs stretch far into the aisle, where his big feet float on air and his arms sprawl everywhere because he has nowhere to put them. He should sit up, I think.

And then a bunch of them say, "Black History Month!"

"Who wants to tell Angel what Black History Month is?"

And then all the kids talk at once, like I care about what they have to say. They fight to say it. They want to name it. Their faces go bright with meaning. Their shoulders fall back and their chests go broad. I hear the energy, the rhythm of the phrases, and the way they punch each syllable. I still don't understand, but I can feel it.

THIRTY-ONE

We turn away the winter light by shifting all the blinds shut. My class gathers round a big television monitor. Most of the students pile on top of each other like throw pillows. I sit at my desk in the back of the room and I watch. Ms. Anderson inserts a videotape into the machine and hits play. There is no color on the screen, only shades of black and white. The images blur, like they've been played so many times they're rubbing right off the video. Like memories, the figures are present but distorted.

There are lines of men in darks suits, white ties, and black, plastic-rimmed-glasses strolling down a wide avenue. There are women, but not many. It looks like they are on a Sunday afternoon stroll. What's different is the way the men's elbows clasp together and the way their fingers link like one long human chain. Hundreds of men walk and the sun is bright and raining down upon them in columns of light. Nobody smiles. Sometimes the camera shows the masses. Yes, I recognize that there are millions of people, tiny little images of thousands of people, walking. There are signs, but the signs are in the distance. For a minute, I think it may be a march, a demonstration, but the people are so finely dressed and their manner so peaceful. It is Sunday afternoon, I think, after mass.

But then he speaks. I don't know who he is, but he is handsome and well dressed and standing before a statue of Abraham Lincoln—that man I recognize—and behind him are several men in suits and hats, all standing before a big white statue of Lincoln sitting in an armchair. When the man speaks, I lean forward. Not to hear him, but to understand him.

He delivers words as if each one is a treasure. He speaks each syllable as if the letters hold a sacred power, as if gathering those words and giving them to these people will unleash an unimaginable freedom. I hold his words and let them travel, circling through my bloodstream, arranging and rearranging themselves like a thousand cells, feeding my core, touching the center of my heart. I don't understand everything—just enough. It is unclear to me where this is happening, and if it were not for the statue of Lincoln, I would have placed this moment in another country. So many black people. No others. Some white. Where is this? When is this happening, I wonder. Why are they discriminating against Negroes? I try to picture the people he speaks of, but I don't know. His words pulse, and even though he speaks slowly and calmly and even though the words come to me intermittently like half phrases on a shortwave radio, I recognize the feelings.

He declares war on injustice, on poverty, on discrimination. There is a nation mistreating its people and he is standing up to that nation. America? I know it treats third-world countries inhumanely, using and abusing us, but its own people? I'm not sure I understand.

His fire is so strong he doesn't have to shout. He doesn't have to use anger, though his words fall like heavy burdens of accusation. I know this talk. I know this heart. As he speaks, I am suddenly marching down EDSA Boulevard with my people, our arms raised and our voices loud. We bear signs. We do not walk calmly. We do not wear fine clothing. But we are marching and I know his words. I recognize them. Nobody should have to live this way. And even though the fight is new to me, I know this corridor of injustice. He says that one hundred years later, the Negro is still not free. How is that acceptable, I want to know. There is a story there and even without knowing, I know.

When the lights come back on, I am ready to raise my hand to ask where I sign up to join the next march, but Ms. Anderson speaks quickly, handing out copies of the speech.

"This is the historic 'I Have a Dream' speech that took place in August of 1963. How many of you have heard it before?" Almost everyone raises a hand. I sit alone in the back of the room. "How many of you think that Dr. King's dream has come true?"

That was Dr. King? The hands stay down. One hesitatingly wants to rise, but then falls back to the student's side.

"Dr. King may be talking about the whites and Negroes, but I hear him talking about all of us—whites, blacks, Asians, Native Americans, and Latinos. It's our obligation to make the dream come true." And when she gets to me, handing me the white paper with black words on it, she says, "So did you study our civil rights movement in the Philippines?"

I take the page and I start reading it and I think, CAPITULATIONISM: The tendency to surrender to the class enemy.

We barely covered our own history of resistance, I want to say. We barely know our own fight. When would we study yours? They never taught us this. I feel the tears welling up inside. I stare at the paper and see that Dr. King repeats himself so many times. Now is the time. I have a dream. Now is the time. I have a dream. I have a dream. I tell myself that I will read each word. Before the end of the week, I will know this story. Understand it with my whole body. I am learning fast that America is not the dream. It is not the dream. I have so much to learn.

THIRTY-TWO

Ináy is a figment moving through the house, leaving evidence of a life we are not witnesses to. I walk through the rooms and pick up after her—a hairbrush in the sala, a pair of slippers in the hallway, her half-finished cup of instant coffee, a dog-eared magazine lying in her favorite easy chair. It is as if I am just missing her, walking into spaces still warm with her breath. She leaves me notes and lists of things to do. When I discover them, I crumple them up, the anger rising from a place I cannot name. At least when she abandoned us for the States, we were able to set her memory aside and live a life without her. At least back then I found ways of forgetting. Now she has taken me from my life, dumped me in her house, and left me again. This was not the plan, I want to shout, but I can't talk to her for five minutes—let alone tell her what I'm thinking. She charges me with her child, who speaks half-words with her accent, who mimics her insane laugh. In this way, she is ever present and never here.

I place Danny before the TV screen, handing him a plastic cup filled with milk. Then I seat myself before the television to fold towels, warm from a machine, soft and fragrant. Sunlight heats up the room and reveals dust floating like snow. Danny shakes the cup and tosses it back at me like it's a game of catch. The lid flies off, spraying the wood floors.

"Danny!"

"You have to tighten the top before you give it to him," Manong Jack says as I grab a towel and wipe the floor dry.

"Opo," I say obediently.

The boy runs to the cup and tosses it at me again, and when I run after him, he squeals in delight, running around the room and climbing into a cabinet full of electrical cords, tape players, and machines. I drag him out of the cabinet and he runs in another direction, diving hands first into Ináy's plants and uprooting them. The boy gets dirt all over the front entrance. I squat to sweep the dirt away.

Ináy works from seven at night to seven in the morning. I'm in the shower when she gets home from work. I'm out the door as she collapses into her bed. Maybe she looks up from her cooking when I come home from school, but often she is too preoccupied to notice me, to talk to me, to say, "How do you like your new school, anak? Have you made any friends?" By five-thirty she is out the door, walking back to the elevated train.

I feel like I have left Manila to be a maid in the first world, a yaya who runs after the child and raises him until he is old enough to care for himself. I am not the daughter. I'm not the one living the dream. It is a nightmare.

I grab the boy and set him on my lap, hold him tight to settle him down. He smells of sour milk, of baby powder. He smells of my mother.

"Look," I whisper, drumming on the tops of my legs with his. "Play the drums," I say. "Play the drums." He laughs again, this time settling back against my chest.

"Naku," says Manong Jack, "I'm too old for this."

I struggle with Danny, his squat legs kicking in the air. The old man rests his hand on Danny's leg and, leaning over, he kisses it.

I would run away, except that I am in a foreign country where everything is the opposite of what I know. When I look out the window and see the hot sun burning on a bank of white snow, I expect the sun to warm my skin. I step out the door and the wind is so cold it freezes my lashes together, burns my cheeks cold and red. I look at my mother and I see a stranger. I see a strange boy and he is my brother. I would run away, but where would I go? How would I do it?

I pretend to be watching the television. "Do you like being here," Manong Jack asks me. "Being in America?" I pretend he is not talking to me.

Danny stands on my legs, locking his arms around my neck. He presses his nose against mine. "Danny," I say. "Sit still."

"I hated it at first," Manong Jack says. "Americans can be so arrogant. Think they're so much smarter than you. Son of a gun, they think we want to be like them. Naku! Can you believe it?"

His stories fill the air, but they do not land anywhere near me, they do not plant seeds of thought or feeling inside me.

America has stolen my mother. Now, I'm living in her house, but she is never here. What kind of shit dream is this?

"Danny!" I shout, and just as I am ready to spank him, he opens his mouth and kisses my face. "Stop it!" I yell.

The old man doesn't say anything for a long time. I watch the boy's hands and my heart aches.

Manong Jack says, "Every night I hear you." He watches the boy as he describes the silence in the house, the sounds he hears when he's waiting for my mother to return—the hum of the computer, the heaters hissing, screen door rattling, and my cries. At exactly midnight, every night, he hears me mewing like a cat, the sound flowing through the vents. "I worry about your mother," he says. "Now I worry about you. You have nightmares?"

I don't tell him that when I sleep I travel to the other side of the world and I sit in the trees, hovering over my Lola Ani and my sister as they go about their days, moving among the masses from the convent to our little house in our city barangay, riding two jeepneys and an LRT in the middle of rainy season, in the heat of the summer and in the dead of a moonless night. In my dreams I step before them when they are crossing the streets. I keep a hand on their backs and I guide them through the crowds. But at night, I have a hard time seeing them, especially when the moon has yet to rise. Every night I witness Lola Ani and Lila walking to the jeepney stop, stepping around potholes, scurrying fast between the light, and the thieves are about to descend on them and I am ten blocks away, close enough to see them, but too far away to stop their thug bodies. The thieves jump my grandmother and sister all over again. Night after night, they hold the blade of a sharp knife at the thickest artery of their throats. They toss my family about like vegetables in an old frying pan and all I can do is watch, is scream. Is wake up and see that I am much farther away than ten city blocks.

This dream returns with such regularity even Danny, who sleeps at my side, has come to expect it. I wake with a start to find my eyes wet, my throat sore, and Danny holding on to my face with his small hands. "Ate, o.k.?" he asks me every night. "Ate, o.k.?" Midnight here is noonday there, and when the clocks between the oceans strike, I am the alarm, I am the cry, the one who says, "Wake up, there is danger over there." I fly the same path, hover and watch, slip like a shadow, and when the moon fails to rise and the thieves make their move, I wake tired, dreamless, angry.

But I say to the old man, "Who will watch over Lola and my sister?" The sadness escapes before I can stop it. I don't want him to know.

"Don't you worry," he says, laughing. "You'll see, it's going to all work out."

Danny squirms in my arms, calls me in such a baby voice, "Ate! Ate!"

And then the old man asks me, "Why are you so angry with that boy?"

That night, I look up the words *emancipation*, *manacles*, and *the fierce urgency of now*. I study the shape of them, the sound of them. I look at the construction of each word. I try to use them in a sentence. I look up the phrases *words of interposition* and *invigorating autumn of freedom* and *tranquilizing drug of gradualism.* My finger grazes each line and I read them out loud. They feel bulky in my mouth. They feel unnatural. I furrow my brows. *America has given the Negro people a bad check.* My heart is beating so loud it feels as though I have pulled it from my body and placed it on the table next to me. I look up the word *Negro.*

Ms. Anderson has asked us to study the speech and answer the question: Dr. King's dream is deeply rooted in the American Dream. What is the difference between Dr. King's dream and the American Dream? Can you define yours? Is it the same as the Dream?

The words rattle inside me and I do not know how to arrange them. I do not dare. They feel charged like bullets. I don't know who to aim them at. I spin a pen above the page. I stop. Reread the words. They make little sense to me. But they feel familiar. I cannot explain it. After an hour, I give up.

Next to my desk, Danny lies in bed, whimpering softly. He burrows under layers of blankets. Behind him, the large window frames the full moon. It seems so faraway, that moon. So small. Write about my dream. I know what the dream is not. My dream is not living with my mother's replacement family. It is not giving up the revolution for this so-called better life. This is not the dream.

Danny shivers and kicks hard into the mattress. I crawl to him and watch the way he sleeps. He looks just like me at two—

all that curly hair, those cheeks fat and ruddy as plums, and skin the color of earth. I run my hands over his forehead. He's twisting about and whimpering just soft enough to let me know: his is a bad dream. I put my ear to his mouth. Yes, he is calling ever so softly for Ináy.

"She's at work," I whisper. "She's at work." She is always at work. I hold my hand to his heart. I keep it there. I wait for him to settle down, to sigh, and find his way to peace.

THIRTY-THREE

I run down the stairs, dragging my hand along the wall, sliding into the kitchen where I find my mother asleep at the table. She is slumped onto her side, leaning on her arm. Moonlight kisses her. In my place, a plate of rice, eggs, and corned beef waits for me. I look at her and then the stove. The frying pan is still popping with grease. She wears scrubs from the night shift. What's gotten into her, I think. I sit before the food and I spoon the rice and eggs into my mouth. The food has grown cold, but the taste of garlic is so good. I hear her stirring next to me, but I ignore her. When I look up at the clock, she is watching me. "Alam ko, anak," she says. "But you must try and forgive me."

I stare at my plate. I think about the flavor of the corned beef and onions. How the soft tomatoes make the meat moist and tasty. I keep eating.

"Manong Jack is a good man. He is not your Papang, but he is a good man. You have to try to forgive, anak. You have to try to be happy."

She doesn't say that she loves Manong Jack. She doesn't call him mahal. She doesn't say a word about Danny. She doesn't apologize. She just asks me to forgive. Ano ba iyon, anyhow? She watches me eat, reaching out her hand to me and I get up and put the plate in the sink.

"I was happy," I say, running water over my dishes. "Now every minute I breathe, malungkot ako. I miss my sister, my lola, all my friends, I miss my life. And for what? I don't even have you. Anong dream ba ito? " I tell her. "I hate this life." I look at her and wait. Her mouth trembles and I can't stand her. I leave the room and dress for school.

In homeroom, I can't sit still. My mother's voice plays in my head louder than Ms. Anderson, who is standing right in front of me, gesturing at some diagram on the green slate. Chalk dust covers her hands, flies in the air when she thumps at the boards. But it is my mother I hear. "He is not your papang, but he is a good man." I bang on my legs with the drumsticks. I keep them low and under the desk. I bang on my shins. Her words are trapped inside me, crowding me, and making it hard for me to understand anything. I can't think, her words are so loud. So I bang, bang, bang.

I bang so hard I drop my stick and it rolls across the floor. I reach down, keeping my head up, looking toward Ms. Anderson, who seems to be counting off the problems on the board, naming numbers and equations like a song or a poem or a language that is too foreign for me to comprehend. My fingers stretch and feel around the floor, looking for my stick, only to find another hand. Fingers thick and bony grab hold of me. When I look under the desk I see the boy from the hallway, looking at me upside down. Then his fingers reach around and hand me the stick. He winks and I catch a flash of green in his eyes. I drop the stick and have to scour the floor again. When I come back up, Ms. Anderson has stopped talking and she is leaning over my desk.

"Is everything O.K.?" she wants to know.

The boy and I answer at once. "Yes."

"Is Jordan making trouble?" she asks.

"No," I say. "No ma'am. May I go to the comfort room, ma'am?" She doesn't answer me right away and then I say, "The bathroom?"

Once I get to the girls' room, I lock myself in a stall and I peel my jeans down and I sit down on the toilet and stare at the little red marks emerging under my skin; indigo bruises shaped like ancient tattoos. "Not your papang," is what I am thinking, and then in my mind's eye I see Ináy and not my papang sitting at our dinner table, holding hands and laughing about the day. I see him teasing her and smiling that wide old man smile, and she is blushing right before us. This image haunts me all through the morning and right into the noon hour. So distracted am I that I spend most of the hour banging on my legs, drowning out that voice. Playing beats that are hot and regular like heartbeats.

After lunch, Ms. Anderson calls me to her, has me sit across from her big desk. She has my paper in her hand and I am watching her read. She mouths the words on the page. I hear *oppression*, I hear *imperialism*, I hear *bourgeois populism*. Back home we never called it a dream. Ináy called it a dream, but it was only a plan, a way out, a life outside of poverty. That was the plan, but a dream? No, this was never a dream. And when Papang died the plan got turned inside out and upside down and now I am sitting across from my American teacher. She says, *capitalism, careerism, feudalism.*

I hear the students outside, their indiscernible English bouncing off the white snowbanks, the sound of basketballs hitting brick walls. Ice cracking. I hear it. I hold my sticks to my legs and I hit lightly, count the sounds, and play along.

She pulls her glasses from her face and looks at me intently. "Do you know what you are saying here?"

I nod my head.

"Do you understand these words?" She picks up a dictionary. "Because I had to look them up."

"Isn't this what he's talking about?" I ask her. "Isn't Dr. King questioning America, isn't he saying not everyone is a part of the dream?"

"Yes, in a way—"

"Me too. I am questioning America. In my way."

I'm drumming on my legs by now, I'm hitting each leg as I speak, the words are like rests and the sticks are banging away. Boom. Boom. Bang bang, boom.

"Angel," she says, peering over her desk at my body. "Stop." But I only play harder. "Angel, please," she says. "Please stop."

But I can hear the way the wind blows and the ball breaks against the wall, I can hear the bell sounding in the courtyard and the students marching back into the corridors and this is what sets my rhythm going, what guides my count, my beat, my inner boom.

When Ináy abandoned us and I threw myself into the movement, I was searching for my heartbeat, I was looking for my papang. When the people and I, when the old lolas and the student resisters and the farmers from the provinces, when the people and I marched, I found my rhythm, so steady. We walked the streets and our feet would stomp the earth like drumsticks on a big bass drum. And all the voices would clamor together— Ba-Boom! Ba-Boom! Pintig, pintig, pintig, and I'd see Papang's bright light swirling in the sky, reflecting on a jeepney roof. I felt the heat of his white light pounding in my chest and I could move through the rest of the day and know that I was living my life without Ináy. And when the movement got in the way of Lola Ani and Lila's health, I found the beating of the heart when I put my hand to their chests, when I listened, and I fed them the heat from the palm of my hands. I found that music in the routine of our day, knowing they were safe. I knew for certain I was Pinay, that I was of the people, and I would never abandon Las Islas Pilipinas. And now this.

Ms. Anderson invites my mother to meet. Ináy and I sit like students in detention. The classroom has wide windows and snowdrifts on the sill, fat and white and waiting. "What about your job," I whisper in Tagalog.

"This is important. They'll understand."

I roll my eyes. Since when, I think. The pipes of heaters bang, rhythmless and out of whack. Ms. Anderson enters and seats herself at a student desk facing us.

"Angel is an outgoing young woman," Ináy says. "Back home she's a youth leader and an activist. She loves school."

When they turn to me, I stare at them as if I am on a bus or a train and they are strangers. I don't move. I don't breathe. I am hoping they stop looking.

"Perhaps Angel needs more time to assimilate," says Ms. Anderson. "Warm up, learn English."

"She knows English," my mother says. "Anak, tell her," she says to me, but I look at her like I don't know what she's talking about.

"Well, she definitely has a command of the written language." Ms. Anderson hands me the paper and asks me to read an excerpt. So I do.

My experience with the American Dream is to capture, oppress, and discriminate against the Filipino in order to fulfill President William McKinley's order to educate, civilize, and Christianize our people. This U.S. imperialist ideology was first made popular in the Philippines during the Spanish American War and is still widely practiced throughout the world. That is the American Dream.

Ináy glares at me and says, "She's been disrespectful."

"It's not so bad, really," Ms. Anderson says. "It's natural for lots of students, but the language and the ideas here indicate so much more." And then she points to my legs where the drumsticks roll to the beat of the clock. "I'm concerned."

Ináy says, "She won't do this again." She hands the paper back to Ms. Anderson and asks her if I should do it over again.

"Are there problems at home?"

My mother looks startled, slightly offended. "I will talk to Angel," Ináy says.

At that moment, Sally Tucker struts into the classroom and sits in one of the desks behind us, waiting. I've seen her around school, standing on the top of steps, or perched high on lunch tables with her posse of girls. She's the president of the debate club and a poetry slam champion. I've seen her reciting her poems, swinging her arms, rocking her body, words ticking like hands on a clock. I have no idea what she's saying, but there is music in it. I can hear that much. It is so easy to be invisible when Sally and her friends walk by.

"Hey, Angel," she says, nodding her head at me. "Sup?"

"Sally's a senior and one of our brightest students. She's a poet."

My mother and I turn to look at Sally, who is leaning back against the desk, her long legs stretched and her belly button hanging out from under a rag-wool sweater. A shiny rhinestone sparkles on the side of her nose.

"I think it would be a great idea for Sally to mentor Angel," Ms. Anderson says. "Help her out with her homework, show her around."

Sally's skin is so pale it is translucent and I can almost see the blue veins under her skin. Her eyes are lined with dark blue liner. I think she scares my mother and that is sort of nice.

"That's a great idea," I say. Since these are the only words I've said through the whole meeting, my mother has no choice but to allow it, to try it, to give me into the hands of Sally Tucker.

THIRTY-FOUR

Sally Tucker sits with me, her blonde hair falling in streaks before her eyes. Words come out of her flat, like flowers that have been pressed between the pages of a dictionary. Her mouth is small and pink and thin like her words. When she talks, Sally's hands curl in and out of the sleeves of an oversized sweater. Scars, fine as threads of silk, peek from her sleeve.

"Don't you want to be with your friends?" I ask her, pointing to a group of girls walking through the cafeteria.

"Sure I do." She waves at them and they make their way to our table, gathering around us.

They are so different from one another—tall and short and fat and skinny. Some in makeup and glittery eye shadow, others plain-faced and boyish. She introduces me to them and they speak so fast I can't match their names with their faces. Lindsey, Rachel, Jenny.

"Angel's from the Philippines," Sally tells them.

"My grandpa's nurse is from the Philippines," says one girl.

They tell me every single thing they know about Las Islas Pilipinas, like I have never been there. They rattle stories fast like rain, their voices cascading over one another, their words scattering everywhere. I don't understand much of what they say, but I feel their energy and even though some of the things they say are weird or just plain wrong, they make me smile. They make me realize how different they are than those rich girls back home, the ones with voices soft and cloying as cans of sweetened condensed milk. Back home, Papang had to die before those girls talked to me. But these girls, each one different as a candy in a box of mixed chocolates—these girls talk to me like we've been friends forever. They don't notice that I am catching every other word they speak, that their voices clamor in my ear like notes played out of tune. Or maybe they do and they don't care. After awhile I let their words wash over me. I nod at them. I smile.

Sally points to my sticks and says, "You play?"

I pull Papang's drumsticks from my back pocket and hold them up. "Sometimes," I answer. "They were my dad's."

"He died?"

"Stop it, Jenny. You're so embarrassing."

"What, I'm just trying to get to know her. I'm sure she knows we know."

Jenny's big mouth makes me think of Karina's big mouth. I tell them not to worry. I know how it is. New girl, foreign girl.

The following morning, my mother comes into my bedroom, fresh from her graveyard shift at the hospital.

"Anak," she says, shaking me awake. "We have to talk."

I groan into my pillow. I do not move.

"If not now," she says, "when?"

"Ewan," I moan, "you're the one never here."

I pull the blankets over my head and feel my breath warming the space under the covers. I continue to sleep, and I am trying to remember what dream I'm having, but she is rocking me and her voice goes from a soft whisper to a hiss, and rising high-pitched and angry, she pulls the covers down.

"Walang hiya!" she tells me, as if I am the one who should be ashamed. "Wala kang galang."

She was embarrassed at my school, she says. She's more worried that Ms. Anderson thinks she's a bad mom. She is a bad mom. Pulls me out of my life, out of my work, away from my only real family. Throws me into a school of capitalists and consumers. "Don't you know how hard we've worked to bring you here?"

I listen to my breath instead, to the slow rise and fall of it and the hum inside my head. I listen to the alarm clock ticking away, and to the sound of shovels scraping at the cement as someone clears a driveway. Danny whimpers, resistant like me. All she ever cares about is how she looks. I have embarrassed her. I have shamed her.

And when her words overpower the beating of my own heart, I sit right up and I tell her, "And what do you think this looks like, Ináy? You married to an old man, you making a baby with him, our Lola Ani almost dying because you are here, and

206

me and Lila still crying for our papang! I thought you loved him!"

Then there is silence. Everything stops. She looks at me like I am a stranger. She waits the longest moment and then, without a word, rises from the bed and leaves.

THIRTY-FIVE

We stroll the dark hallway, past clumps of students leaning on lockers or pulling on giant parkas and slamming metal doors. Conversations rise like heat. Boys nod at girls. Shout out. Sometimes they wave, but they never stop talking. By the door, six or seven boys, big as men, stand guard. They plant their feet on the floor and fold their arms across their chests and nod as we begin to parade past them.

"Hey, Sally," calls out a boy. "Who's the new girl?"

She points to me and announces, "This is Angel."

"She Afro-Japanese or what?"

"I like sushi!"

When Sally walks past, she shoves the boy in the shoulder and he breaks into a smile. "Filipina!" she says.

"What's that?" asks the boy again. "Chinese Cuban?"

That's when I see Jordan right behind him. A slow curl rolls across his face and the dimples crease and frame those white teeth. I look away before he sees me looking, but it's too late. "Another idiot," says Jordan. "Ignore him."

Sally hooks her arm around my arm and whispers, "He thinks you're hot."

I follow the girls out the doors and sun hits us, shines right in our eyes. There is nothing but white now. The parking lot is packed in heavy snow and mounds of white line the fences. We sneak around the building and shoot down an alley, our boots crunching on the snow. A patrol car cruises slowly past us, rolls a window down. My heart holds on, waits a beat. The pulis is a woman with yellow hair pulled back and a thick fur collar on a black leather jacket.

"Good day, ladies," she says, driving slowly enough to catch each of our faces.

The girls all greet her and Sally turns to me and says, "Officer Jane. She's cool."

"Don't be late for class," Officer Jane says, waving her hand out the window.

We all wave and they tell me she watches out for them, lets them walk around the block if they need to.

"She's really cool," Rachel says.

We stand behind a dumpster, five girls wrapped tightly in sweaters and down coats and heavy scarves, puffing smoke after smoke. I think about how this is the first time I have felt relaxed since I've been here.

We smoke for a while, until the clouds build and billow over us like thoughts. And then Rachel says, "So you liked that speech?"

I nod my head. I hold the cigarette to my mouth and breathe. "What's a bad check?" I ask.

They giggle. "Oh, that," Sally says. "He's talking about injustice."

Lindsey says. "Want another smoke?"

I hold my hand out and say, "I know about injustice." My ear must be getting used to the sound of their voices. I hear the breath between the words. Under the sun, with an Arctic wind blowing, I feel a wave of electricity shooting from somewhere deep below the snow, from the center of the earth through my rubber boots and up my spine, a connection that I had thought was lost forever.

That night, after I put Danny to bed and Manong Jack sits before his computer, surfing news from the Philippines, I pick up the phone and I call Karina on her parents' landline. It is so easy. I just plug the numbers in and there she is, as if she's down the street and I am in the convent.

"It's like being in prison," I tell her. "It's like walking upside down on earth. Everything is so baliktad."

"But you have your mother," she says.

"No, I don't. She works all night and sleeps all day."

I don't know what makes me call Karina. Maybe spending time with Sally and her friends, maybe standing around the dumpster with cigarettes hanging from our mouths and talking all at once. Maybe hearing my mother's voice inside me all day. I don't know, but it suddenly occurred to me that I could call home.

"and . . . I saw him," I tell her. "I saw him on a video."

"Who?"

"Dr. Martin Luther King."

I don't tell her how the footage took me by surprise, how I had no idea who he was. We had always heard of him in the way you hear about faraway heroes so faraway you don't know if they're real or myth or what. But we had never seen a photo, we had never read a speech. We had never seen him. I don't say the speech is confusing and that some of the words are in disguise. I say he is powerful. "He gives me hope," I say.

"What kind of hope?"

"Not sure yet," I tell her, but I definitely feel hope.

Something happens when I am on the phone, talking overseas long into the night. I feel like I am breathing again. Karina asks me questions about America and mostly I talk about the cold or I talk about how wild the students are. "Sex seems to be the number one priority," I tell Karina. I don't talk about my mother's marriage or how my new little brother's tuft of unruly hair makes him look exactly like me as a toddler. I don't talk about how Manong Jack is living in this house as my mother's new American husband, healthy and happy and telling love stories I refuse to listen to. I tell her I made a new friend, even though she's a senior assigned to mentor me. I don't mention the cuts on her arms, how they leap out at me every time I look at her. How I wonder how she got them.

THIRTY-SIX

Sally Tucker invites me to her house, where she takes me to her room and pulls out stacks of notebooks. "These are my diaries," she tells me. She opens one up and I see blue ink scratching at the pages, heavy and wavy like a storm. "I put everything in here. Do you have a diary?"

I tell her no, but I tell her about Karina and her revolutionary love poems. "Whenever her parents quarrel and she doesn't want to hear it, she writes love poems and leaves them places for strangers to find."

"What for?"

"To change the world, she says."

"What would she change?" Sally asks me.

I think about that a second and I know that Karina thinks she's writing about land rights and overseas workers and victims of World War II, but I think she'd change her household. I think she'd change the way her parents speak to one another. She'd change the way they don't love each other. She'd change the way they love her. But what I say is that I think Karina would like to change the world—the way she sees it and the way it treats her.

"Now that," Sally says, "is a revolution."

I pick up one of her notebooks and she says, "You can read it." But I don't want to read it. I want to hold it in my hands and feel the bumpy words. She must press so hard on the page that the words sink to the back of the notebook and the paper rises like high tide. Her writing is big and sloppy. Her words grow distorted as they move from one line to the next. She is shouting on the page.

"You must've been mad," I say.

"Totally pissed off."

"Your mother?" I ask.

"How'd you know?" she says.

I don't know how I know, but I point to her wrists. And she offers them like a prayer up to the window so I can see them better—the fine scars layering her skin like vines of green sampaguita stretching out along her long thin arms, swirling around her wrists where the blade has sliced her and scarred her over and over again. She talks about the way her mother was a woman of God, how she used to hover over her every moment of the day like a guardian angel, her mother would say, but Sally says it was more like a prison guard. "Guardian is the word, all right," she tells me. Sally was an only child, a special child, a gift from God, and she was not allowed to step on dirt, or to eat food that was not sanctified. She had no friends. No playdates growing up. No babysitters. Only her mother, who was constantly praying

213

over her. "I was dying," Sally says, "I was holding my breath and I was dying."

She started small, picking at her skin, slicing little bit by little bit. Until the night she hid inside a closet, a razor blade in her back pocket. She exhaled. She cut. She let the blood run, felt her spirit slipping, and she was free. "But then they caught me," Sally says. "She's better now, but I still can't stand her too close to me."

"I know what you mean," I say, but really I meant she was lucky to have her mother love her so much, to be with her like that, to never lose sight of her. But what I said was, "I hate my mother too."

And then I think of all the little bruises on my thighs. Little marks of anger bursting out of me. Every time Ináy makes me crazy, I bang the drum. I bang drum. I let the beats flow out of me sometimes fast and low, sometimes slow and syncopated, sometimes banging, just banging.

"Do you want to hear a poem?" Sally asks. I nod my head. And then closes her eyes and speaks. The words move around us like little trains, her emotions all lined up and falling into place, leaving her calm and rested. As she speaks, she swings her body like a giant clock, tossing words out so easily that I am jealous.

THIRTY-SEVEN

I spy on my mother lying on her bed under piles of heavy blankets. I watch her breath rising up and down, moving through the curves of her body, coming out in snorts and whispers. I am looking for something to love. For something familiar and mine. I am wondering why I cannot be happy with what she has given me. She sleeps despite the bright sun intruding through all windows and cracks of the house. I feel closest to her when she is like this, off in a dream, her body relaxed and unaware of my gaze. I almost feel something, but then I see her holding hands with Manong Jack, laughing until tears stream down her face, and I forget who she is. It's when she leans over to kiss him on the mouth, the two of them smooching like newlyweds that I think I'm going mad. In those moments, though she laughs and her whole face goes bright, she is most like a stranger to me. I cannot recognize her and if I look too long, I want to burst with anger.

In those moments I pull the sticks from my back pocket and I drum on the tops of my thighs, rhythms so complicated and loud that I cannot feel the bruises burning under my skin.

Once I walked past her room and saw Manong Jack lying in bed while she stood next to him with her hands on his heart. I stood behind the doorway and I watched her healing him, his body shivering as the energy flowed from her hands to his chest. That is how this whole thing began, I thought, healing that old man's heart. I wondered how often she still worked on him, how much he needed her, and then I started getting mad. What about us? I thought. What about Lola Ani? And then I felt hot, remembering my old lola lying in a hospital bed blue as midnight, her body swelling with pain from the beating of street thugs. Where were you, I wanted to scream.

But now I'm looking for my mother and I sneak into her crowded room, walking around a maze of objects—discarded shoes, nightstands, a television, little dumbbells, and a rowing machine. I tiptoe around the bed and I sit on a chair by the window and I watch her like she is a telenovela. I study the lines of her face and the way her eyebrows rise in crescent moons. I look at the veins that are popping out from her hands like blue roadways to her heart. I think about the way she smells, the way my sister and I used to curl up next to her and nap away a rainy afternoon.

The last time my family was all together, we were dancing at my cousin's wedding, swirling around under the canopy light of a full moon. My parents were so young and beautiful. They could have been the bride and groom. They could have been high school sweethearts, the way they were hanging all over each other. Watching her like this, I am hoping to see something from the past. A sign. A word from my father watching from the other side. But nothing happens. The sun moves around the room. Ináy shifts under the heavy blankets and disappears. My daydreams put me to sleep and when I wake I find a flannel blanket covering me. The room has gone dark and my mother is still sleeping.

THIRTY-EIGHT

When the bell rings, I lean back and stretch my legs. I pull my hood over my head and keep my eyes focused on the desk. Ms. Anderson's telling us she has a surprise. She sounds so damn happy. I tap tap lightly on the tops of my legs. I tap. I tap. I tap. The door creaks open and feet shuffle in. Then people start to shout good morning and hello and wassup. I shiver, a remnant of sadness running through me.

"Hey, Angel." It's Jordan.

I examine the wood grain, how the patterns flow like water.

"Morning," I say.

I feel myself drifting off, my head nodding, the teacher's voice in the air like a dream but then I hear the heavy beats of a boom box. When I look up, I see four teens looking Chinese or Filipino, maybe Japanese. Ms. Anderson calls them Haiku House. The girls are in tight sweaters and long black pants with beads and bangles hanging all over them. The shorter one has dyed her hair purple and Valentine red. The taller one's hair flows long and loose like bolt of black silk. One boy has skin smooth and yellow, has eyes that have disappeared in the folds of his face. The other boy is as big as the full moon and bright too. The boys hold their hands to their mouths, feeling the beat, rocking and swaying.

The complicated rhythm mesmerizes everyone, anchors all of us to the same heartbeat. And then I figure out, there is no boom box. The beat comes from their mouths. They spit and boom and moan and click their tongues. Wow.

And then the words. Each of them has their own set of words. The girl with purple and red hair has words that flame up like fire, lashing out at the world, accusing everyone of every crime. When she speaks, her pretty face clenches up all sour— her mouth, her eyes, her ears even—like she's straining to hold it in, like any minute she might explode. The boy with a yellow face closes his eyes and spins a series of words into the air. The words are spoken, but they are flowing out of him like a song. They are the kind of words that take over his whole body. His black-and-white high-tops rock back and forth and the knees give way in a syncopated fashion. His shoulders collapse over his heart, drawing his arms to the ground like a large rag doll. I cannot stop watching him. Sometimes he rears his head back, the chest open and the heart pumping and I think of Karina marching alongside me, howling at the moon. The boy aims his heart at the sky and light shines all around him as words burst into the air. He is a song, that boy. And the girl with the long hair holds her tongue, lets this birdlike yawp resound between the words.

She keeps her eyes open and she looks out at us, and even though her words are fragile like glass and full of pain, she is smiling, cooing. She makes me think of operas. She dances around the others and her voice sails high above the pitch of anger and confusion. It is the way I imagine my own pain, light and sharp and waiting to attack.

What is this, I think? What are they doing? The words roll out all at once and I understand nothing, but I feel the letters vibrating in the center of my chest. The release of each syllable seems to lighten them.

The bigger boy whispers and I sit quietly, waiting to hear what he has to say. He tells the story of an old manong pulling doors open for white Americans. The old man stands at attention, no matter the weather, waiting for the next man or woman to enter his building. He smiles at the white Americans. He nods. He welcomes them home. He stands at attention all night long. He talks about the way people ignore the old manong or talk loudly like he's deaf or insult him because they have had a bad day.

A voice that is not mine comes to me when I imagine the old manong standing in the middle of a snowstorm, opening doors with a wide, welcoming smile for two dollars and twenty-five cents an hour and a tip jar full of insults. And I don't know why, but suddenly I hear it: *One hundred years later, the Negro still is not free.*

For the rest of the morning, we listen to Haiku House poetry, banging on our chests like fists on a door. I close my eyes and I am lost in the music, my own head bobbing, my sticks hitting at my lap. I don't catch all the words, but I feel them enter me from the crown of my head and move down my spine, coursing through all my veins. Now and then, I open my eyes and I catch Jordan smiling at me, nodding at me, whispering in grunts and humps and knowing affirmations.

At the end of the performance, we split up in groups and each of us gets one of the Haiku House members.

We get the girl with the purple-red hair, the nose ring, the tongue ring, the twenty-seven piercings in her ear. She talks with her hands and her eyes go big and wide like two black moons. She wants us to talk about our past, where we came from. I smile at Jordan. Naku, I think, that's all I talk about. Where I came from. Las Islas Pilipinas. Pamilia. City of aktibistas. Province of green hills. She asks us to conjure up objects from that time, something you can touch, you can taste, something you can feel. I think Papang's drums. Ináy's healing hands. I think Lola Ani's purple wounds. The girl with the crazy hair spins around us and we're supposed to be writing these things down, but I cannot seem to move. I look over at Jordan and he is scribbling all over his paper; his words crawl off the page the same way his limbs sprawl from the confines of his desk—the arms, the legs, the feet, shooting out in all directions and winding all over the room.

"You O.K.?" says the girl. Her eyes are so big and round. She looks almost Pinay, except for the hair, except for all the silver coming from her face like stars twinkling at night.

"Yes," I answer. "Thinking."

When she asks the group to share, only Jordan raises his hand. "I come from New York, via Jamaica, via China. When I open my mouth and speak, I taste meat patties and plantains and ginger ice cream floats. When I close my eyes, I hear sirens, and dogs barking, and if I'm lucky, sometimes I hear the ocean roar." I watch him pulse the words out into the room and I think, who is he?

Officer Jane and her partner, Officer Dave, cruise by in a squad car, flashing their blue and red lights at us. We wave at them and turning back to the dumpster, we continue our after-lunch ritual. A blaze of light bounces off snowbanks. We smoke in a circle and a halo protects us, rising in one big breath to God.

"So Ms. Anderson brought in Haiku House," Lindsey says, inhaling deeply. She holds the smoke inside of her and then dramatically tips her head back and releases.

"Oh, yeah," Sally says. "I like when she does that. How were they?"

"Hot as ever. What'd you think, Angel?"

It's not what I think that stays with me, it's how I feel. After a while, I closed my eyes and felt the pulse of each syllable, the way the sound rolled around the tip of the tongue and kicked its way out of their teeth. Sometimes the fat boy tossed out a word in Tagalog, and while the vowels were a little longer and the tongue a little slower than I was used to, I knew what he was saying and the whole experience made me want to cry.

Ms. Anderson had asked them what they wanted their words to do, and the girl with the red-purple hair said, "What do you think?"

I want my words to bring me home. I want my words to bring my Papang back, to help me remember how much I love my Ináy. I want my words to sew my family back together—Lila and Lola Ani, Papang, my mother, and even little Danny boy. I want my words to help me find my own beat.

"So what, Angel," Sally asks. "You like them?"

"They were O.K.," I say.

And then we sit in silence, puffing on our smokes, watching the way the breath dances up to the sky and dissipates into blue.

THIRTY-NINE

The house smells like home and I find myself in the kitchen with my mother and Ate Gina, smashing garlic, chopping cabbage, slicing thin bits of carrots. We make egg rolls, taking mouthfuls of ground pork mixed with eggs and vegetables, rolling them tight in wonton wrappers, and holding them together with dabs of water.

"Your mother has invited the whole community," Ate Gina says, rolling lumpia thin as her old fingers.

"I won't know anyone," I say.

"But they all know you," Ate Gina says. "My gosh you should hear how she talks about you! My anak the drummer, my anak the aktibista, my anak the grade-A student! Everyone is dying to meet you."

"Billy Morgan's family is so excited," Ináy says. "He's been a good friend to you, no?"

"He says he met you before he left," I tell her.

"Yeah, he knows Mother Mary from before kasi he was working on this project. So sabi ko, my daughter can help you; she loves People Power."

"You asked him to include me in his project?" I say, wrapping an egg roll so tight the skin bursts, and ground pork, carrots, ginger, and scallions squirt out everywhere.

"Yeah, good idea, no?"

"No," I say, though I don't know why I say it.

"But you love that project."

"I hate that project," I yell, and I storm out of the room and run up the stairs. My heart thumps so loud I think it has invaded my brain.

Upstairs, I search my bedroom for my drumsticks, but they are nowhere. I look under the beds, between the sheets. I throw open the closet and dig through piles of shoes and dirty laundry. I can't find them. I can't find them. And this only fuels the fire inside me. The confusion. I pull a cigarette out of a drawer and I don't even bother to leave the house. I open the window and let the cold rush in and I light up right there. February in Chicago barges into my little space and I offer it a pack of smokes. My breath blows and ashes swirl, mingle with snow drifting in from the open window, scatter in the room, settle. I smoke almost every cigarette in the pack. Smoke until the alarm goes off. Until there is nothing left inside of me and my whole body goes numb.

The doorbell rings several times. Boots stomp at the front door, announcing families loud and friendly. The mothers and fathers shout their greetings and the children chase one another. Their bodies thump up and down stairs, across hallways. Small hands pound on the walls like feet running up the steps. Every few minutes, Ináy calls out my name from the living room and Manong Jack makes excuses. "You know teenagers. They spend more time in the bathroom than they do at the parties!"

I ignore them. Soon the house is so full of people that the walls vibrate with their voices and words begin to seep through the floor boards—not just English words either—there is Tagalog and Ilokano. Now and then a little Visayan and some Kapangpangan creep under the door. The conversations dance in the air, flirt with my ears. I don't want to admit that I am happy, but I am. It's been such a long time since I have heard these languages bouncing off each other, prompting one another to bellow and cry and shout with such joy. The jokes are generally stupid, but they make everyone smile. The laughter is so Filipino. I think about sneaking down to take a look at everyone, but I can't. Alone in the room, I wonder if there are any teens my age down there, if any one of them was born in Manila too.

Ináy comes to my door. She knocks but doesn't enter. She calls to me from the other side, asking me what is wrong. "Why is everything so hard with you, anak? Can't you see we love you?" I can hear her standing there, breathing. I can feel the weight of her on the other side of the door, but I cannot seem to move, to get up and walk to the door. I look at the room, the way the wind has blown everything out of place, the way the sheets and the little rugs are damp with winter's breath. But instead of getting out of bed, I lean back into the pillows of my bed, pull the comforter over my head, and I rest.

In another moment, Manong Jack walks in. No knocking. He sits at the foot of my bed and very calmly he says, "Tama na. You stop acting like a spoiled brat, ha? You are breaking her heart. No daughter of mine has ever treated her mother like this and you are not going to start. Do you hear me? You stop this. You get dressed. You come down and you enjoy, ha? I will not have you hurting her again. You stop it or I will."

I say, "You are not my father." I don't move out from under the blankets, but I say it loud enough for him to hear. I can feel the weight of his body at the end of the bed. He sits there long enough for me to understand he is not going anywhere. So I sit up and cross my arms. "Give me five minutes," I tell him, wiping the tears from my face.

After surveying the room, he walks to the window and slams it shut. The curtains fall silently into place. "The heat is on," he says. "You're wasting energy. If you have to smoke, you go outside." And turning, he leaves the room, the window rattling behind him.

I get up slowly and stand before the mirror. My hair stands on end, curls flying in all directions. The tears have swollen the lids of my eyes so they seem small and slanted like Karina's eyes. My lips are swollen too. I pull the hair together and tie it at the base of my neck, the curls popping from the end like a witch's broom gone wild. I scrub my face clean. Dry the tears away with a towel. I wear jeans that are too big for me and I pull on a thick gray turtleneck. Before I run down the stairs to join them, I lift the window frame up one last time and I light a cigarette and, poking my head out the window, I blow smoke up into the white sky.

The house is so noisy, nobody looks up when I come down the stairs. In the living room two card tables have been set up. Men and women reach into the center of the tables, mixing ivory cards and stacking them up like walls around a garden. The mahjong tiles click and spin and tumble in a rhythm of their own.

Manong Jack sits like a king on his recliner. Grandchildren from his first marriage climb him, nestle into him, tickle his old face with their sticky fingers. When he sees me, he pulls a child off of his chest and calls my mother. "Milagros!" he yells, "the birthday girl is here now!"

My mother comes out of the kitchen carrying a tray of food, and when she calls my name everyone pauses for a moment—the games stop, the children freeze, and everyone begins clapping wildly. I wave at all of them, because I don't know what else to do, and then I run into the kitchen and busy myself, washing dishes and wiping countertops.

"You go talk to the guests," Ate Gina says. She pulls the rag from my hands.

But I tell her I can't. I don't know what to say. In Manila, everyone talks about coming to the United States. People are always dreaming about it, coming to open a restaurant or be in a movie or save lives in high-tech operating rooms, but all I ever wanted to do was stay in the Philippines. I wanted to start a revolution. I wanted to live in Manila, the right way.

She tries to take the broom from me, but I push her away.

I reach into the corners between the floor and the base-boards. I scratch at the rim and sweep, focusing on the vinyl tiles and the little bits of food—pieces of garlic and onion, uncooked grains of rice, vegetable peelings.

Then my mother charges into the kitchen and, hissing at me, grabs the broom and sends me down the basement steps. "Naku!" she says. "We worked so hard and you act like this! Go downstairs with the other kids."

I stand at the top of the basement and look into the dim lights—dark red and blue lights flickering bodies without faces. I can feel the beat of the bass vibrating up the stairs. This doesn't feel so bad, I think, stepping slowly.

There is a room full of teenagers lounging all over the floors, on low couches and folding chairs. In the corner, a DJ has set up two turntables and giant speakers. Nobody talks, though some of the girls whisper into one another's ear. The room smells of boys' sweet aftershave and girls' flowery shampoos. I think the girls are my age, but they have painted their faces and slicked their hair back or curled tight into long ringlets that fall between their eyes.

Their fat cheeks give it away. Their skinny hips say they're still girls. Their just-becoming breasts say they are new to this scene, too. But they don't act that way. Like the kids at my school, some of the girls hang on boys like ornaments on a tree. The boys take up lots of space, their too-big jeans spreading wide on the sofa and trailing well past their feet. I can't see their eyes under the brims of their baseball caps. I can't see their hair stuffed into the knitted caps that are fitted to their skulls. The music is so loud my skin vibrates. The words of the song slur together, hiccup and skip in and out of the beat. It is so dark I nearly trip over a strobe light. That's when I see a Filipina hanging all over the DJ, reaching around him to mess with the toggles of his soundboard.

"Hey," she says when she sees me. "Wassup?"

I shrug, not really hearing her words over the slow bass. I hear sirens and whistles coming from the record. I hear grown men grunting.

"You're Angel?" says the girl. I nod and she tells me her name is Liza. She says to the boy, "This is Angel, Tita Milagros' daughter from the Philippines."

I wave to him, but he turns his back on me, digging through a stack of records.

She points to the boy and yells, "This is my boy, Tommy Morgan—you know his brother, Billy?"

In the dark it takes me a moment to recognize him, the Filipino boy from Haiku House, fat and more Chinese than his brother Billy. "Did he just bring his stuff?" I ask Liza, as if he can't talk for himself.

"Naw," she says. "Your mother hired him to spin some disks." She doesn't have a lot of makeup on like the other girls, but she's wearing a hooded sweatshirt and it's zipped down to reveal a little bit of cleavage.

"Oh?" I say. "My mother?"

"Sup?" Tommy says. "Saw you in the classroom the other day."

He runs his fingers along the edge of a record, pulling it against the needle, scratching against the record's grooves. The sound is abrupt and loud like a shotgun.

"Happy birthday, girl. You like rap?"

I tell him yeah, though I don't know what he's talking about.

Tommy spins a record and as soon as the first notes ring from the speakers, the girls in the room leap up and start dancing. "I love this," Liza says, waving her arms in the air. Silver bands of bracelets shoot up and down her arm, sending off little sparks of light. She tosses her long hair and more silver dangles from her ears. I feel like such a tomboy down here. The girls move their bodies like snakes standing on their tails. They place their hands on their hips, on their rib cages, looking down at the ground. I feel like everyone is so much older than I am.

I sit down on an empty love seat and watch how they lean into each other and whisper, how they chant along with the songs, songs that sound mean and aggressive and foreign. It is the most horrible birthday of my sixteen years. I lean into the cushions and I become invisible. And just as I am finally blending in, my mother and Manong Jack flip all the lights on and start calling from the top of the stairs.

"Time to open presents!" Manong Jack yells. Each footstep bangs on the wooden stair, warning the kids to let go of one another, to make themselves presentable. In the light I can see how young everyone really is. Tommy, who was looking so cool and gangster, is nothing but a big teddy bear, hiding behind his turntables. Some of the girls' faces are breaking out with pimples. Probably from the oil of all that makeup. The goatees on the boys' faces are stray hairs, desperately trying to grow into beards.

A herd of adults follow Manong Jack and Ináy down the stairs, several carting gifts wrapped in colorful paper and glittery ribbons. Stacks of presents pile at my feet and people smile at me like they've known me my whole life. Ináy lights the candles on a sheet of birthday cake. The people sing at the top of their lungs and I am so embarrassed that this group of strangers is being forced to sing to me. They are loud and happy. Their Filipino accents rise in short vowels. "Nakakahiya, naman!" I tell my mother, who insists I blow all the candles out.

"Angel de la Luna, for your sixteenth birthday," says Manong Jack, "your mother and I wanted to get you something really special." He gestures at the sky with his hands and then to my mother, who stands before a huge tarp with a red ribbon on it. Ináy yanks the cloth and reveals a full set of drums. The whole room goes quiet, waiting. It's all brass and silver and my drumsticks rest on top of the snare drum. Papang's drumsticks.

That night, after everyone leaves, I sit on the stool and hold the sticks over the skins and hover like that a moment, feeling the energy with my eyes closed. I count the beats out in my head. I picture Papang standing in the corner with a set of drums of his own, clapping his sticks in the air, and on the downbeat I bang the tom-tom, I hit the cymbal, I bang the tom-tom. I kick the bass drum. I kick the bass drum. I roll the sticks over all the skins, one right after the other. I crash the cymbal and as much as I want to hate this gift, I lose myself in the rhythm, I find my way to my father and I play with all my heart. I play my way back home.

FORTY

We keep the drums in the basement and I find myself running down the stairs to bang on them several times a day. I like to play to the radio, to funky tunes with offbeat rhythms. I like to lose myself under all the bang bang banging. Half the time, Ináy is not here, but her words stay with me, echoing and vibrating against the walls of the house.

I want to love her and I want to sit with her and stroke her hair or kiss her on the cheek, but there is always Manong Jack sitting between us. He is like a giant block of ice stuck in the middle of a Chicago snowstorm. He makes it hard to see her over him, to see her all by herself.

Sometimes early in the morning, before anyone is awake, I hear them arguing about me. He is the one who plants all these ideas in her head. He says I'm not grateful. He says I was rude to the guests. He says I did not smile enough. He says I am not a feminist at all, but a spoiled child. Even though I come home every day and pick up where she left off with the vacuuming and sweeping and laundry and childcare, he says I am spoiled. I know he says he wants me to act like his daughter—kiss him when I greet him, make mano, offer him glasses of water or little snacks. I won't do that. He's not my father.

I can barely hear her answers through the howling winter wind. I think she defends me a little bit, but she doesn't silence him. I hear her telling him the story of Papang's death, of how she went mad when we needed her the most. I hear her say that he should be patient with me.

Her voice is soft and moves in circles, like snow drifting in and out of clumps. When she sees me, she turns his words around and dresses them up to sound like her words. I don't want to hear it. She begins and I run down the stairs and I drown her out. I bang so loud, the whole house echoes with my rhythm. I bang so loud, not even the winter storm silences me.

After a few weeks, he wants to take the drums away, but I hear her say, "We can't do that to her. We can't give her something and take it away like that. It's the one thing that makes her happy." So I bang the drums and the silences between them grow. First the silence comes from their bedroom. Then silence appears at the dinner table. And then in the car. Silence invades the house and quiets almost everything. Sometimes the only sounds in the house are Danny's squeals, the beating drums, and the television game shows. Sometimes Manong Jack's computer beeps. But the words have left the house. The voices go low.

Nobody speaks. Until one Saturday, when flurries of snow block the sun from our windows and Manong Jack rages into the room, himself a blizzard of anger.

"What do you think we are, made of money? You think dollars just fall from the sky? Have you ever worked a day in your life?"

He is crazy, rambling on and on at the air and pacing back and forth across the kitchen. Ináy leaps to her feet with her hands up, hushing him. He brushes her away like a man fleeing bees. He slams a fistful of papers before me.

"Are you responsible for this?" he says.

I look at him and then back at my plate. I spoon rice and eggs together and I continue eating.

"You see? She has no respect!" he yells. "I thought you were going to talk to her about this? In one week she throws away all your wages on what? Phone calls to the Philippines!"

He sits across from me, staring me down, but I continue to eat as if he doesn't exist.

I hear his breathing, steady and forced. I hear the click of his syllables. His round, short vowels. I find a rhythm and I stay with it, ignoring what the words mean. Danny runs from the room, scared of his father. Outside the storm pounds at the windows.

"What is the matter with her?" he demands, sweeping all the dishes off the table. Everything comes crashing—the plates of longganiza sausage, the rice, the glasses of orange juice, and mugs of hot coffee. Everything. When I look at my plate, there is nothing there but the plastic tablecloth.

"We cannot go on like this!" he yells at me.

"I'm eating pa."

"Angel!" my mother yells. "Stop."

"That's it. Send her back!" Manong Jack yells. "Send her back before we all get deported. Before I get sent to jail for killing her! Send her back." He reaches out as if to swat me but Ináy grabs his hand and swings him to face her.

"Huwág, old man! She is sixteen!" Ináy is shaking when she says it, her hair falling in long black and sliver strands across her face. It is the first time since Papang has died that she looks familiar to me, that her face softens and her eyes sparkle. It is the first time since Papang died that she has raised the vibrations of her heart up so high that I can feel it in the air. She loves me.

FORTY-ONE

During our next workshop I write with my eyes closed and I picture Papang holding his drumsticks and beating that drum—the skins vibrating and booming and shaking my insides so that the words fall out of me for once. I push them onto the page: *Indy climbed aboard that plane, even as the cramps were swelling in my belly, even as I was doubling over and calling her name. She was adjusting the cushions on her seat. She was buckling up and I was throwing up for three days after that.* It comes to me easier than I think. And when the Haiku House kids say, "Who wants to share?" Jordan stands and I watch him. He has memorized his poem and he dances with it, his arms swaying gently, his feet rocking up to tiptoes and down again. A dimple creases down the length of his square jaw. His blue eyes pop against that brown skin. Like he is talking to me about leaving home. "I'm off the island now," he's saying. "I'm off the island."

Me too, I think. I'm off the island too. And when they say, "Angel, you go." I say no, I shake my head though inside I am dying to stand up. I say, "No, not today."

We wave french fries at each other like swords, gesturing with burgers in our hands. We cram our bodies into a booth, our words lapping one over the other like the tide. And then a gust of wind blows through the burger joint, the glass doors swinging wide open, and several seniors from our school saunter in, their jeans dragging wet on the tiled floors, their bodies bringing with them the cold winter chill.

I scan the crowd to see if we know any of them and see Jordan and his friends strolling in like it's warm and breezy outside. They hang their big hands in their front pockets and walk with their chests wide open, broad like the continent of Africa.

"Sup?" they mutter one by one as they shuffle past us. "Sup?"

I look away just as Jordan slips by, but then he takes a step backwards and he lingers at the corner of our table. I feel my cheeks go bright red and my palms sweat like we're in the middle of a rally.

"Sally's crew, wassup?" he says.

The girls sing his name like bells chiming one at a time. I glance out the window like something has caught my eye. There's so much traffic out there, rolling in the mush of ice and dirty snow, but unlike Manila it is moving and constant. People are going somewhere. It doesn't matter that the snow is falling from the sky in one continuous breath, piling up and covering everything white, white, more white. Where is the color of the earth? I watch Jordan's reflection in the mirror and focus on the caramel texture of his skin and the way his eyes dart from the window to the rest of the girls. "Hey, Angel," he says. "What's going on?"

Slowly I turn around and smile. I keep my eyes on his shoes—work boots layered in slush—long and wide and falling apart. "Hey, Jordan," I say.

"You look good, Angel." He leans on the table with his forearms and peeks up at me, catches my eye. "I wanted to hear you read today."

I look up at him.

And then he smiles that way he does and I feel my throat go dry. We stare at one another for what seems like forever and he says, "Looked like you wanted to." And that's when I see all his friends are waiting for him, standing there, listening to our conversation. They laugh loud and hard. I look back at the window, how their bodies take up the whole room and their images go fat and wide. Boys with hoods on and sunglasses. Boys with knit caps and pea-green parkas. Boys wearing pants so big they could fit two or three boys in there. Boys acting like men. They stand together like an army, laughing, hovering, making me feel small and stupid and foreign.

Jordan doesn't even turn his head when he addresses them. He looks right at me and yells out, "What are you fools laughing at?" And they raise their arms up like questions marks, muttering, "o.k." and "My bad" and "All right then." And turning away, he waves and saunters back to his circle of boys. The chaos at the burger joint goes up, the girls' voices ringing after him, the garble of boys slapping each other on the back, the cashier shouting "Two burgers, three cokes, extra-large order of fries" all compete against the roar of winter blasting through the automatic doors, blowing us away.

Outside, a horn honks down the alley and a car sidles up to the burger joint, its tailpipe blowing smoke all over the parking lot. The doors open and Tommy and Liza emerge from either side of the car. The bass from the car speakers makes the car throb. They wave at me and the girls. "Come on," they're telling us, "let's go." And so we do.

FORTY-TWO

Tommy has one arm thrown over Liza's seat and the other stretched and barely touching the wheel. I sit on Liza's lap, my back hunched over, head hitting the ceiling of the car and hands splayed out on the dashboard. I watch her slowly knead the top of Tommy's leg. The other girls cram in the back, giggling as their elbows poke one another, or their knees bump their bottoms. The music dominates, pounding like a giant heartbeat. Tommy guns the car down the alley and spins us out into the street. We scream.

He takes us down deserted neighborhood streets, sliding on ice and spinning at four-way intersections. Tree branches, naked and brown, wear a coat of ice, shine like crystal. We almost hit a dozen trees as we coast Chicago boulevards and zip down alleys with stacks of green plastic garbage cans all lined up at attention. The buildings are so sturdy—red brick or sand colored, stacked like children's blocks. Here, there are no people on the street, not like in Manila, where everywhere people are walking about, stepping around each other. Here, the cars only move during certain hours of the day. It is amazing to me that we can find a whole neighborhood without a single living soul on the street.

We follow the sun, shooting through neighborhoods, passing cars parked under layers of snow. We chase the shadows on the streets, racing them to the edge of Lake Michigan. Tommy parks the car in an open lot, shuts the engine off, and says, "We're here!"

We crawl out of the car and start climbing icy rocks, jagged and dusted in frost. The lake waves surge, blow fierce like the wind howling at the sky. It is beautiful and cold and slowly going gray out here. We huddle in pairs and threes and fours, folding our bodies over to keep the warmth from escaping. Liza and Tommy sit with their arms around each other, staring out at the white waves. I'm sitting next to them, my hands cupped around a smoke, trying desperately to light it.

"Good luck with that," Liza says.

"I'll get it," I say, turning away from the wind. A little spark hits the paper and I inhale fast. The girls from my school sit on a picnic table under a dead tree.

Tommy leans in closer to Liza and kisses her on the cheek and, turning her face up to his, he kisses her on the mouth and I watch like I've never seen this before. I bet that it was like this for Ate Rosalie and J.R. I bet it was like this for my ináy and papang. To be so caught up in the other that you cannot help it. You cannot help your hands, your mouth, your bodies.

I turn away from them and breathe in the winter air.

"You adjusting better now?" Tommy asks. "You and your moms? Manong Jack?"

Since the birthday party I watch my mother move silently around the house. Her body is often bent as if it is broken and her footsteps drag. Every now and then she catches me looking at her and she smiles. Sometimes I think she feels like the mother I knew in Manila. On days she's not working, she and Danny like to sit at the window in her room, under a big blanket rocking and watching snow fall. She sings him songs she sang to us—funny songs about Philippine vegetables, island birds, and nipa huts—songs out of place in a world where arctic winds whistle out your window.

I have been watching the way Manong Jack treats her. He isn't so talkative these days. He has stopped making stupid jokes. But she is still very malambing to him, rubbing his back when she passes him. She cooks for him, places dishes of steamed rice before him, and hot bowls of chicken tinola, and sinigang soup with big bunches of pechay leaves wilted in the broth. She holds his hand and tells him clever stories. But he just looks at her, mouth closed, without that sense of humor.

In the distance, my classmates chase one another, laughing loud as the wind. Snow dusts all of us—our hair, our lashes, our scarves and coats. We look like old people scattered in white landscape, slowly becoming one another, the white sky, the white ground, the white breath. I turn to watch them and I wonder what Lila is doing now. I picture her asleep in the bed next to

Lola Ani, the sweat clinging to her skin and hair, the sound of roosters crowing in the distance, the vendors pushing carts up the hill by our house, calling food out to no one in particular, their voices stretching from Malate to Makati, from Quezon City to Parañaque, the warm air filling up with good things to eat.

At the dumpster, I take a long drag and after a moment, I ask the girls if there are political clubs in school. They look at me like I'm crazy. Since I have arrived, I have lost the direction of the sun, the sound of the ocean, even the light of the moon. I watch my batchmates and each day I realize how little we have in common.

The earth is different here. I cannot seem to reach it. My feet slide too easily on ice. Since I've gotten here I haven't even seen the ground. I miss the dirt-path roads of the provinces. I miss seeing carabao on the street. I miss the mais cart. The palengke and barrels of bright-colored vegetables. I miss being able to barter for something sweet to eat. I wonder if there is an American sisterhood here, a feminist group for youth. I scan the *Chicago Tribune* and the *Sun-Times,* looking for a sign. Where are the protests? Where are the resisters?

My face feels hot, even under this winter sun. I feel it flushing red and swelling with embarrassment. "Have you heard of the Freedom Women?" I ask them. I inhale a smoke and hold it in my chest. I wait.

"Who are they?" Lindsey asks. The curls under her hat frame her face like one of those dolls that close their eyes when you lay them down.

"You don't know?" I ask. They step a little closer and the heat of our breath comes together, waiting. I say, "They are heroines of the war."

"What war?" Jenny asks.

I try not to roll my eyes. "World War II," I say. "We call them the Mahalaya Women."

I whisper, and the words escape me like the smoke of my breath, soft and practically invisible to the ear. They step closer to me, link arms with one another, lean toward me. I speak so quietly they close their eyes to hear better and the winter sun bathes their white skin with noonday light. I draw them a picture with my words, of the tree with branches that reached out like arms. The bark so rough and sturdy it could hold a hundred women. I set the bodies of the women on branches, perched like singing birds, their legs drawn to their knees and their arms folded across their chests, or rooted to the bark. There is a soft breeze. No sun, but there is the moon. And little sprinkles of light flash from the night sky. There is no sound except the boots of the guard walking just below them, his bayonet held upright, the sword shimmering like stars.

In the camps, the little yellow men tear their own clothes off, ravaging the arms, the legs, the breasts, and bellies of the imprisoned. The stink of the men fills the air. The women held down cry out and their voices tear the sky open, slice the moon to pieces.

I search the faces of my batchmates, see their eyebrows wrinkle up, their mouths turn downward. Jenny's face is wet with tears. I take my glove and wipe her cheeks. "Shhh," I tell them. "Not so loud, they will hear you crying. They will kill you."

The circle of girls tightens up, our arms reaching around our shoulders. We bow our heads and lean on one another.

In the dead of night, when only the owls are singing, the women in the trees whistle night songs to guerilla warriors who are waiting just beyond the hill. They let their hair down and their tongues slip through the trees, reaching into the camps, pulling the gates open.

"You're making that up," Lindsey says. "You make that shit up."

I look around the circle. I look right into their eyes and I say, "I have met the survivors. They are old women now. Like grandmothers and old aunties."

Sally leans closer to my face and she whispers, "They told you?"

I take a drag from my smoke and I squint up at the sky, holding the warm air in my chest, imagining the old lolas marching for justice, and I say, "They told everyone."

"That's so sad," Rachel says. "My mother says sex is a beautiful expression of love."

I shake my head. The voices of the lolas are so strong inside me. Sally takes a drag on her cigarette and blows the smoke high into the sky.

We're quiet again, thinking about it, imagining it, then Jenny sighs long and low and says, "I love these after-lunch smokes. They're so enlightening."

FORTY-THREE

One night I invite my American classmates over and we sit in front of the television and watch Billy Morgan's video. They've been asking so many questions about the movement that I have given in and they are all slumped over on couches under big blankets, waiting for the videotape to roll. I decide to sit in a big easy chair all by myself, and when Liza and Tommy arrive, they find a place on the floor on top of huge cushions.

"I can't wait!" Jenny says, chomping on a handful of popcorn. "I've always wanted to see a revolution."

The girls kick up their stocking feet and set them on the coffee table, all lined up and waiting.

I hit play and go back in time. There are bright flashes of color and the faces of people I love. The story goes back and forth between the excitement of the protest, the chanting of the people, the marching down wide boulevards, and the pulis cloaked in riot gear against the quiet lives of the poor working in rice fields, living in makeshift shacks and half-built houses.

Between the marches there is a wide shot of Smokey Mountain, the giant landfill right outside of Dagat-dagathan, and a toddler bathes in an old rubber tire, his lola squatting next to him and rinsing him in dirty water. And then the people begin talking and I see my people—Mother Mary and Lila and all the aktibistas sitting around the council table, debating the merits of the new president. It is my life, but it is not my life. It is what I know but not the way I know it. Still, just the images are enough to soothe me. I have never imagined the story so big and so dramatic, so full of music. Billy captures the rhythm of the city and this is what I love best—there is the city of the rich and the city of the poor, and it is obvious that it's supposed to be one city, not two. The movement pushes on to the screen with our screaming pink banners, our signature T-shirts and scarves.

Liza's yelling things at the screen. "That's my ate!" she says. "She's my cous!" Lindsey falls off to sleep, her breath deep and heavy underneath the blanket. I am so lost in the video and the way I show up on the screen, running around, waving my hands, pounding on plastic buckets with Papang's drumsticks, I don't even care when Danny climbs up the easy chair and settles in my lap.

"That's you!" Jenny says. "I told you that revolution was cool. Look at you!"

I hardly recognize myself and then I see my best friend. "Karina!" I whisper. We are running right up to people and singing protest chants to their faces. We dance around the children who are walking in perfectly straight lines, bearing banners bigger than their four-foot-tall bodies. We are so alive.

Danny points to the screen and even he is yelling. "Ate Lila! Ate Lila!" I turn to look into his face, the way the light from the television fixes a blue glow on his little body, and I can hardly believe he is calling out to my sister. On the screen, Lila hands out plastic bags of food to the old women protesters, sometimes hugging and kissing them as she moves through the crowd. Her figure is small and moves easily through the tight spaces between people, like she's been doing it her whole life. Danny laughs as if she can hear him and blows her kisses. I wrap my arms around his body and I squeeze.

"You know Lila?" I whisper. And he laughs again, not paying any attention to me at all.

Nobody hears Manong Jack shuffling into the room and dragging a chair with him. Nobody hears him cracking peanuts and tossing them loudly into his mouth. Nobody notices until I hear him shout, "You know they pay people to show up at those rallies. They're paid protesters!"

That's when I turn around and I see him sitting right next to me, his feet spread wide apart, his hands on his knees like he is at a fight. I toss him a look to shut him up but this only makes him say it again.

"Didn't you know that? Half of those people on the streets— maybe more—are getting several hundred pesos to stand in the street like that. No kidding."

"That's not true," I say, glancing at the couch to see if my friends are listening. They probably can't understand his accent anyway. "This is the people's will right here."

"Angel, don't be so childish naman. You think all those people really care about politics? They're poor." His fingers gesture to his lips and he says, "They are just concerned with putting food on the table."

"You don't know what you're saying," I whisper to him.

And he shouts back, "Is that any way to talk to elders? Of course I know what I'm saying."

"I'm sorry po, you have not lived in the Philippines for many years, but I was there. I know. I was an organizer."

"You are seventeen and disrespectful."

"I am sixteen."

I don't care if he thinks I'm rude, because I know my movement and my people. I know that there are some corrupt people, even in the masses, but the majority of the people are fighting for their lives and he has no right—no right—to fight me, especially now in front of my friends. I begin speaking to him in Tagalog, telling him that he is embarrassing me. "Why?" he asks me, breathing so hard I can smell his old breath. "I'm only speaking the truth." I ask him to leave, and this is when he stands up and walks over to the television set. He hits the power button off.

"Tama na! Umalis na kayo!" he yells, waving his arms in the air.

Sally Tucker jumps from the sofa and calls to the girls, who are slowly waking or so stunned they don't know what to say. She's at the door, pulling on her shoes.

Manong Jack yanks the blankets off of Liza and Tommy, who are lying in each other's arms. "Ano ba ito?" yells Manong Jack. "You're Filipinos, you should know better. What do you think my house is, a brothel?"

He thinks he's Jesus in the temple of thieves, casting demons out of the house. Arms go reaching for jackets, scarves are thrown in the air. The girls are so startled and I am up and shouting, "I'm so sorry, but he is crazy!"

"Hey, no worry," Liza says. "We've all been there."

Jenny says, "My old man is the same exact way."

"We'll call you later," Rachel says.

I have never seen an adult act like this. I cannot believe he is married to my mother. When they are gone and the doors are shut tight I turn to him and I start shouting.

"What do you want from me, old man?" I wave my arms at him like he is a plane and I am directing him to land. "I finally make a few friends in this crazy place and you drive them away! Ano ba iyon?"

This time the words come out of me so fast I don't have time to check them, to hear them in my head before they come out of my mouth. I know that when my mother comes home I will really be in trouble, but I cannot help myself. I throw words at him. I go for his head, his heart, his stomach. The old man waves his hands like he is indestructible. I haul out words like God and damn and fucking and shit, words I've learned from my new friends, words that bite the tongue and spin everything angry and black. I hold them over my head and hurl them with all my strength. I know I want to hurt him.

"Go to your room!" he shouts, pointing in the direction of the stairs.

"No," I say.

"I said go to your room!"

And I run for the basement steps and I sit on my stool and I play every drumhead, every cymbal. I smash every bell with my sticks. I kick the bass drum. I kick the bass drum. I play until my mother returns, hours later, as the sun is coming up and the clouds are parting, and the whole neighborhood is deaf from all that rhythm.

My body has curled itself at the foot of the bass drum. I don't know how long I've been sleeping. I don't know if fatigue caused me to sleep or if the drumming cast a spell on me, drawing me to grow quiet and full of sleep, but I know I have been resting here for a while, clutching the sticks. I wake to their voices in the kitchen—Manong Jack and Ináy—talking loudly. I cannot make out what they're saying. I only know that they are in the kitchen and it is Ináy who is shouting. She never shouts. Stretching, I slowly rise, creep up the stairs, and press my ear to the door.

The voices sound angry but mottled by the walls, by the frying sausages in the pan, by the wind howling above the house. Even the lights humming in the kitchen contribute to the din. I close my eyes, thinking that if I focus, the words will become clear.

"I was speaking the truth," Manong Jack says. "She shouldn't answer back!"

Anger colors Ináy's voice as her pitch rises and falls in a rhythm of admonishment. The words blur, but it is clear she is protesting his behavior.

And then I think I hear her say, "Why did you lecture her in front of her friends?"

"She's seventeen—sixteen—whatever! Bata pa siya!" he says. His voice is clearer than I want it to be. Underneath their banter, I hear my mother sighing. I want to believe she is sticking up for me, reminding him of how hard it must be to move to a new country and leave it all behind. "Don't you remember, mahal?"

"She should be grateful. She has us."

Naku, I think. He's really got a problem if he thinks this is a good deal.

"That video is her life," Ináy says.

"She has no respect. Wala talaga siyang galang."

"Ikaw rin," my mother answers back. "You are so busy talking, being charming-charming naman—you don't listen, mahal. That is her life! We've taken her from everything she loves. You must be patient."

"You too?" Manong Jack says. "Is there no respect in this house?"

"Anog gusto mo, Jack? I care about you and I know it has been hard taking on a second family—Talagang grateful ako— pero you forget. She is my daughter. Anak ko! And she is six-teen. She has a mind of her own na." My mother, who never raises her voice, now bellows like a storm that has blown into town, full and loud and powerful. "Ano ba iyon?"

There is silence. I drop one of my drumsticks and it rolls down the steps as loudly as if I were beating each step myself. I wait a long while before I climb up the stairs and place my hand on the door. I close my eyes and I let her voice move through my body like air, like blood. I don't know what to do. I don't know what to feel. I know I must enter the room. I take a breath and open the basement door, peeking my head around the corner to see if they are sitting at the table or standing on opposite ends of the kitchen. But when I look, there is only Ináy and her empty cup of coffee. Her hands hold her head up, covering her eyes so she doesn't see me walking up to her. On the other side of the house, Danny and Manong Jack sing to each other, their voices, haunting and low, vibrate gently from the walls and open vents.

"Ano," my mother says as I reach down to kiss her cheek. "Your bedroom is not good enough? Now you're sleeping sa basement?"

"I wasn't sleeping."

"So I'm told," she says. "You should know better than to play those drums at night."

I help myself to a plate of eggs and rice. The eggs, sunny-side up, look right at me. Ináy pours me a glass of Ovaltine milk, sweet and chocolaty on my tongue. "You must be patient with him because he is your elder," Ináy says.

"But you should have heard him," I say, pulling on my mother's hand. "He was insulting the whole movement."

"Even if he's wrong, anak," she tells me. "He is your step-father."

I must be dreaming, I think, I must be hearing things. I look into her eyes and I search for the truth. Her face is haggard, the lines pulling her skin downward, her eyes red from crying.

"He is not my father."

"No, he's your stepfather and my husband. He's an elder, Angel."

The kitchen is silent now. No pans frying, no wind humming through the drafts in the windows. Just the sounds of furniture creaking in the other rooms, of footsteps moving in other parts of the house, of old men and young boys greeting one another.

"He's not your husband," I say, not looking at her but at the eggs. I break the yolks and let the yellow ooze into the garlic-fried rice. "He was your ticket to America."

I don't hear her hand coming. I don't see it. But somehow I know to brace myself, to blink upon impact. My cheek burns. My eyes tear up. I slowly shift my gaze from the broken egg yolk and greasy sweet meats on my plate to her face—her face blown up big with anger, framed by stray silver and black hairs, by fine lines where age and worry have marked her. She waits for me. But I sit perfectly still, looking at her like she should be the one to apologize. My hand wants to touch the skin where she has slapped me, but I hold back. I watch her. I let her know. I meant it. I'll say it again. I think it. He was your ticket to America.

She is the one who breaks, who sighs as if it is her last breath. Tears run like rain, wash her soft and blurry, wash her away.

FORTY-FOUR

At school, the girls and I spin stories about the Mahalaya Women, flying in the night, opening doors, freeing the imprisoned. We sit in a corner of the cafeteria, scribbling poems on paper bags and cafeteria napkins. We block out white noise—teenage babble, rattling food trays, and teachers walking by with whistles. "Their hearts were heavy," I say, "because they knew that men were plucking women from the floor and using them."

I close my eyes and I imagine soldiers moving women around like furniture—a couch, a table, a footstool. Deaf to the women's cries, the soldiers threw themselves down and collapsed on the women, drenching them with sweat and the blood of other dead men. And the women held their breath, their arms locked down above their heads, their legs pried wide apart.

Sally pushes her tray away. It's half gone and half there—three tater tots, the last bite of her sloppy joe, and a pile of yellow lettuce leaves and carrots. She pulls out her notebook and scribbles blue ink all over her pages. "O.K., Angel, are you ready? Let's do it."

"Angel wrote a poem?" Lindsey says, her eyebrow rising like a question mark.

I hold my sticks up and hit, marking time, and then I play something like a march on the cafeteria tabletops. Sally rises up and slinks her body to the beat, fake marching, hips hitting the downbeat. Her free arm goes up and her words start to play with the rhythm of my sticks. Every now and then I hit a food tray like a cymbal, I hit the bench like a bass. I hit the bottom of my shoe. Her words dance around my beat. They mean to establish the islands on the other side of the world, they mean to place white America at its shores, they mean to show the struggle of what it means to call yourself big brother to a people who never wanted you at all. To show that your so-called little brown brother isn't so little, isn't your brother, isn't your sister.

She's using her words to tell the story of the occupation. I'm using the beat to show the resistance of the Philippine people.

The girls dance in their seats. As our poem fills the cafeteria, crowding out the white noise, pushing at the air around us, we close our eyes and move back in time, going back to the war, back to the women, back to the villages, and just as we are arriving with our rhythm, with our words, with our poems, there is a disruption.

I open my eyes and I see Officer Jane and Officer Dave combing the cafeteria, their bulky bodies layered in leather and heavy black sweaters. The police move their way through the sea of tables, shifting their bodies left and right, not walking forward but zigzagging. Like the other students, we stop everything to watch them. The officers move to a table on the other side of the room. To a table of black kids. They single out a girl and a guy. Selma Smith and Devon Fox. The pulis make them stand, grab their arms and move the couple through the field of students. Everyone is standing now on their tables, waving arms and shouting into cupped hands. It is the first time I see the students unite—the black and the brown and the white and the yellow. It is the first time we rise to our feet and we come together—when the officers take two of us away.

Voices move like wind across the room, a soft whisper that says the two were seen walking the streets earlier that day, truant and holding hands blocks away from the school. They were seen leaving a White Hen Pantry, armed with doughnuts and hot chocolates, smooching as they walked, their breath rising silently.

Over the P.A. system, the school principal tells everyone to settle down, to take a seat, to remember to respect the cops.

"I thought you said Officer Jane was cool?" I say to Sally.

"She is," Sally says back.

The principal's words only cause more cries of dissent. The teachers walk in twos and threes, waving their arms, palms facing down as if to quiet us. As Selma and Devon walk out the door, students call to them in a last hurrah, like they are warriors sacrificing their lives for us.

"Then why is she taking them away?"

Sally shrugs. "Who knows? Maybe they were truant."

"But we're truant every day," I say.

"Not really," Lindsey says. "We go to the alley and we smoke. We come back."

"We go to the White Hen Pantry," Jenny says. "Sometimes we just walk over, grab more smokes, maybe a Coke."

"That's running an errand," Rachel says. "That's not being truant. They weren't gone during lunch hour. They were gone during second, third, and fourth period. That's truancy."

Selma and Devon are a quiet couple and everybody knows they are in love. She is tall and lean and likes to wear her hair pulled up and cloaked in pretty scarves. She wears golden hoops that dangle about her dark skin, and just a little gloss to make her lips moist. I think she's the prettiest girl in our school. And he's always hanging on her, whispering some sweet joke into her ear as she breaks into a smile, shaking her head. She rewards his bad jokes with kisses. Devon's a stocky boy three times her size and dark skinned with long, black lashes. He's not as tall as some of the other boys, but he's one of the starters on the basketball team and so everyone knows him, how quick he is, how talented and humble he is. What did the police want with them?

Word gets around that this is the third time Devon and Selma have cut classes and been caught and that this time they are facing suspension. I look the word up—suspension—and I see the two of them hanging in the middle of the sky like two bright angels, wingless and lonely. It doesn't make sense to me. I see kids cutting class all the time. We cut class. We even wave to Officer Jane when we see her on the street.

"Something's not right," I say to Sally on the way home from school that day.

"That's just the way it always is," Sally says.

"What is?"

I let my mind rest here, let myself get worked up about the injustice of charging Selma and Devon with truancy. Don't you have to catch them in the act, at least that? I think.

Sally doesn't seem upset and that bothers me. She just keeps saying that's how things are. "But just because that's how things are doesn't mean we got to settle," I say.

"What's the point? And besides, they must mean business. If Devon is suspended, then they won't let him play ball, and we're tied for first place right now."

The sky has gone dark early today and we are walking with flurries of snow swirling around us. The wind howls and sends a chill through my body. I feel hot inside; I feel my anger rise.

"What do you want to do?" Sally says, wiping her running nose with her sleeve. "Start a revolution?"

I stop walking and I turn to her and smile. We look into each other's eyes and I say, "Yes. That's exactly right. We start a revolution."

FORTY-FIVE

That night I am so excited I call Karina's landline after the rest of the house has gone to sleep and my mother is well into her shift at the hospital. I sit at my window, punching the buttons—the zero, the one, the one, the sixty-two, the rest. I wait, I listen. She'll be so excited when she hears that we are starting our own revolution. The sound of it makes my heart beat fast, makes my hand go tight into a fist, to be cast to the sky. I get a weird busy signal so I cut the line and begin again, hitting the zero, the one, the one, the six, the two, the two, the nine and all the while I am already beginning the campaign. There are posters and flyers to make, and meetings to organize. We'll have to get student leaders to approach the principal. I get another busy signal. I figure I am so excited that I am hitting the wrong buttons.

Wait till Karina hears that here, instead of using class to divide the people, authorities use the color of skin. I'm sure she won't believe it. I try again, but this time, a recording comes on and tells me that I cannot dial international calls without a calling card. I try two more times before I give up.

An operator tells me that I cannot make calls on the local line.

"But I always make international calls, I always call overseas on this line."

"Maybe that's why you've been cut off," says the operator. "Have you paid the bill?"

Of course they've paid the bills, I think—and then I realize they have cut me off. How could Ináy do this to me? I place the phone back onto its receiver and even though it is nearly midnight, I run through the house, with my sticks in hands, drumming as I go through doorways, down stairwells, through hallways. I pound on the doorjamb, on the walls. I knock on the railings. I drum my way to the basement, to the top of the stairwell, and to the light switch that will reveal my beautiful set. The sticks click as they hit objects in search of the skin of snare and tom-tom and bass drums. They swish at the air, and when I come to my corner of the house I see an empty space, a hole where my drums used to be. There is a note hanging from the light bulb:

Dearest Angel,
We're sorry to have to take your drums away.
We don't know how else to make you listen.
Love, Papang Jack and Ináy.

Papang Jack? Are they crazy? Ano ba iyon? My heart beats in offbeats, feels red and hot and syncopated. It cannot seem to find a rest. It cannot rest. I sit down where the stool would be and I begin drumming on the tops of my legs, looking for a four/four, half time, bearable beat. I cannot find the beat. I cannot hear the music. I pray that my father finds me, that his spirit moves me out of here, but nothing comes to me. I drum and I drum and I drum so hard that my legs ache under all the pressure. The blood vessels threaten to rise and pop. I call Liza in the suburbs, I beg her to come and get me, to steal me away from this house, but she and Tommy were caught kissing in her room again.

"I'm grounded. But I'll tell you what," she says. "I'll see if Tommy can come to you."

"No," I tell her.

"It's better than nothing," she says. "He'll understand."

For a long time, Tommy and I don't speak. I feel like I am on an alien planet. The air is so cold the stars shiver. The moon is an icicle. Tommy drives toward the water and pulls the car's nose up to the shore.

We listen to hip-hop beating in tandem with the lake's rebellious tide. Tommy's big body shifts to the subtle beats and he whispers rhymes under his breath. When Tommy spins words, he closes his eyes and shifts his head like a metronome. That pulse comforts me, lulls me, lets me find that rhythm my drumsticks have lost.

"So you really think all those kids are gonna walk out?" he asks.

"Yeah, but not because they care about injustice," I say. "They're going to protest taking Devon off the team."

"That's crazy. Sure you can get all those kids to walk out? Crazy."

I ask him how he and Liza got caught and he smiles and says, "Aw that was messed up. We weren't even doing anything. We were cuddling and fell asleep in her bed—our books were still open when her moms comes into the room. BAM—the door goes wide and BOOM the lights go on and she's yelling at me like I just killed her daughter and I'm running out of that room, my hands pulling at my clothes and my socks in my pockets an shit. Man! It was the worst!" And even as Tommy is talking I am picturing the two of them, skin pressed against skin, woozy from sleep and dreaming something sweet when words loud as firecrackers pop in their ears. I imagine Liza's mama wrapped up in her blue robe and her hair up in rollers and her face all greasy with night cream, chasing after Tommy like an aswáng fallen from the limbs of a magnolia tree, slapping him with the back of her slipper and all I can do is laugh. He has his hands on his belly now, laughing like he's going to pee in his pants. "Then Liza is all screaming and crying like it's my fault we got caught. Shoot dang I think that girl is grounded for life!"

"Where was her dad?"

"That cat? Who knows!" Tommy says. "I'm just glad I didn't see him on my way out! Thank you, Mama Mary!"

Tommy says you got to laugh even when it's ugly, and I think maybe he's right. His girlfriend has been grounded for life and here he is, sitting with me next to a frozen lake, cranking his music when he could be home, sleeping under piles of warm blankets.

"Ain't no big thing," he says. "Sometimes you need your peeps to keep you going. Don't be too rough on old Manong Jack. He was a widower for years before your moms came around—always jokin' everybody—but you could tell he was lonely. You could tell he had lost the love of his life when Manang Betty died. He'd act all tough and tell his badoy jokes to all of us—man, they sucked—but you could see it in his eyes. He was sad. So it was good for him to meet your moms, you know?"

I shrug, not wanting to seem ungrateful. I think about how Manong Jack can't stop talking, hiding all that sadness with the noise of meaningless words. "Yeah," I say, "don't expect me to feel for them. I hate them."

"But you don't hate Jordan."

"Shut up, Tommy," I say, and even as I say it, I feel a little smile growing.

We sit until the sky goes from opaque to transparent gray to blue. He chants meaningless words all night long and soon I am grunting too, making up syllables, arranging them in the air. Bumping consonants and stretching vowels, rolling my tongue to the beat. We sit until the sun taps the moon on the shoulder and the night becomes day.

When I enter the house, Ináy is sitting at the kitchen table with her coat and hat still on. She's watching me through the back window. "Where were you all night?" she asks me as I shut the door.

"Where are my drums?" I ask her.

"This is not a hotel."

"Where are my drums?" I ask again.

She looks at me for a long time and then turning away, she takes her hat off, then her coat. Hanging them by the door, she says, "You'll get them back when you start acting like my anak again. When you respect your Papang Jack. When you return, my darling girl." And then she disappears up the stairs, like a ghost haunting an old house, moving lightly like a whisper.

FORTY-SIX

I write Karina. I press the pen down hard and words sink into the paper, blue ink clotting across the page. I draw my life, my crazy stepfather, my white friends, the tsismis about Tommy and Liza getting caught in each others' arms. I write what I cannot say, wonder what it's like to lie with a boy, to sleep with his skin pressing up against you, to breathe with him. My native tongue scores the pages, the vowels fat and round as lychees, the words rich with multiple syllables. I season the stories with hot consonants and sparks of bright accents. It's almost like drumming. I tell her about Officer Jane and Officer Dave. I tell her about Devon and Selma and how there is a rumor going around that tomorrow during the big game we are all walking out.

For days the halls have been humming, vibrating with a kind of electricity and protest. Suspending Devon jeopardizes our Spartan's first-place standing. I don't hear anything about injustice—oh, I do—but it's mostly connected to the beat of basketballs hitting the court, to the swoosh of nets and three-point baskets. It's connected to the fear of being second place. I listen to the hum and I buzz too, but my song is so out of tune. I am thinking of disparity, of the wrong done Selma and Devon. I am thinking of racism and that so-called American Dream.

On game day, Ináy drops Danny off on her way to work. She hands me a backpack with a built-in baby seat, so he can ride piggyback wherever we go.

"You watch your brother, ha?" she says as she places him before me like a prize. "Don't get distracted."

"Opo," I say, holding onto his hand. Danny squirms to be free.

She kisses us quickly, a habit without any meaning. One and two and then she's gone, driving through the parking lot and out of our day.

I take him to my locker and peel the winter right off of his two-year-old body. I unwind the scarf around his face, loosen the hood and pull off the coat, the snow pants, the boots, the double sets of mittens, and the hat. Underneath all that, Ináy has placed him in a little green T-shirt and purple pants. Even as I am freeing him from clothing, he is squirming and squirming, giddy with the energy in the school.

"You stay near, O.K.?" I say to him. "Don't run away from Ate." He laughs in my face and leans over and plants an open wet mouth on my cheek. "I need you to be a good boy, O.K., Danny?"

Meanwhile, kids walk by the locker, patting him on the head and calling him cute. "Don't distract me, O.K., Danny?"

I kiss him on the forehead and then, yanking him up in the air, I seat him in the carriage strapped on to my back. We walk as one unit and when we enter the gym, he squeals at the sight of the crowd, waving like he is the star, the center, an athlete of great magnitude. I'm hoping all this excitement will keep him occupied.

The cheerleaders line the floor, leaping up sporadically, their skinny white legs splitting in the air like wishbones, their perfectly blond curls bouncing like hair in a shampoo commercial. The bleachers shake as I climb them, placing my hands on each step like Danny and I are crawling up a mountain. There are so many people in the stands and when I look across the gym, all I see is green.

When I get to the top, I give my brother away. "O.K.," I say to Lindsey, "Liza and Tommy should be here any minute. So can you watch him for awhile?"

"Love to!" she yells above the crowd.

"You have to keep him on your back, or he'll wander off and you'll never get control of him."

"Got it," she says.

The girls coo as I lift him off my back and everyone treats him like a live teddy bear. "He looks just like you," they say. "He's a little Angel," they say.

"Danilo," I say, stern like he's in trouble. "I have to go, but you watch me, O.K.?" There is a roar and we look down and see Sparky the Spartan enter, a purple cape of velvet trailing after him. Danny squeals and claps his hands.

The revolution is a winter storm swirling white noise in our tiny gym. Two hundred voices burst like thunderclaps, banging up against steel beams and glass ceilings, vibrating on thick walls of concrete. In this sea of green and purple, people tiny as grains of sand swirl and spill from bleachers onto wide, waxed floors. Students march in place, moving to the buzz, the energy circling like wind, a monsoon waiting to happen. The band's brass instruments point at the nets, at the rim, at the backboard, trombones sliding, tubas groaning, teasing the crowd. The drums slam-dunk the beat. Bum bum bum.

A couple of teachers guard the doors, arms crossed and smiling at all this positive energy. Jordan, Jenny, and I scatter across the length of the basketball court. On either ends of the floor, news cameras, set on tripods with legs long and awkward as spiders, stand by. Print photographers crouch low to the ground, holding onto cameras with their too-large lenses. This is a big game.

When the Cougars and Spartans go bounding onto court like warriors, the students jump, cupping palms like megaphones, shooting words like bullets from a gun. I tilt my head back, howling, eyes closed, full moon flashing in my night sky. For a moment my body is transported into the middle of EDSA Boulevard, surrounded by a thousand resisters, bringing down Estrada. All the blood shoots from my heart to all the limbs, spinning round and round and I am nearly dizzy from all the adrenaline.

MAKIBAKA!

DO NOT FEAR!

I nearly forget that this is not the same. I nearly forget how cold it is outside. I nearly forget that I am no longer marching on the streets, holding on to old comfort women, singing resistance songs with the farmers. No, now I'm a sophomore in America, standing in the middle of a court, screaming b-ball cheers. I nearly make the mistake of thinking this is the same damn thing. I realize that I am holding my breath and if I want to breathe, better do it now. Better give it all I got, 'cuz I've been turning blue for months holding it.

WE BAD, WE KNOW IT, AND WE KNOW HOW TO SHOW IT!

Everybody is clapping, dancing on those bleachers, chanting like this is a celebration.

COUGARS THINK THEY GOT IT ALL, BUT THEY DON'T—UH-UH, WE DO!

I get so lost in the voices, in the way the words build and move me, send me flying. Each letter pushes something in me, a vibration that gathers other vibrations, other letters, words, and I am ready to explode.

I run off the baseline and I grab a plastic bucket, swinging the straps over my shoulders and grabbing my sticks. I go BANG BANG BANG, like a mad lady. BANG BANG BANG! The women's locker room flies open and a line of resisters marches onto the floor, weaving about the basketball players like a long caterpillar with dozens of legs, kicking up at the knees. They use their hands, pounding their buckets like tight-skinned bongos. They march in a figure eight. They march in a zigzag. They march until referees chase them off the floor.

I lead them with my sticks, I feel each pulse and I release the energy into the air with a bang. Holding the silence between each beat of the drum, the space between the words, I lift the stick up in the air, exaggerate the movement, dare to hesitate and then, at the very last moment, I bring the stick down, I make a sound. I breathe between the beats. I rest. I summon Papang from my heart and let him explode on the scene. He is exactly what this revolution needs. He is the spirit of the revolution. Papang.

The lights go down and suddenly all the players have disappeared and there is only one spotlight flooding the gymnasium's wood floors. The students make snake sounds as the announcer calls out the Cougars' starting lineup. Boys skinny and awkward run into the light and, hitting center court, they go blind with so much brightness. The Cougars are mostly white kids of Polish and Russian descent whereas our team is mostly made up of African Americans, a couple of Latinos, and one or two white kids.

When the announcer calls out the Spartans, the noise is so loud our voices merge. We are the noise. The speakers crank the same disco music that the Chicago Bulls use and it makes the students go nuts. The man sings the boys' names like he is God and he himself has named each boy, his position, and in fact fashioned his very soul. When they fail to announce Devon Fox, I run into the spotlight and crack my plastic drum so loud the lights flash. Off court, the snares have joined me, the bass drums too. They keep my beat and when the lights go up, our plastic-bucket drum corps marches around the court, fast like speeding through an obstacle course, banging drums, and all the kids rise to their feet. The drummers stop. I hit my sticks together and they march in place, like soldiers.

And then it begins. They move. They walk. They march their way across the court and out the door; the students in the bleachers rise up, fists punching at the air, voices clamoring. The drum corps yells and the rest of the gymnasium responds, and as we march out the doors, the students follow us, spilling out into the hallways and then the parking lot and then the block. Every Spartan leaves the gym, marching and hollering until finally there is no one left but the players and the Cougar fans, rivals caught off guard and amazed; rivals stunned to silence.

In the parking lot, we continue the protest, pulling out poster boards and signs, marching around the entrance of the building and calling to one another.

HOW WE GONNA STAY ON TOP WHEN PLAYER'S GONE, YOU GIVIN' UP?

Each word floats on the white cloud of our breath, crowding the sky and the cold Chicago air. The wind tries to drown us out, but we just get louder. To stay warm, we jump up and down, dancing in place, waiting for the media to grab their coats and come and join us. My toes have already gone numb in my boots. The skin on my fingers feels cracked and dry. I refuse to wear gloves. I can't afford to let my drumsticks slip.

HOW WE GONNA STAY ON TOP WHEN PLAYER'S GONE, YOU GIVIN' UP?

A sharp wind blows and the crowd moans like maybe it wants to run back into the building. I glance up and I see Lindsey waving at me, calling me. I wave back. Jordan slips next to me, and leaning into my ear he whispers, "This is so dope, girl." And then he kisses me right there, right on my ear. His breath smells like peppermint, hot as Manila heat. It seeps into my skin and ignites something I don't recognize. So off-guard am I, I go red and the sticks slip from my hands and slide across the ice and I have to scramble to pick them up.

Just then, the gym doors burst open and three television news crews descend on us. Jenny, Jordan, and I keep the crowd chanting. My friends raise their placards to the sky and I beat the drum. I beat the drum.

We are hot with fire now, all chanting and cheering for the cameras, waving our signs, dancing to the beat of our plastic drums. We do it for the cameras, the public eyes that are sitting among us, marching with us, holding our signs for us. We stand out there, the sun slipping completely away, the moon nowhere in sight. The snow falls again, falling and falling, trying to hush our voices, trying to blanket us with such a chill we run for cover.

"Angel!" Lindsey yells across the parking lot. The light has gone and all I see is her tall figure, arms up and head cocked like she's tired.

"Hold on," I yell back. "The team is ready to come out."

That's when I see Liza and Tommy walking underneath the parking lot lights, hand in hand. I take a step toward them, and they call out, "How's it going?"

"Sorry we're late," Liza says. "We got caught in traffic. There was a huge pileup on 295."

"You just got here?" I ask, looking back at Lindsey. "Hey, Lindsey!"

But she's no longer standing in the shadows with the rest of the kids. I run through the crowd, calling her name, and someone says she's back in the building. I drop the drum. I drop my sticks and I run into the hallways, calling out to her. There is a wave of heat that sucks me in, swallows me whole. My wet boots slide down the corridor past reporters and cameramen. "Lindsey!" I shout. "Where's Danny?"

I fly into the girls' room and knock on every stall. I stumble back out and run up the stairwells, calling out Danny and Lindsey's names. There is nothing. There is no one.

Above the first floor, the halls are long and dark. Blue light comes from the windows. The shadow of falling snow casts ghost figures onto walls. I run laps on the second, third, and fourth floors, and all I hear are my own footsteps. My feet, blocks of ice, slow me down. The world freezes. Nothing moves. And then I hear the voices down below. I hear the teams in the locker rooms. I listen to my heart. It beats louder than all the drums of our protest. I breathe. I listen to that rhythm, the pulse of it, the open and close of it. And then I'm running back down the stairwell, through the hallway, and onto the basketball court.

I can hear him crying, lost in a wild nightmare. His small figure, no larger than a teenager's winter coat, lies underneath the bleachers. He rests his chest on his knees, his face too. His arms lie limply at his side. It is the wailing that breaks my heart. Still wrapped up in sweaters, scarves, and thick boots packed with ice, I crawl to him, trailing slush behind me. He doesn't see me. He doesn't hear me. He doesn't feel me pick him up and put his head to my chest.

"Naku, sweet boy," I whisper in his ear. I wipe the hair out of his eyes and I make him look at me. "Here I am, sweet boy. It's Ate. Here I am." He sees me, but doesn't recognize me. I place my arms around his whole body and embrace him as if the act of holding on will help him remember. I put my hands on his back and I rub. My palms go hot. I cradle him and place one hand on his heart. I say nothing more. He hiccups. I rock him and he quivers. The tears fall and fall until the heat of my body quiets him and he is calm.

FORTY-SEVEN

That night, Danny will not sleep unless I lie next to him. I cover his skin in baby powder and bundle him up in flannel. We snuggle under a mound of blankets. He pulls at my fingers. He tugs at my hair. When I give him a kiss on the nose and roll away, he cries. I roll back. I look into his big cow eyes and they are glossy with tears. What did I do, I think. What happened to you? I embrace him and he sniffs at my skin. "Time to sleep," I say, and I sing him a counting song in Tagalog. I name him the stars in Ilokano. "I'm sorry," I tell him. "I was distracted."

I look out the window, searching the empty limbs of trees for women dressed in white, guarding me and waiting to break me of this prison. But it's only me and the moon and the barren trees. It's too cold even for the stars to come out.

Even after he has drifted off, he cries in his sleep and I find myself next to him, holding him, brushing the damp hair from his forehead and letting the palms of my hands hover above him, blessing him. I have not told Ináy what happened in the gym, how I gave him away to a friend to watch and how she set him down for two seconds and he was gone. Maybe the noise scared him. Maybe the drums. But he was out of Lindsey's arms and running. She could not keep up with him, the way he weaved his body through the many legs, the way he crawled between the bleachers. She spent most of the rally searching for my little brother. And I am not sure what he did in that time. Was he simply lost and scared? Had someone found him? Hurt him? When I gathered him up and held him, he was hysterical with tears, but there were no signs of injury, no broken bones or bruises. His clothing was all intact. What could cause a boy to run? To cry like that? Between sleep and wakefulness, he is terrorized. But when he sees me and feels my arms and the heat of my hands, he sighs, closes his eyes, and falls back to dreaming.

After a long while, I rise and lock the door. Then I pull out blues records and I spin them low like lullabies. In the giant bed, I stay up all night and write down my heart. Tomorrow I'll send the letter to Lola Ani, the only grown-up besides Papang who ever understood.

Torn ako, Lola. Gusto ko ng justice so I organized the protest. Di ba, justice must be organized? Justice must be won? But then I lost Danny. Scared ako. What did I do?

I let the music roll and my heart opens up, opens up, opens up. This is the blues and it feels good. In two years, I will be eighteen and I can leave this house and all the people in it and they won't be able to do a thing. I won't even need the Mahalaya Sisters.

Mrs. Jackson, our school principal, announces that from now on all students who get caught cutting classes more than three times will be suspended—no matter what color they are. They drop Selma and Devon's suspension, provided that our core group takes responsibility.

We are sentenced to a month's worth of detention and we're asked to put together a responsible presentation on the civil rights movement for the entire school. I smile at this and as I'm walking out, Mrs. Jackson says, "Don't get any bright ideas, Ms. de la Luna. I read your paper."

FORTY-EIGHT

After school, Jordan meets me outside.

"Can I walk you home?" he asks. He pulls my body close to his, so close I feel like I can't breathe, like I don't want to.

I say I can't. I tell him I have to go straight home. I say, "You don't know how much trouble I'm in."

He breathes into my neck, whispers, "But I'm walking you home. You won't be late." His words are soft and warm and I don't know why. Maybe because I want him to stop. Maybe because suddenly I realize we are acting like one of those silly couples in that corridor—I say yes, o.k., let's go.

He pulls me up from the bench and guides me through the parking lot. We shuffle our feet through the white powder dusting the ground and make our way out onto the streets.

"Nothing clears the head like a walk," he says.

I look over my shoulder at the school, at the kids still standing against the walls, and he tugs at me and says, "Don't worry, Angel. We're good."

We walk east on Addison, moving toward Lake Michigan. It's a long walk from Western to the lake and it seems we are heading right into the freezing winds. We don't talk. I breathe in and move along the wide avenue, looking at the sandstone three-flats standing like little castles with wide picture windows. I tilt my face up to the sky and let the snow melt on my cheeks.

For a while we talk about the walkout on the Cougars, how hot that was, how dope. "I haven't felt that way in a long time," I tell him.

"Like what?"

"Alive. Like I got something to fight for."

When we get to Clark Street, we take a left and move north, peeking into small shops and boutiques. We pass a storefront window displaying Mama Mary with open arms, plastic flowers, and a neon-lighted sign that says, Abierto.

"In the Philippines, my mother was a healer," I say.

"She's a nurse," he says. "Right?"

I nod my head and imagine the long lines of people snaking through our living room, waiting their turn before the makeshift shrine to my saintly papang. "It was different back home," I say.

We walk past windows where mannequins gesture at the air, their fingers webbed together like aliens. On the sidewalk, people wrapped in scarves and heavy coats storm past us, breath rising from them like smoke from house chimneys. People walk with eyes cast down, searching for their path, holding on to their privacy. Yeah, this is the American Dream, I think. Keep to your own path. Do not look up. Do not make contact with the bodies around you. Stay warm. But Jordan pulls me close to him, and at intersections where the red hand flashes STOP before us, he leans in and kisses my eyelashes.

"Where are we going?" I ask.

"You'll see."

Above us the sun is still trying to break through the haze of snowfall. I look up and see the white shadow of its moonlike body lined against the white sky. I breathe and the cold air rushes through me and sends energy jumping from my skin.

We come upon the high, iron gates of Graceland Cemetery. Angels tall as buildings guard the dead; their wings span the width of the cemetery entrance and their hands gesture us to come in. We stop for a moment and I gaze up into their faces, green from weathering so much rain and snow and wind. Their eyes are big and wide and vacant. Their cheeks, fat copper globes of green, remind me of Lila. They are dressed in white gowns of winter.

"They're beautiful," I whisper.

We walk under their wings and step around the graves. Above us, the skeletons of trees and their ice-plated branches point to the sky, to the east and west. The sun comes out of the fog and suddenly it's as if there are crystals everywhere. The graves are underground, so different than in the Philippines where bodies live in little houses rising up from the ground and stacked like city buildings, one on top of another. I tell Jordan about the last time Lola Ani and I cleared the weeds and branches from my Lolo Ninoy's tomb, how we lit candles and watched the flames rise high and were so sure he was blowing on those little votive candles.

We find an iron bench and Jordan brushes the snow from the seat and we huddle close to one another. I take my gloves off and peel the mittens from his long fingers.

"What are you doing?" he says, laughing.

"Nothing," I say. "I just want to hold your hand."

It is so cold out, but I feel warm next to him. I feel good in the company of all these saints. The stories escape into the winter air. First it is the story of my life at St. Magdalena's. "We could not afford it after my Papang died," I tell him. "I had to stop and work as a maid and my little sister would go to school half-day and then she would work right next to me."

He doesn't say anything; he just pulls me closer to him. "Do you think that's bad?" I ask him.

"Why's that bad?" Jordan wants to know.

"We had to sell our house," I say. "We moved into a convent," I whisper. And his eyes go big and then I smile and say, "With nuns!"

"Nuns?" he says. "Man, I could never be a nun—they can't have sex, right?"

Talking to him is so easy. Slowly I pull the words that have been piling up in the bottom of my heart and I cast them out into the open cemetery. And I remember. I see myself sneaking into the hallway, peeking into Ináy's room. She is collapsed on the bed and Lola Ani is lying next to her, holding her, and they are crying together, whispering Papang's name over and over like a prayer to God. Lola Ani says, "Huwág ka na umiyak." But even still, all they do is cry. "We will find a way to pay for everything. Ernesto is watching over us," she's telling my mother. "He will find a way." I see myself running to the bed, joining them, crying too but not knowing why I am crying and so devoted to their sadness.

"What do you think would be harder?" I ask him. "Losing your parents or losing your country?"

"That's crazy," he says, smiling. "I can live anywhere as long as I got my family. Why?"

I shake my head, say I don't know. Say I lost both my parents and my country.

"No, you didn't. You got your mom. You got your sister and brother. You got your grandmother and a stepdad and you might even have me."

I smile because for a minute it sounds so true. I say, "You think?"

"I know."

"Well, I don't have a stepdad. So you can stop there."

Visions from my past paint the skies at Graceland Cemetery. Jordan watches them, nodding, holding me closer with each image. I talk so much that sometimes I slip into Tagalog, but he doesn't stop me, he lets me tell the story anyway, and I feel that there is more room in my body to breathe. I tell the stories until the sun melts into the white sky and there is nothing around us but the night. I cannot even feel my toes, but inside I am so warm and lighthearted. I think I might even be happy.

"Man," he says putting my palms to his face. "Your hands are hot!"

"Yeah," I tell him. "That happens sometimes." I put my hands on my face and feel the heat of them penetrating my skin.

"How do you do that?" he asks.

I shrug at him and say, "It just does. I get it from my mother."

In between the stories there is a pause like the earth breathing wind everywhere. In between the stories and the silence, Jordan begins talking and what I hear opens my heart.

"My old man and I are always fighting. He doesn't think I see how hard he works. How he comes home defeated and broke even though all day long he's been riding up and down that elevated track, calling out street names. It's all good, he works every day like that and I feel for him, but he doesn't know what we go through either. He thinks we're spoiled."

Jordan's face goes soft when he talks about his dad. I see how much he loves him, even though his dad is always yelling at him. I tell him I know, that my mother is the same way. She only has to work three days a week, twelve hours a day, but she works every day for the extra cash.

"What she gonna do with all that money?" Jordan asks. He knows they pay nurses pretty good money, so I tell him she wants to buy the American Dream, bring my whole family over here and put us into fine schools and clean houses.

"That's what she thinks, anyway," I say. "Sometimes I miss her."

"Yeah," he says, holding on to me. "I hear that."

I reach into my pouch and pull out my stacks of letters. I hold them up to the rising moon.

"What are those?" he asks, looking over my shoulder. "Love letters?"

I shake my head and the tears start to fall again.

"Aw," he says, don't." A sharp breeze blows through the cemetery and I hold on to the letters like they might fly away.

"Looks like they've never been opened."

My whole body shakes no. He says, "Why not?"

And I shrug that I don't know.

"Don't you want to know?" he asks.

I riffle through the envelopes, counting them and sorting them by date. There are over fifty letters on onionskin paper folded over, blue and fading. I tell him that when she sent them to me, I wanted to light them on fire.

"But you didn't," he said.

And I say to him, "I know, right?"

My hands are burning right through my gloves. I peel them off, the tears coming down my face so fast, so hot, and the wind blowing them frozen at once.

"Hey," he whispers, kissing me. "Hey."

I let the tears mingle there on our lips. I let our breath warm our mouths. There's something more I want to say, but I don't know what—only that this kiss feels so good. He moves with me, his hands following mine, like music. Like beating the drum. Like he knows what I am feeling.

"This is it," I think out loud.

"What?" he wants to know.

"The American Dream," I whisper back.

And he laughs out loud like I might be crazy, but he knows what I mean. In a single afternoon of walking the city, he knows what I am talking about. I feel it and that's when I remember. "Patay!" I shout, pushing away from him. "I'm so late!"

We run out of the cemetery, careful not to step on people's graves. The night has turned so cold that we dance on one leg then two, waiting for the Montrose bus. The big city bus rolls to a stop right in front of us, its brakes squeaking and hot. We hop on and run to the back of the bus, the stink of the city mixed with the heat coming out of vents. Holding hands, we watch the neighborhoods go by us, the moon shining down on us like a guardian angel. I count the stops going west and by the time we get to my block, an hour has gone by and I am rushing to get out. I don't even stop to say good-bye or thank you. I know I'll see him soon. I know that a fight is brewing at my house and I don't care. I haven't felt like this since before Papang died. Free ako. Free.

FORTY-NINE

At home, Ináy's so mad she's blowing words from her mouth and spewing them in the air and they are settling around me like ashes falling from Mount Pinatubo. She dances madly around me as I sit at the kitchen table eating, waving her arms at me, and scrunching her once-beautiful face.

"You are only in the U.S. for three months and you are causing riots?" Tears begin falling too. "What are you trying to do to me? Ano ba ito?"

I stop eating. I don't look at her. I sit with my arms crossed and my shoulders held back like a warrior. I catch glimpses of her tirade at each revolution around my chair.

"Why are you always making trouble? Why are you always kontrabida?" She sounds like an aswáng gone mad. "I understand that Lola Ani and Tita Mary Matthew put ideas into your head, I understand why you would rebel against me by taking to the streets back home, but what do you care about basketball? What do you care about two strange kids?"

She leans into my face and examines me. I stay perfectly still. I stare straight ahead and I focus on the sky, on the flurries of snow wafting down. I think about standing in the middle of the street with my arms stretched out and my head flung back, catching the little white flakes on the tip of my tongue. I know the snow would sting my mouth.

"I give up! I don't know how to be your ináy anymore!"

It's not like you ever did, I think.

"And how do you think you're going to fulfill this month of detention? I need you home! I need you here!"

I continue eating as she moves around me. I pretend she isn't there. I scoop the rice and meat onto a tablespoon and carefully slip the food into my mouth. I close my eyes. I chew. I taste the sweet meat, the salt of the toyo, the soft grains of rice.

It is her fault, after all. She insisted I be here. She insisted I leave my sister and my grandmother. She insisted on this American Dream. From here, I can't even think about visiting my Papang's grave. So I have started my own revolution. I want to go home. I want to leave this place, this so-called dream, and get back to my reality. I think that soon, she'll cave in. I think Manong Jack will be happy when she does.

"Walang hiya!" she's yelling. Like she should know about shame.

Where did she go when Papang died? What did she think the neighbors saw when she would float right out of the house and into the trees? And how long did she wait before she married this old man? Papang was still warm from the sun, from the fire of the van that burned his body on the Cordillera hills. I take a sip of my water.

"Your Papang Jack was right about you."

I finish off the rest of my rice and meat. I peel a banana and I eat it slowly.

"Anak," she yells. "I am losing my patience already."

I give her a look and then I clear my plate, rinsing it in the sink, and then I leave her there, rattling around the kitchen with Danny, loud and crazy.

Late one night, after she has gone to work, I open the back door and I let Tommy into the house. We sneak down the stairs to the basement and settle into the overstuffed couches. I turn the television on and keep it low. Blue lights flicker off the walls as images move and roll around on the screen. He doesn't talk much.

"Where's Liza?" I ask.

He shrugs. "At home, I guess."

"What's wrong?" I ask.

The light hits his face and makes him look so blue. "Nothing, I guess." Then he tells me that Billy called him that day. "He asked me if you saw his video and I told him—Oh yeah, she did!"

"Did you tell him about crazy Manong Jack too?"

He nods. "He wants to know if you saw the whole tape."

"More or less," I say.

"He says there are messages for you at the end of the tape."

I put the tape in and we watch it from the very beginning and it's like I am seeing it for the first time. The images come to me slow like a memory that returns after a long, deep sleep. A clip of the old women protesting with their mouths gagged and their hands tied in yards of hemp rope stirs something inside me, a kind of truth. Perhaps the school walkout was dramatic and effective, but the cause was so tiny compared to the plight of the comfort women, so forgettable next to the old farmer with nowhere to go, or the overseas worker who comes home in a pine box after months of physical abuse.

I think about the protest and the way I lost my brother, and while I won't say it to Ináy, I wonder about what we did. I mean, we knew what we were doing, but the rest of the school thought it was about the game. They walked out for the game, not for the injustice toward black kids. I should be happy. I should be feeling at home in my role as a fighter. But now that it is over and all that's left is this: a boy who wakes in the middle of the night with eyes wild and breath shallow and small. I want to sleep forever. I want to fold up like a dying blossom and let the wind carry me away.

"You think the protest was worth it?" I ask him.

"Hey," Tommy says, smiling at me. "You made a change, didn't you? And you now know you got the power to organize if you need to. That's something, right?"

"Messed up my little brother too," I say.

"You didn't know."

At the end of the documentary, the tape goes all scratchy with noise and the images garble up and then Lila pops up on the screen, smiling. She stands under a banyan tree, tossing a mango in her right hand, her hip jutting off to the left.

She says, "Hey, Ate, how's it going?" She's filling out her body now. Her breasts are swollen and her hips round like the curve of a bass guitar. Red splotches of rouge streak across her cheeks. Shimmering blue eye shadow dusts her eyelids.

"Oh, my God," I say. "She looks like a tart."

"We miss you," she says, her eyes filling up with tears. "But don't worry about us. Lola Ani and I watch over each other and we don't ride the jeepney anymore."

Lila wipes her eyes dry with the hem of a tight T-shirt. After a second she says, "Jun drives us. Mother Mary makes him."

She talks as if we are standing under the same banyan tree; her voice sinks into my skin and travels right to my belly.

"Wipe that stuff off your face," I whisper to her in Tagalog. I want to run my hands under her eyes and stop the tears from coming down. I want to embrace her and stand quietly like that—just Lila and me under the banyan tree. How long has it been? I feel my own eyes tearing up when just as suddenly as she's there, she's gone and standing under the same banyan tree is Karina.

I'd forgotten how small Karina's eyes are, how light skinned she is. Her hands move as she talks, and her legs shift from side to side like she cannot stand still. She blabbers on and on about school and how everything is the same but feels incomplete. "Something's missing," she says. "It's so tahimik."

"She's hot," Tommy says.

"I'm sure she'd appreciate that," I tell him, punching his arm. "Liza too."

"You're the one that's missing!" Karina blows kisses into the frame. "Mahal kita!" she says. "Love you, love you, love you!" she sings.

She has a million things more to say, but when she ends, her body goes suddenly still and her face grows serious. No smile, no shiny eyes. She takes a breath and ends by reading one of her poems:

> Ikaw ang puso ko.
> Ang hangin mo, ang hininga ko.
> Ang lupa mo, katawan ko.
> Ang diwa mo, ang buhay ko.
> Wag ka matakot. Nandito ako.
> Wag ka umiyak, wag ka magulan.
> Laging nandito ako. Laging lalaban ako.
> Para sayo, Pilipinas ko.

Tommy shakes his head and says, "That's so deep. Look at her, man. What's she saying?"

"How do you know that's deep?" I say.

"Can't you just feel it? What is that, a love poem?"

"Love poem to the Philippines," I say, a little amazed at how he got it. "Is that a tear?" I say, reaching over to his fat cheek and wiping it clean with the palm of my hand.

"What if it is, you don't think I can feel or something? I'm a poet, sister."

When we turn our attention back to the television, Lola Ani is sitting on the church steps. My sister fusses over Lola Ani, brushing her hair while Lola waves her away, scolding Lila, who simply kisses her. The camera zooms in on Lola's eyes and focuses, the lines of her face fill the screen, the fading color of her jet-black eye shimmers softly.

The frame settles on her small face and her hair of white. She looks tired and the skin hangs off her bones like clothing on a hanger. Her mouth trembles as she speaks and I see she has aged one hundred years since I've been gone. Her voice has grown scratchy and teeters in the air like any minute it may fall to the sala floor and shatter into a million pieces. When I close my eyes and listen to her, I cannot find her—only a shadow of her, a faded imitation.

"Ano," she begins. "Kamusta?" she wants to know.

I answer her under my breath. "Eto na ako," I tell her. Look at me, I think, and you can see how I am.

She is trying to smile but the muscles in her face resist, and all the trembling in her mouth and face and head releases tears. She starts by speaking in Tagalog, greeting me, missing me, sending love to me, and then her voice hardens a little when she begins her lecture. It's no secret that I have been difficult. It seems the whole community back home knows it. "You're a woman," she's saying. "You are a feminista. You should know better. How hard, how painful it is for your ináy." And for a while I can feel Lola's hands on me, holding on to me and rubbing my arm as she speaks. I can feel her breath in my ear, the smell of her baby powder wafting from her skinny neck. Her voice gets shaky and full of static, like something is in its way—something in the throat, something in the heart. But she pushes the words out and the words change from Tagalog to Ilokano, a dialect from her birth.

I lean forward and Tommy rubs my back, like he can sense the change too. It's a little strange being this close to him, having him touch me in such a familiar way, but it feels kind of nice, too.

"After the war," Lola Ani says. "Many husbands abandoned their wives when they found out. Disowned them. Many husbands acted like their wives agreed to participate in this war and they stopped loving their wives, but your lolo was different. He wasn't even married to me when he found me, when he learned of my past, but he loved me just the same."

She paints a picture of their family home—burnt to the ground, the charred bamboo foundations, the roofless flooring, the lack of walls. She was only seventeen, but lost and in search of her family. She had been walking in circles for days. Her face was covered with dust from the road and her skin smelled unclean. Her feet were swollen and sore from walking on the hard, cracked earth, scorched with sun. She had wrapped the soles of her feet in leaves and had finally crawled her way to where the house should have been standing. When she found no one there, her heart stopped altogether and she went mad. Collapsing on the site, she sobbed.

Lolo Ninoy didn't know who she was, but he heard her weeping from the main road. He followed the cries and found her lying like a fallen angel, her clothing like wings tattered and soiled crumpled about her.

He took her to his family home and he nursed her back to health. His sisters had been taken by the soldiers, his aunts too. He pitied my lola and he found her beautiful even in her madness. He saw something glimmering inside of her, a fire. "Nawala ako sa sarili ko."

It didn't matter to Ninoy that she was mad, because he understood the nature of her illness, and he knew what the Japanese soldiers were capable of. He had lost his sisters to them.

First, he bathed her and gave her clothing that was not ripped or stinking of blood and body. He let her sleep for what felt like months, till her bones strengthened and her skin healed and he thought he saw the inkling of angel wings where her shoulder blades protruded. And after she was strong, he nursed her heart, holding her when she asked for it and leaving her alone when she needed it.

Sometimes her madness spewed angry words—senseless words, spiteful and dangerous—aiming them at anyone who was near. Sometimes she was silent for weeks, seeing nothing before her. She'd ignore him and she would ignore herself, forgetting to eat, forgetting how to sleep and soiling herself. The silence was uncomfortable and it would have been easy to leave her then, but he waited until the episode passed. Sometimes the words and the pain met in the center of her being and she would tell him the stories of her life in the garrison. This was hardest for him, for in these moments he had to picture her lying with her legs strewn apart, the angry men filed in neat little lines, waiting to attack her. He had to know what happened. He listened to her and did not judge her. She learned to trust him, to be his friend. She opened up and she told him everything.

"Angel," Lola Ani says, "I have not told you everything. I have not told many people because it is my business what happened to me. But you see how dedicated I am to the plight of the comfort women, you must have suspected, huh? Anak, people have their reasons for making choices you cannot understand, and if you love them, no matter how much you cannot understand, you trust them. You are patient with them."

I knew that my family had suffered during the war, I knew that we had lost family members and that Lola Ani was blessed to have survived, but this I didn't know.

Every time she was chosen by a little yellow man, her spirit was slaughtered, her body beaten. "Sometimes," Lola whispers, "they come to me seven times in one day. Seven times I die in one day, seven times for thirty days, for twelve months. I cannot believe Ninoy still wanted me after knowing that."

I can hear Lila crying next to her, sighing as Lola Ani speaks. "O.K., La," Lila whispers. "O.K."

"O.K., La," I chime in too. "O.K." I am weeping now. And Tommy, who has no idea what Lola's words mean, is crying with me.

"That is why you have to listen," Lola says. "Your ináy has been through so much. Your ináy has tried to share with you her heart at every step of this journey—and you refuse her. We did not come this far to have you destroy our family. Listen to her, anak. Love her, anak. Be kind to Manong Jack."

"What are you crying for?" I ask Tommy, wiping away my tears. "You don't know what she's saying."

"I don't know, I just am. She's so sad," he says. He leans over and he kisses me on the cheek. "You're so sad."

"You're not so tough," I tell him and we embrace one another, Lola Ani's words settling in our bones, the meaning revealing itself slowly and painfully to the both of us.

Tommy and I let our bodies collapse and we hold one another for a long time. I focus on the breath, how at first the weeping robs us of our breath, but in time we begin to fall and rise together, holding on a little tighter.

"I'm sorry," he whispers.

"About what?" I whisper back. He smells a little bit like the wind, like the outdoors.

"You got all that pain inside you."

"Thanks," I say.

We stay that way for a long time and it doesn't feel like we're doing anything wrong. It feels like for once, I am lying with someone and my whole heart is right there and I feel safe.

We're quiet for a while and then I say, "Tommy." The moonlight showers the dark room. I see shadows on the walls, an aswáng with long arms and a very skinny body dancing on the ceiling, casting spells on the moon. The television still glows because we've let it keep running even after the tape was done. "Why are you so sad?"

I wait for him, but he just wraps his arms around me tighter and buries his face in my chest, sighing loudly. I don't know what's wrong, but I know what to do and I run my hands over his scalp, holding him gently, and I feel the heat of my hands vibrating as they move from his head to his back, to that place that is parallel to his heart. I let my hands rest there and his weeping subsides. My hands are itchy right in the center where the heat is coming from and I know that he has pain in the heart: I know it's real and that in this moment, my hands are taking it away.

We fall asleep like that. Me on the couch and Tommy on top of me and my hands resting on his back. We fall asleep, but not before he tells me that Liza hasn't gotten her period in a few weeks. She hasn't been feeling so good.

I tell him not to be scared. I say, "God will protect you."

He laughs and says, "Oh yeah? What makes you so sure?" Instead of answering him, I breathe. I close my eyes and I breathe. And for a few hours we sleep.

FIFTY

The breeze laps against my skin. My head tilts to heaven and limbs rise, wafting gently at my sides. I am gliding like a blossom flowing to the sea. A spattering of stars float past like jellyfish in the Pacific. I move toward the light of the moon, and when I return to the land I know I'm home. I am in the Philippines years before my birth, before my Papang's birth, before his parents were married for one entire year.

I slip onto the shore, pulling my wild hair up into a high ponytail, the curls sticking straight out of my head like exclamation points. I walk barefoot on sand, moving across the earth, as if I know exactly where I'm going. The songs of crickets, frogs, and out-of-tune birds haunt the skies. Mountains rise up like gigantic walls around me. I push my way through big, green leaves—banana trees, magnolia trees, banyan trees. And along the banks of inland waters, stalks of kangkong grow from the bottom of the river, their leaves waving at me like little hands.

I walk the hills, looking for the houses, and I see a thatched roof, a nipa hut with hemp-woven walls and a staircase made of bamboo poles. There, I think, go there. I can hear the voices from the red soil footpath. A woman screams in Ilokano, "Can't I keep my own thoughts? Why are you always asking me? Why do you want me to give them away?"

I crawl to a glassless window, lift the thatched covering, and I peek inside.

"Sorry, my love," says the young man. "I just want to help."

They are facing the wall and I cannot see them, but it's clear I know them. Their voices sink into my skin, so familiar, so unforgettable. He is lean and muscular, dark from the sun. Maybe he is a farmer. Maybe he is a vendor at the local palengke. Handsome. Her slight figure hides under wild curls that fall to her waist, beautiful and out of control. Fish steams in a pot of vinegar, tomato, and ginger on the floor, in the center of the room. I smell it, nearly taste it. I hold my tummy like I haven't eaten in years. Her hands pour through a rice bin, scooping the hard, uncooked grains into a pot for supper. She holds a handful to the light and the grains fall through her fingers like rain.

I hear her weeping, her breath irregular and sighing in broken spurts. He approaches her, and gently leaning down, he wraps his arms around her and she throws the pot of rice up into the air, the grains scattering on the thatched floor like broken pieces of glass.

"Why are you touching me?"

"Last time I left you alone and you were mad. Can't I win, Ani? Now I want to embrace you and you act like—"

"Act like what?" she screams. She turns to face him and that's when I see. "Are you going to say it?"

"No, mahal," he says.

She is so beautiful. Her dark eyes burn hot with fire.

I say, "Nandito ako. It's me, Angel." But she doesn't hear me. I crawl through the window and I walk right up to her. "It's me," I say, but she doesn't see me.

"Why don't you say it, I'm acting—what—crazy?" she says, walking right past me.

He is so young. I never knew you, I think. I tiptoe around them and find my way to a corner of the hut and I squat. Why do you let her treat you like that, I ask.

This is the illness, not Ani.

Why don't you leave, I want to know.

Some days, he says, but my heart knows better. This is a phase. She only needs to find her heart again. She only needs to remember.

But how do you know? I ask.

I don't, he answers. I hear him, but he is not speaking. And she is oblivious to us. He understands that he will never know what happened when she was in that place. She cannot speak about it. Sometimes he has doubts, but her light is brighter than her anger. Brighter than her madness. He tells me, I'll take her away from here. I'll bring her to Manila where there are no memories chasing after her.

Watching him, I think he's the crazy one, but then I remember how things turn out. I thank him for loving her, for taking such good care of her.

I cannot help myself, he answers.

And just as the dream is starting to make sense, a heavy moan intrudes like a gust of hot wind and I am blown awake by the grumblings of old Manong Jack, who has stumbled down the stairs to find me asleep in Tommy's arms.

"You jackass!" he yells, slapping Tommy awake with a rolled up newspaper. "What are you doing having sex with my daughter? In my living room! And you!" he scolds, swiping me too. "Upstairs."

He doesn't give me time to explain, to say, "Wait a moment. This is my friend who is scared and sad." He is too busy shooing us into the night. I run up the stairs, not looking behind to see if Tommy makes it out of the house safely. I can hear the old man screaming at him in the yard, even as Tommy's car door opens up. From the window in my room I watch the old man throwing snowballs. I hear the engine roaring. White explosions flash in the night, snowballs hitting the windshield, the hood, the bumper. Snowballs shatter in midair. Manong Jack stands like a baseball player in the middle of a white field, his sockless feet sliding around in slippers, his bald head shining like the moon.

I go on hunger strike. Ináy won't listen to me. She won't hear my side of the story. Manong Jack's words paint Tommy and me thrashing about on the living room floor, half-dressed and moaning. Ináy shuts the door on me.

The incident bonds them, makes them fall back in love. They sit in corners of the house—in the living room, in the kitchen, in the tiny bathroom that they share—holding on to one another, whispering. Their words, like spells, travel through vents and under doors. Walang galang, they say, walang hiya. They rename me Angel-Has-No-Respect de la Luna. No-Shame de la Luna. When the three of us are in the car, or sitting in the sala, their eyes shift between me and themselves. Over this incident they reunite, reaffirm their vows, and this makes my heart shrink small and dark.

The morning after, when I woke up dreaming of Lola Ani suffering in a Japanese war camp, confused and sad, my mother and Manong Jack brought me into the kitchen and sat me down.

"I've tried everything," she told me. "I gave you space to be angry. I let you call overseas. I bought you drums to express what you cannot say. I let you gallivant with wild Americans who have pierced every part of their body. But you resist. You contradict. You defy."

"You don't listen to me," I say. "You don't hear me. You're never here!" But she walks away from me like I am not speaking.

I am not allowed to go anywhere after school. I am not allowed to sneak out of the house at night. I am not allowed to have friends over. I am not allowed to use the phone. I have been charged with a crime I have not committed.

I follow her around the house for days. I wake her in the middle of her rest, thinking if I catch her off-guard, I can reason with her, make her see how twisted Manong Jack's version of the incident is. I try to tell her that I have learned the truth about my Lola Ani and I am aching from what I know, but she won't hear me. So now I am on a hunger strike. This is day three.

The family gathers around the table. The plates travel in circles, hover over the table—rice and vegetables, noodles, lumpia, and crispy-skinned lechón. I sit with them so they can see I am not eating. I sit with them to make them feel guilty.

They pile food on their plates like this is the Last Supper. I sit with my empty plate before me, the porcelain shining white under the kitchen light. My silverware guards both sides of the plate, spoon and fork bright as two stars. They slurp and moan. They send the aroma around the tiny kitchen, the flavors rising like spirits—garlic and jasmine, ginger and pork, fried wonton wrappers and sweet-and sour-sauce. My mouth waters, but I say nothing. I don't move. It is day three. I am a resister. I am making a point. I take a sip of water.

"What did you learn in school today?" Manong Jack asks.

"Things," I answer.

"What subjects?"

"Truth. Justice. You know, liberty for all—ay wait—maybe you don't know."

"Angel," my mother says, "wag ka mag disrespect."

"Then why won't you let me tell you my side of what happened?" I ask, my arms falling to my sides in exasperation.

"Enough," she says. "Or else—"

"Forget it," I say, throwing back my chair.

"Angel," Manong Jack shouts. "You haven't been excused."

"You're not my father!" I yell as I run up the stairs, slamming the door behind me.

My stomach is hollow, but the ache inside is too painful. I refuse to eat. I pull out my records. I crank the blues, drumming on my thighs with the sticks, marking myself with each beat, blue, black, purple beats. I hit and I hit.

In the next few weeks, I find rest in the letters I write. I send my love to Lola Ani in new ways. *How come you never told me? I want to know. Didn't you trust me?*

I tell her I know what it feels like to be a prisoner, though I cannot imagine how brutal her life must have been in the hands of the Japanese. *Don't you hate them?* I want to know. *Aren't you angry?*

Her shaky penmanship crawls across the page, creates a landscape of mountains and hills that I eagerly enter and explore. *I was protecting you,* she writes. *I was too busy with our life to dwell in the past. Didn't you feel my heart? Don't you feel it now?*

I stack her letters in the sock drawer, next to my mother's letters. In weeks, the pile grows fat with her words, with her stories of the war and the courtship with my Lolo Ninoy. I begin to see how he stuck by her no matter how mean she was. *I don't think I could have done that,* I write. *Not what he did, not the way he loved you and not what you did either. I might have killed myself,* I write. But she tells me that if I had walked the path of war, I might've found things out about myself, a strength and a will to survive I might never have known existed. *That is why you must learn compassion, anak. Look inside yourself now, anak. In this war with yourself, you might still find it.*

I'm not fighting with myself, I write, *I'm fighting with her.*

You're fighting yourself.

I don't know what she's talking about, but it doesn't matter to me. At night I close my eyes and visit her, a young girl in those garrisons, strong and feisty. I see that even though they win her body and her mind, she owns her spirit. This is what she has and it is what carries her.

I look at the dreary sky and the ice melting so fast I think the earth is weeping. The birds flit from tree to tree, pecking at buds sprouting from skinny branches—branches that were barren only a week ago. I find a bench just outside the cafeteria windows and I pull out my paper and pen. A warm breeze blows in my ear. The sun weaves in and out of clouds and shines on the wet pavement. *The earth is melting,* I write Lola Ani. *There is water everywhere.*

I like the smell of wet earth. I like knowing that this freeze is finally over and I can experience my first spring. In my last letter to her, I asked her when she lost herself. *Kailan, Lola?* And she told me that while she was in the garrisons she was too angry to lose her mind. *Every time ginagamit nila ako, I would get so mad and that kept me strong. At nagdadasal ako.*

For a week, I've been thinking about praying when angry. When I am angry the last thing I want to do is talk to God. When I am angry, God is just a character in a book. When I am angry, I want to scream and not whisper sweet words. I want to hit something. I want to beat the drum. I want to surround myself with the rhythm of Chicago blues. How did Lola Ani do that? Be angry and pray.

Sometimes, when I'm reading her letters, I see the younger version of Lola Ani sitting in a classroom with fifty other pretty girls. She is not sitting at a desk, but squatting on the floor, barefoot and soiled in a dress she's been wearing for months. The other girls huddle around her on the dirty floor, some of them awake and fearful, some have passed out, some are crying. Outside the sky flashes with bombs, rains bullets. Smoke in the sky is a sign that another plane has crashed. I imagine the girls holding on to each other and every time the classroom door opens, the fear. Who will it be? What now?

I grew up hearing other women tell their stories. I grew up consoling them with the palm of my hand, massaging their war wounds as they released the history that damaged their bodies. I would ask, "How did you do it? How did you survive?" And they'd say, "Sa awa ng Diyos." What kind of God does that, abuses girls too young for sex? What do they mean by the mercy of God? After awhile, the stories numbed me. An old woman would tell her story and I would still hold her, still wonder, still look into her eyes, but it was part of what I did, holding them, loving them. I expected them to say it. "Sa awa ng Diyos."

The old women would talk and Lola Ani would come quietly into the room, setting up our meals. She left rice and fish for us. Baked us cassava cakes. Squeezed hundreds of little calamansi to make us juice. She'd come and go, and I wouldn't think anything of it. She fed us, even as the old women were crying and Lila and I were painting banners or marching alongside of them. I never suspected it was her story, too. I never believed the old women when they said that God is what got them through it, even though that was always their answer.

A sharp wind suddenly blows through the school courtyard and sends a flurry of snow down from the roof. I hold my hand up to my face and brush cold away. I pull Lola's letters out of my pocket and choose the latest letter from the Philippines. Carefully I lift the delicate flap of the envelope and I unfold the page like it is a sacred text. I read it again, the third time today:

Anak, I did not go insane while I was in the garrison. I could not afford to go mad, so I asked God to give me strength. I asked God to show me how to do it because all around me, girls were dying. Sometimes when they gathered us up at the schoolyard, they'd move us about like toys and distribute us and right there, in the open air where everybody can see, they take us and they use us. So I asked God, what am I going to do? So God plants a seed of anger to make me strong, to remind me that my body is not who I am. My body is just the house where my spirit lives. Di ba? You know this? Sometimes, the soldier is right there, on top of me, and I want to throw up, but if I do, I know he will beat me and so God says it's O.K. to be mad. It makes you strong. So like that, I made it through, knowing my spirit is larger than this body, is more beautiful than anything these soldiers will ever see. They cannot touch that. Even now, old ako, skinny like dried ginger, pero, do you see my spirit? I did not know the Mahalaya Sisters, but I heard about them. I dreamed about those women. They come to me and say, be strong. We are with you. God is with you. You are more than this body. Where are you? I asked them. Why are you not calling the guerillas? I want to know, but they say that I can do it. I can free my own self. And then I think, ah, the freedom is in the heart, di ba? As long as I have my heart, my spirit. Free ako.

I lost my mind afterwards, when the war was over, when I could not find my way back to my house, when I could not find my family, when they told me everyone had been slaughtered with the bayonet. My mother, my father, my handsome brothers. Wala na. I lost myself when I lost my family. Hindî ko tintiis. Imagine, you lost your father, how painful that was, but you still have your mother and Lila and me. Imagine losing all your family like that. Only my sisters survived, and that is because they were taken by another set of soldiers and placed in the town hall. Ginamit din ang isa. The other, your Mother Mary, was just a baby girl. No one touched her. Baka my heart broke in too many places. Mabigat ang dibdib ko. And all the crying I did not do during the war, all the tears my heart held, broke through the walls as if it were a dam holding back the sea.

You must soften your heart, anak. You must forgive your inay. Forgive yourself.

The words on the page go blurry and I cannot see beyond my tears. A cold front sweeps down on me and snow begins to fall again. I fold the paper up and file it with the others, carefully placing it into my pouch of letters. I go back to the letter I am writing Lola and let the pen circle just above the page. Imaginary words fall from the tip of the pen, hover over the paper, do not land. I don't know what to say.

Soon my whole body goes numb. The snow is falling so fast now, covering the ground and muffling the sound of the cars on the street, making the voices of my classmates in our parking lot a distant memory. The sun burns through the clouds, but the fog is so thick even it cannot penetrate the blinding snow.

After Ináy came out of her trance, she hid her tears from us. She was so busy grounding our lives that we barely saw her smiling or crying or sad. But thinking about Lola and how she lost herself to herself—nawala siya sa sarili niya—I have a memory coming back, of Lila and me lying in our bed. Of the moon infiltrating the room through the thick blinds and women arguing with one another. Sometimes they sounded like wounded animals. Sometimes the words were so clear that my whole body would double over, as if the words were rocks being hurled at me from afar.

Was that a dream? Back then, it was as if we had lost everyone. No mother. No father. Only Lila and me. Only Lola Ani.

When I look down at my pad of paper, the sheets are wet. Jordan is sitting next to me with his arm around me. I'm not sure when he got here or what he's doing here, next to me.

"What's the matter?" he's whispering. "What's the matter?"

His eyes are so green I cannot stop looking at them. I don't move away from him when he leans his forehead on mine. I don't mind when his lips settle on my own and he tastes the tears running down my face. I try to speak, but he is kissing me and it is the only warmth that I feel. I kiss back. I hold on. I taste.

FIFTY-ONE

At two in the morning, when I am still writing my life down, Jordan and Liza and Tommy toss stones at my window and I sneak off into the night with them. We cruise south and west down Milwaukee Avenue to an old house that's been turned into a corner bar. Tommy nods at the bouncer, who slurs a "Wassup, T?" and waves us through. Outside the air is crisp and the windows of the house-bar are fogged with winter's breath. Inside, red light colors everything and smoke hangs above our heads like guardian angels. It's hot like island hot, the air humid with human sweat. A long bar with a thousand bottles of booze shoots through what must have once been a living room and dining room, and near the fireplace a band of old black men lean over their instruments and jam.

"Now dis," Tommy says, indicating the band with his hands. "Dis is the blues."

It sounds like a lot of noise to me. Lots of whining guitars and stubborn drums stuck in patterns, lost keys, and harmonicas coughing and wheezing like they've got bad colds. It doesn't sound sad and mournful and heavy, but happy, bouncy. This is the blues?

The place is packed and we have to squeeze our way through bodies soaked in cheap perfume and drugstore cologne. Some of the bodies smell like protesters' bodies, overworked and sweaty. Alcohol rises from the pores of the people around us.

We find space on a windowsill at the rear of the bar. We crawl onto a thick ledge covered in floor cushions and we lean against the walls and let the music roll. After several songs the musicians rise and slowly people from the bar get up and take their places.

Despite the fast guitar riffs, the quick beats and scratchy voices, my body pulses with melody, my heart opens up. I summon my Papang. I know he is here. I can feel it.

The bass is slow and heavy like a man's voice when he's just come home from work. The sax runs up and down the scale, looking for a place to rest, squawking high and low. An old man sits on a chair with his eyes closed, kissing the microphone, his words pushing one into the other:

YoudamnstraightIgotsdablues.
YoudamnstraightIgotsdablues.

I can't understand, but the way his old voice rattles and sighs makes my chest ache. "Are you here, Papang, can you feel that?" I whisper. The whole room vibrates with the slow drag of the drum. The man's voice is so sad.

This is the blues, I think. This is the blues. Tears fall down my face and for once, though I am seated in the crowd, watching the players on stage, it is me I see up there. It is me. My fingers find the rhythm of the old man's ballad and I tap lightly on my thighs.

"Are you O.K.?" Jordan asks me as he hands me a bottle of light beer.

I nod and wipe the tears from my eyes. "I'm great," I say. "Thanks."

Jordan puts his arm around my waist and brings me close to him. I look over at Liza and Tommy. She rests her small head on his expansive chest.

"You like this, Angel?" Jordan whispers in my ear. "Makes you cry?"

I tell him I like the rhythm, but I can't understand the words, I can't understand the song.

"Don't need to understand the words," he says. "Just feel it."

Even as my eyes are closed and my whole body feels like it's releasing sadness, Jordan whispers, "This one is about a broken heart."

I let tears fall and it feels good.

Another song is letting go of the love of your life, another one is loving someone who doesn't love you anymore. In another one someone cheats on you and you don't know why, but you still love him. I know this not because Jordan tells me, but because I begin to understand the language of the music, the way it slides and pushes at the body, the way the voice breaks up in the middle of a phrase, the way the heart is slow to beat. I know from the bass.

Papang knows what I mean. He's been watching for some time. He knows how his absence breaks my heart. But it's Ináy's face that I see. Every time the song feels like someone has ditched someone, someone has hurt someone, someone won't listen to someone, I see Ináy embracing that old Manong Jack. I see her holding Danny. I see her pushing my little-girl self away from her and walking onto a plane bound for America. Every time the song's about letting go of someone you love, I see her floating out of her body faster than Papang's spirit did when he died, leaving Lila and me lying in our convent beds, crying. Alone.

That night, while musicians take their turns on the little stage, I feel myself blooming out of a hard shell. I feel all that pain that I have been growing just rising to the top and, like smoke from my cigarette, it floats right out of me and joins the red lights in the house, the fog on the windows. I know the blues. I know the blues. Oh, yes. I know the blues.

I stumble up the steps, the blues still vibrating in my skin, my ears pounding with its bass. And stinking of bar smoke and spilled beer, I slither out of my pants and sweater. I slide under the covers. I'm so tired, but I can't sleep, thinking about Jordan and the people in the little bar, how each of them had a story to tell, something sad and achy in their pockets, under their hats, in their thick and overstuffed purses. They'd climb the stage and, digging deep into their secret places, they'd pull their sorrows out and release them like doves.

Yes, I think, pulling out a pad of yellow paper, this is the blues. Under the covers I scratch the rest of the night onto the paper. I write down the music, the ache of each beat. I press hard, drag the pen, slide it across thin blue lines, and when I hear the birds in the distance, and when the sky changes color, I fold the paper up and seal it.

FIFTY-TWO

When Manong Jack yells at me for staying out all night, I don't answer. He rants about Tommy and Liza, how they are a bad influence. How Tommy was only using me, coming here late at night, holding on to me like that. I don't answer him. I know the truth. Tommy is my friend

I take my spoon and fork in my hand and I feed Danny. I say, "Is it yummy, baby? Do you like mama's cooking?"

I try not to close my eyes or think too hard, but it doesn't matter. The tears fall anyway. I think about that winter cemetery, those green iron statues, those angels standing with their wings spread, with their fat cheeks, with their powerful gaze. I try to remember how they made me feel just like one of them, but I can't. It's useless.

"What is wrong?" he asks. "You're feeling guilty, huh? Finally. Maybe there's still hope for you."

I stand from the table and unbuckle the baby from his high chair, brushing off the sticky wet grains of rice from his overalls.

I wash his face with my napkin and I hoist him onto my hip. The abrupt movements startle Danny and his face goes wide and he begins to wail and I am grateful for his cries, for the way he breaks up the silence and fills the house with noise.

I wrap my arms around him firmly and Danny squirms—legs, arms, feet, hands, head. He moves everything at once and in all directions. But I am the older one. I hold on tight and I kiss his fat neck as I run him up the stairs. As soon as I am gone, Manong Jack starts up again. The words float up into all the rooms of the house, big and clunky and full of mean spirit. There is nowhere to hide, to find solace. In the bathroom, water rumbles in the tub, rising higher and higher. I bring the little boy close to me, pulling his shirt over his head, exposing his fat little belly. He's still crying. The shirt collar snags around his ears and I pull and pull, which only makes him kick his legs harder.

"I know, baby," I say to him, tears falling down my face too. "I know."

The old man's standing at the bathroom door now. His voice reverberates against the uneven doorjamb and it feels like the whole room is rattling. I don't know what he's saying but I am feeling so smothered, so crowded. Danny embraces me and leans his head into the crook of my neck. He wraps his arms about me, and hooks his legs around my waist.

"Go away!" I say to Manong Jack. "You're scaring him!"

It is as if a thunderstorm is bursting from the center of the house. I put the child down on the cold tile floor and I calmly pull the door open. "I said you're scaring the boy," I hiss.

Manong Jack raises his hand and I whisper, "Go ahead. That would be perfect." And growling, he lets his arm fall to his side and stumbles back down the stairs, away from the door, leaving us alone, finally.

It takes me a long time to calm Danny down. I sit him in the center of the tub and he kicks water to all the walls. I don't even bother to roll up my sleeves. He douses my t-shirt and soaks my pants, pulling me closer to him by the strands of my wild curly hair. He kisses me. I make a face at him and he stops for a moment, examining my hair and my face, the dampness on my skin.

"Who did that?" I say, smiling, and he smiles at me. "Who did that?"

I sing Danny all the songs Lola Ani ever sang to me. There are only three of them, but I sing each one like a lullaby. I sing them under my breath as I soap each toe, as I dry his back, his belly, and his Tootsie Roll legs. I sing as I cover his whole body in baby powder and wrap him up in flannel pajamas. I softly chant lyrics into his ear. His eyes flutter, resisting these hypnotic rhythms. He sips a warm cup of milk and he too begins to imitate the shapes of vowels and the snapping bite of soft consonants. I whisper the melodies as we lie in our big bed and spin away into some dream. His eyes cannot stay open, and he has fallen into his sleep ritual, holding on to his foot and kicking at the air while pinching my elbow with his free hand. We fall asleep to Lola Ani's songs, drifting off to some place where there are no angry words, where the snow falls but in raindrops on tropical soil, in ocean warm and blue. I hum the songs in my

sleep and they stay with me until that moment I wake and realize I am still here.

The house has grown dark and only the moon shifts in and out
of all the rooms. I open my eyes and watch the way Danny's
belly moves with his breath. Perspiration gathers at his temples
and his long black lashes rest on his face, so beautiful. The
rooms still echo with the old man's tirade. The walls are stained
with his words and I think I actually hear them in the middle of
the night. How is that possible?

I creep out of bed and look at the hallway clock. It is nearly
midnight. The old man snores in the room down the hall. I
wonder if he would wake in the middle of the night. If there
were a fire, or an alarm, or if Danny woke up crying, would he
hear? What did they do before I arrived? Every object in the
house reminds me of the old man and my mother—the chairs,
the curtains, the slippers on the floors. Every smell reeks of her
perfume or his old-man smell. I find myself opening the windows in the house, airing the spaces with the sharp February
breeze. And still, I feel like I am suffocating. I need to go.

I watch the moon settling on the trees and I think of the
Mahalaya Women waiting on the boughs of trees, waiting for the
enemy to lie down and sleep and dream with their fat bellies
sticking straight up in the air. How quiet the nights might have
been, I think, listening to the clock in the kitchen softly clicking,
to the minutes falling off the shelf. How beautiful the moon.

FIFTY-THREE

I wander the neighborhood and find myself standing outside a large cathedral. This house of God is made of gray marble. On a cement mini-plaza, concrete Mama Mary stands with her arms stretched and her palms to the sky. I wonder if she was a healer too. I walk right up to her. I look her in the eye, but there is nothing there. No glimmer of light. No sign of life. Not even a glass eye. Her face is void of expression. No wonder she stands alone on the mini-plaza.

The mahogany doors stand as tall as trees. I yank the copper rings, use my whole body to get the doors open, but they don't budge. Locked. There are two more sets of front doors. Locked. I try all the doors and in the back I find a little entrance, insignificant and made of aluminum like any back door. This one I step through.

The church has high ceilings and is two city blocks wide. Images of the Bible stain the windows in brilliant blues, greens, yellows, and reds. My steps echo, make me sound bigger than I am. I find my way to the front and I sit right on the steps that lead to the altar. I cross my legs. A giant Jesus hangs his head, dying before me, arms spread like angel wings waiting to take off. He is pinned to the cross. His body is unable to fly anywhere. I close my eyes.

I try to find words to speak to God, to ask for something, though I am not sure what I am asking for. Perhaps God thinks I have some nerve, showing up like this. Where've you been, Angel? Why now, Angel? I breathe. No words. I sit in silence. The colors of the morning swirl around me, warm me in the cool hall. Without opening my eyes, I place my hand into my pouch, fingering the books and stacks of papers and old quizzes, feeling for my stack of letters. There are two stacks. I pull them out. I offer them to the giant Jesus, eyes still closed.

There's a leak somewhere, I hear water dripping, echoing. The pews creak like old bones. I open my eyes and look around. Behind me, an organ and a bass sit next a full set of drums. My heart goes weak looking at those shiny rims, at the skins pulled taut. I want to play those drums. I want to play the blues. I want to escape into the rhythm of my heart. I wipe my eyes with the sleeve of my coat, and then I remember the letters.

I turn back to God and I hold them up. One stack is worn, wrinkled and torn, read and reread like the palm of my hand. The other stack is older but orderly, pressed. These are letters sealed and untouched. I have no idea what these say.

I hold them up, I say, "I want to read these. Will you help me?"

I wait. Nothing. After a minute, I get up and I go visit the Holy Family—Joseph, Mary, and Baby Jesus—painted lifelike in every way. Joseph holds the baby up like they are having a family photo taken. Mama Mary's lips are the color of pink blossoms. She's smirking at me.

I light the candles at their feet, three rows of them. I light them all and I watch the glow of a hundred flames. I ask them, "Will you help me open these?"

I can feel my body pulsing, breathing like it is separate from me. The air flows in and out, and I ache. I think I might be having chest pains. My heart is on a string and it is swinging like a giant pendulum. Woosh, and woosh, and woosh it goes. I close my eyes and the hundred flames burn inside me. It is very bright. Blinding even. Woosh, woosh, woosh. My heart cracks, and this time when the tears fall, the pain also falls out of me, spilling like sweets in a broken piñata.

"Open them, anak." It is my father's voice, coming from inside me. "Go ahead, open them." I think about dropping the letters and running to the drum set at the front of the church. I think about pulling out Papang's sticks and just playing my heart out, but I hear him again, whispering inside me soft as a hundred flames, "Open them, anak. Open them."

The sun shifts its vibrant colors across the church. I pull a tea candle burning at the feet of the Holy Family and I place it on the ground next to me. I search the stack of letters, examining the postmarks and perfectly carved letters drawn by my mother's hand. On the back, her lipstick marks the boundaries of the envelope. I see her sealing each letter with a swift kiss. Too busy to speak me, to hold me, to kiss me on the cheek, she left with all her things thrown in a box, waving good-bye, in a hurry. The palms of my hands go hot, like they are going to heal someone, but I cannot imagine why.

And then I do it. I tear them open one by one. I sit on the marble floor with my books falling out of my pouch, my drumsticks rolling down the aisles of the church, and my coat thrown to the side. I hold a candle to the pages and I read:

Anak ko,
I pray someday you understand. Even though I know your heart will break one day, hindî ko kaya. I don't want to think of it. Maybe I should have told you about that moment when the baranggay captain unlocked the doors. Lola Ani and I followed him through the iron gates. There were five Americans and one Filipino. The bodies were bloated, unrecognizable.

"Mabuti dumating na kayo," said the coroner. "We are still looking for the other families. Good thing you came na."

Anak, I could barely look at them. The men were broken, missing limbs, and growing fat in unusual places and their skins were foul and deteriorating. I could still smell the alcohol rising from their bodies and I didn't name your papang at first because his face had been so greatly disfigured. But then I saw him. I knelt down beside his body and lifting his arm, called to your lola.

"Tingnan mo, Mama," I said.

My hands trembled as I traced a blue-and-purple cloud shaped like a tiny human heart resting on the inside of his arm. You remember this birthmark, yes?

"Look, it's him. It's Ernesto."

The officials handed me a pair of drumsticks with his name carved into the grain. They found them near his body, thrown wide apart and sticking out of the ground.

"It's amazing," said the coroner. "They should have burned in the fire, they should have been charred, pero look! Like brand new!" And that was when I wrapped my arms around your papang and wept. That was when it happened. When your father died, nawala ako sa sarili ko.

Forgive me anak.

Ingat,

Iyong Ina

Her words penetrate all the hard layers that protect me. I imagine her sitting at the kitchen table, shivering as a cold draft sneaks under the back door, writing after one of her twelve-hour shifts. I close my eyes and I take a breath. I read another letter:

Anak,

Talagang wala ako sa sarili ko. At first I thought he had left me for another woman and for days after he was missing we searched—remember, ha? I searched for him everywhere. I talked to his spirit. I tried to get him to come back. If only I could tell you what this was like. Forgive me, anak.

And when I had reconciled his leaving me, I worked to make our family dream come true. To come to the U.S., to bring you all here one by one just like Ernesto and I had planned. What choice did I have? You and Lila are all I have.

Manong Jack is a kind man. And he offered to help us. We were to be husband and wife, but only for the papers. Anak, he is a friend. And when I first arrived, I had gone a little mad ulit. Coming here without any of you was hard. And it was cold. Every night when I cried, he held me, and he brushed my hair, and he let me talk about you and Lila and even Ernesto. He was kind. He was a friend. And yes, I love him now, but not the way I loved your papang.

Mahal na mahal kita, anak.

I wipe the tears away. I pull each memory out, and I see what was happening in ways I could not see then. After Papang died, Ináy stopped eating. Went on hunger strike. Her body grew small and her eyes always looked to the sky, like she might find him there. I lost her then, just like I had lost Papang. I lost them both. And when she returned, hard and distant like a Hukbalahap guerilla, she refused to hold me, be quiet with me, to cry with me. Now I breathe and I feel my heart expanding, the air flowing in and out of me, settling me down. I have missed my mother.

This morning, Ináy came home from work worn from twelve hours of cleaning vomit and spit from some sick patient's bed. She climbed the stairs as if it were the Cordillera Mountains, winding and steep, full of brown rocks. She moaned and she sighed as if no one could hear, but I was in the bathroom, brushing my teeth.

I poked my head out and watched her plop into bed next to the snoring old man. She remained fully dressed in her green scrubs, a winter scarf still thrown about her shoulders. This is her American Dream. Every day, every week—working until the skin begins to separate from her bones, until the hair has gone completely gray—she works when the rest of us sleep. She smells sour like milk gone bad, like the bodies of a thousand dying souls. For what? A paycheck. For what? So she can bring us over one by one and watch her slowly dying before our eyes.

I read each letter and then I read them again. *Forgive me, anak.* I lay them out before me, spread them on the church floor, bless them. As I read, my family joins me. Lila looks over my shoulder, reads the letters along with me. Papang hovers like an angel, drumming on the church pews with the tips of his fingers. Ináy speaks plainly, her voice washing over us, bringing us all together.

I weigh down the letters with votive candles from the Holy Family's shrine. The papers glow red from the glass.

I straddle the floor, my legs spread wide apart on either side of the candlelit letters. I listen to the silence.

FIFTY-FOUR

My mother writhes in pain, a migraine stinging at the crown of her head. I stand in her dark room, waiting. I cannot tell if she is awake. Her small figure is lost under mounds of bedding.

"Ináy," I say.

"May sakit ako."

I move to her side and I run my hand along her forehead. Her skin is damp. Her temples throb under my fingers, steady and strong. Crawling into bed with her, I rearrange the sheets so I can look into her face. Worry lines, familiar and worn like the history between us, track her skin. Her cheekbones slope like hills. I brush tears from my eyes. When did she age? When did her hair grow brittle and dry?

"You want me to heal you?" I ask.

She smiles, eyes still closed. "Akala ko, you didn't believe."

"Didn't you teach me?" I ask her.

"Sige, anak."

I cradle the nape of her neck and wait. I breathe. I let go. And there we are, the two of us marching down EDSA Boulevard, her legs straddled and swollen, her belly full as a helium balloon. I chant from inside the sea that is her womb. I bless the revolution from a dark place where the only light is from my mother's heart. My small hands are in fists and raised up, my mouth wide, wide, open wide. She doesn't know it, but in this moment, when we are marching to that holy place surrounded by a million aktibistas, I am obedient and loving. I am supporting her. In my zeal to right the world I push too far and she faints from lack of water, burns from sunbeams hot as fire.

"Forgive me po," I whisper.

I put my palms on her eyelids. The heat dances over her eyes. I say a prayer. "Eto na," I tell her.

When I move my hands to the crown of her head, a chill passes through me. Though the room is dark, her face grows light and when she looks at me, I see her.

"I didn't understand," I say. "Patawad," I say.

I feel her muscles tightening up then relaxing. My hands are burning. Something small pulses just under her skin. My breath moves like wind. No words, no drumbeats, just silence. Just silence. No words, no drumbeats. Just silence. Just light through lace curtains, delicate as snow.

IN CONTEXT
(OR, WHY THERE IS NO GLOSSARY)

When I was little, growing up in Peoria, Illinois, and Milwaukee, Wisconsin, and for a time, the province of Saskatchewan in Canada, my parents spoke to each other in a language different than the one they spoke to my brothers and me. Theirs was a secret spelled out in syllables—fast and rhythmic where vowels lined up one right after the other—triple As and double Es—rupturing the air like fireworks—where Hs were nonexistent on my father's tongue and my mother rolled her Rs. My brothers Mike and Manny and I spoke our first words not in Tagalog, but in English.

We were born in a time when the "experts" cautioned parents not to confuse their children with more than one tongue. Of course now we know that's far from the truth. I have a nephew and niece growing up in Brooklyn, code switching between English, French, New York slang, and knoting Tagalog. I have nieces who, as toddlers in Santa Ana, California, were asking for water, agua, or tubig—flipping tongues like buttons on a DS video game. I have ten nephews and nieces with midwestern twangs who call their grandparents Lola and Lolo, who lovingly end every conversation with mahal kita even as they learn Spanish, or French, or Mandarin in school.

I have never taken a course in Tagalog.

As a little girl, I watched my parents talking—the way they'd sit across a dinner table and debate politics, or snuggle on the couch watching television, joking with each other in Tagalog. At late-night parties, I spied grown-ups tumbling mahjong tiles and shuffling decks of cards, laughing and eating and speaking in that same secret language. And when my Lola Nikolasa was in the house, she spoke to her son in Kapangpangan, to her daughter-in-law in Tagalog, and to us, her grandchildren, she communicated in kisses, smiles, and little sniffing sounds she made whenever she held us tight. I learned the words from living them. I learned them from seeing them used in context.

By the time I was twelve, I had figured out their secret language. I understood everything. The ladies would come to the house and say, "Dalaga na si Evelina—ang ganda niya." And my mother would warn them, "Naiintindihan niya lahat. Be careful, you'll give her a big head."

And when, at the age of thirty-three, I returned to the Philippines with my teenage and twenty-something Fil-Am students—some who could not speak nor understand Tagalog—I found myself suddenly spewing my parents' native tongue. It was glued together and shaky, but it was Tagalog. And it was coming out without me thinking. I suppose I had been storing up all those words in my head and, finally, had a reason to set them free.

During my Fulbright in 2001, when I began interviewing sur-viving Filipina "Comfort Women" of WWII, women I addressed as grandmothers, I used a translator to ask my questions. I listened to the women's responses.

One day, the translator got it wrong. I knew the answer he gave me was not what the lola had actually said.

"Ask it again," I said. "Ask it this way."

And when he did, the lola answered the same way. The trans-lator looked at me in disbelief. "Tama ka!" he said.

Of course, I was right. I could tell what she was saying, not only by her words, but by the way she was looking down at her skirt, fingering the hem, holding her breath, then sighing like a tire going flat.

Shortly after that I let my translator go and began talking to the women directly. Once someone asked a lola, "Is her Tagalog getting better?" And the lola shook her head and said, "Hindî, pero naiintindihan ko siya." Even though my Tagalog was bro-ken up and turned upside down, she understood me too. We were speaking the same language.

And so *Angel de la Luna and the 5th Glorious Mystery* is drawn of many words—in English and Tagalog, in American slang and in Taglish. There is no Spanish here, though you will see Spanish influence and you will see Spanish words usurped into Tagalog and sometimes redefined. And, depending on who is talking, you will see English spun in circles and rearranged to fit squarely on the speaker's tongue. On the one hand, the words come out of me organically—in the way I see character and place and in the way I hear the characters' voices.

On the other hand, not everyone speaks Filipino. So I made it a point to use the Tagalog, the Taglish, and the slang in context by grounding them in character. I wanted readers to understand what was happening without interrupting the narrative, so I have sewn the definitions into the text. Still, it is not necessary to understand every word—but I hope the energy of the moment, and the emotional content are carried by the words as they are drawn here on the page, surrounded by other words and breathing through its characters.

In graduate school there was only one other writer of color like myself in my cohort—the poet Anthony Vigil. We struggled with the political act of defining ourselves through our words in ways our English-only peers were not asked to do. "If you mean gossip," suggested my workshop teacher, "why not just say it?" He didn't understand the subtext of tsismis—how it is always sitting not so far from hiya that often leads to embarrassment or humiliation. How the weight of that word placed in a Filipino American context means something utterly different than gossip—also two syllables, but quick and clipped by the p—gossip—unlike tsismis, an embarrassment that seems to go on forever—tsismisssss . . . also spelled chismes in Spanish, also means you have no shame. Walang hiya.

In a play between Tagalog and English, words order themselves not only to fit the rules of grammar, but to the culture and the perspectives of a specific people—Angel's people. Characters conjugate, flip, subvert and reverse word order to suggest different ways of thinking, of understanding, and believing in story. A

Filipina "Comfort Woman" giving her abduction testimony may slip from past tense to present tense, from English to Tagalog to Waray, going deeper into her native tongue because the act of telling is the act of reliving, is the act of violence all over again. To translate word for word can be a dangerous thing. You might miss the point if you're too wrapped up in knowing what each word means. And truth be told, the World Wide Web is not always accurate. Just because the internet defines a word doesn't mean the word doesn't change when it's sitting next to another one. Tagalog (taga ilog or "from the river") is as fluid as its meaning. I guarantee words will slip between rocks, go deep into a stream, and come up another dialect like Illokano or Kapangpangan or Waray.

Late in the book when Angel listens to live Chicago blues, Jordan asks her if she understands the lyrics in a song. When she admits she cannot, he tells her, "Don't need to understand the words—just feel it."

I suggest reading the words in *Angel de la Luna and the 5th Glorious Mystery* the way you might listen to a song. Just feel it.

As a girl who grew up hanging upside down on easy chairs with a book in her hand, I often read words—English and other words—that I did not understand. I rarely stopped to define them. Sometimes I wrote them down and looked them up later. (I was a geek, after all.) But more often than not, having stepped into a fiction John Gardner called "that vivid and continuous dream," and driven to know what happened next, I kept reading. Like Angel, I let the words wash right over me, I watched them working next to other words. I listened to them. I tasted them and felt the weight of them in my mouth. I imagined them surrounded by nothing at all. I followed them as they floated down the page, bumping into semicolons, swimming through parentheses, slapping up against em-dashes, evading italics, and falling right off the page. I read the words in context and, right or wrong, I gave the words their meaning.

Angel de la Luna and the 5th Glorious Mystery was born of three major hurricanes. Hurricanes Katrina, Rita, and Wilma. I was supposed to be writing from my more-than-thirty hours of interview tapes, documenting the lives of fifteen surviving Filipina "Comfort Women" of wwii for my book of essays, *LOLAS' HOUSE: Women Living with War.* I was supposed to be transcribing, translating, and writing down history. But the hurricanes came one after the other and my 2005 sabbatical spun fast in the debris of all that rain. I was living at Hecht Residential College on the Coral Gables campus of the University of Miami as a faculty resident master and every week nine hundred freshmen, twenty-two residential assistants, and two other faculty families and I went into lockdown. So I wrote this book instead, a book that allowed me to work under hurricane conditions, a book that was probably brewing for years.

First, I thank the University of Miami and the MFA in Creative Writing Program and English Department for providing me with the time, space, and resources to write. To the 2005 Hecht

Residential College freshmen, to my team of RAs, to my colleagues, and to Leyla Al Monsoori (amazing rock that you are), thank you. To the MFA graduate students who packed up all their perishable foods for every hurricane, who camped in my apartment and wrote with me, thank you. And to my current thesis students, writers who inspire me, challenge me, and always make me proud—gracias a Daisy Hernández, Alejandro Nodarse, y Benjy Caplan. To my colleagues Maureen Seaton, Jane Alison, and Manette Ansay. I send you my gratitude. A special thanks to Lester Goran, for years of good counsel and your ear. Yes, you told me so.

In gratitude to the Fulbright U.S. Scholar Program. There are more stories, histories, and books that will come from your support. The research in the Philippines has been a journey and a gift. And to my Colorado State University professor, the poet Mary Crow, for helping me to refine that proposal. Your dedication to my works-in-progress is often remembered with thanks.

To the staff at Coffee House Press, to Chris Fischbach, Anitra Budd, and Caroline Casey. For your generosity, patience, and kindness. Thanks. And to my editor, Allan Kornblum—what a friend you've been, what an eye, and what insight (and I don't mean just for this book). Thank you for your fellowship and wisdom, Allan.

Thank you Gizelle Galang Jacobs, you fine negotiator, you cousin extraordinaire, you protector and defender of my artist's rights. You are a blessing. To my poet-sister Niki Escobar, for taking the time to read the book, and allowing Angel into your dreams, and drawing these amazing the images. Super salamat, girl.

To the Pinay scholars Allyson Tintiangco-Cubales and Dawn Bohulano Mabalon, for your tireless work in the community and for making time to write a study guide for this book. I give you thanks.

The seeds of this story came long before Miami rains, in the research for a screenplay that was never written—The Dalaga Project. My gratitude to Hugh Haller, Tara Agtarap, Ana Fe Muñoz, Neleh Barcarse Sawsiengmonkol, Lizzie Juaniza, and Mia Habón. To the Lolas of Liga ng mga Lolang Pilipina-Gabriela, your stories are the inspiration for all I do these days. I promise I have not forgotten. LABAN! LABAN! LABAN! To the current and former staff of LILA-Pilipina, especially Rechilda Extremadura, Sol Rapasura, and Celit Imasa, my guardian angels, my cultural translators, my teachers. In gratitude for Nursia Institute of Women's Studies at St. Scholastica College—my writing space, my home. To the women of Gabriela Network, especially Liza Maza and Ninotchka Rosca for leading in so many ways. To Sister Mary John Mananzan, my spiritual and political mentor, my friend. Maraming salamat po. To Faustino Bong Cardiño—You drove me crazy, kaibigan ko! Thanks for teaching me paikot ikot. To my family in the Philippines who housed me, hosted me, and helped me keep my balance, to all the Lopez-Tans, Moraleses, and Galangs, thank you. (I light a candle for each of you—Uncle Armando, Lola Charing, Auntie Goring, Uncle Doming, Ate Baby, and Kuya Vic. You helped me write this book too.) Special thanks to Auntie Pita, Uncle Romy, Auntie Penny, Ate Carol, Ate Menchu, Kuya Joey, Kuya Boy and Ate Ging, and Jing-jing. You gave me writing space. To my nieces Cindy

Ayroso Reyes and Betina de Borja-Relator, my Tagalog editors, my dear ones. Halo-halo when I return!

While writing is a solitary act, there's no way without a community of support. To my barkada, the Kunyari writers—Lara Stapleton, Sabina Murray, Gina Apostol, and Ricco Siasoco. To R. Zamora Linmark, Luisa A. Igloria, Bino Realuyo, Krip Yuson, Barbara Jane Reyes, Allyson Tintiangco-Cubales, Jing Hidalgo, Gemino Abad, Patrick Rosal, Oliver de la Paz. To Chris Abani, Elmaz Abinader, David Mura, Geeta Kothari, Eugene Gloria, Karen Singson. To Adrian Castro, Ana Maria Perez Castro, Edwidge Danticat, Faidherbe Boyer, Geoffrey Philp, Cristina Garcia. To Cyd Apellido, thank you little sister. To Maxine Hong Kingston (for the gift of your insight), Jane Davis, Jose Grave de Peralta, Jacqueline Sheehan Bredar (for your copyedit love) and to my VONA crew (all of you)— Maraming salamat sa inyo lahat.

To my circles of healers. You have found a way into this book. Thank you Judith Spriggens, Carol Lee, Lisa Jacobson. Thank you Phyllis Oreamuno and Jill Yip Choy. Maraming salamat Leny Strobel, for your work building the Center for Babaylan Studies. A profound thank you to mga Lola of LILA-Pilipina who are also hilot, for all the moments you laid your hands on me, and mga Dalaga, chasing off fevers, migraines, bellyaches, and heartbreak.

To my meditation Master—much love, respect and gratitude for your guidance and support in all things. This practice grounds me, centers me, gives me clarity and light.

Always to my family—my parents Miguel and Gloria Galang and to my siblings, my nieces and nephews, and Chauncey Mabe. Mahal na mahal kayo. Thank you for always welcoming me and my many drafts, my distractions, my quirky self home. You feed me love.

HISTORY

- How do historical events—particularly, Philippine colonial history, World War II, and Philippine political history in the eighties and nineties shape Angel's understanding of self, family, and her own possibilities?

- How does the Filipino language of Tagalog, used in this book, create new ways of understanding Philippine history and culture, and Angel's own family culture?

HOME

- Where is "home" for Angel? How does this change over the course of the novel? How do movement, migration, and challenges associated with these moves shape Angel's identity and her family?

- How does Angel react to the different spaces she finds herself in, and the community she is surrounded by—in the Philippines and in the United States?

HEALING

- How do Angel and her family heal from the moments of trauma that they face throughout the book? How do the Lolas heal from the trauma of their experiences during World War II?

- Angel is a budding healer in a long line of healers. What is the role of spirituality and faith in their healing process?

HEART

- Angel experiences heartbreak early with the death of her father. What role does love and heartbreak play in Angel's life? How does this shape her character?

- How is she transformed by love?

HOPE

- How do Angel de la Luna and her family find hope amid the despair in their lives?

- From this novel, what can we learn about hope that can be applied to our own lives?

These guiding questions were developed by Dr. Allyson Tintiangco Cubales, professor of ethnic studies, and Dr. Dawn Mabalon, professor of history. They are both faculty members at San Francisco State University and part of Pin@y Educational Partnerships. For more information and a complete curriculum for *Angel de la Luna* in the classroom, please visit mevelinagalang.com.

COFFEE HOUSE PRESS

The mission of Coffee House Press is to publish exciting, vital, and enduring authors of our time; to delight and inspire readers; to contribute to the cultural life of our community; and to enrich our literary heritage. By building on the best traditions of publishing and the book arts, we produce books that celebrate imagination, innovation in the craft of writing, and the many authentic voices of the American experience.

Funder Acknowledgments

Coffee House Press is an independent, nonprofit literary publisher. Our books are made possible through the generous support of grants and gifts from many foundations, corporate giving programs, state and federal support, and through donations from individuals who believe in the transformational power of literature. Coffee House Press receives major operating support from Amazon, the Bush Foundation, the Jerome Foundation, the McKnight Foundation, from the National Endowment for the Arts—a federal agency, from Target, and in part from a grant provided by the Minnesota State Arts Board through an appropriation by the Minnesota State Legislature from the State's general fund and its arts and cultural heritage fund with money from the vote of the people of Minnesota on November 4, 2008, and a grant from the Wells Fargo Foundation of Minnesota. Coffee House also receives support from: several anonymous donors; Suzanne Allen; Elmer L. and Eleanor J. Andersen Foundation; Around Town Agency; Patricia Beithon; Bill Berkson; the E. Thomas Binger and Rebecca Rand Fund of the Minneapolis Foundation; the Patrick and Aimee Butler Family Foundation; the Buuck Family Foundation, Ruth Dayton; Dorsey & Whitney, LLP; Mary Ebert and Paul Stembler; Chris Fischbach and Katie Dublinski; Fredrikson & Byron, P.A.; Sally French; Anselm Hollo and Jane Dalrymple-Hollo; Jeffrey Hom; Carl and Heidi Horsch; Alex and Ada Katz; Stephen and Isabel Keating; Kenneth Kahn; the Kenneth Koch Literary Estate; Kathy and Dean Koutsky; the Lenfestey Family Foundation; Carol and Aaron Mack; Mary McDermid; Sjur Midness and Briar Andresen; the Nash Foundation; the Rehael Fund of the Minneapolis Foundation; Schwegman, Lundberg & Woessner, P.A.; Kiki Smith; Jeffrey Sugerman and Sarah Schultz; Patricia Tilton; the Archie D. & Bertha H. Walker Foundation; Stu Wilson and Mel Barker; the Woessner Freeman Family Foundation; Margaret and Angus Wurtele; and many other generous individual donors.

To you and our many readers across the country,
we send our thanks for your continuing support.

M. EVELINA GALANG is the author of *Her Wild American Self* (Coffee House Press, 1996) and the novel *One Tribe* (New Issues Press, 2006). She has edited the anthogy *Screaming Monkeys: Critiques of Asian American Images* (Coffee House Press, 2003), is currently writing *Lolas' House: Women Living with War,* stories of surviving Filipina WWII "Comfort Women," and is at work on a new novel, *Beautiful Sorrow, Beautiful Sky.* Galang teaches in and directs the creative writing program at the University of Miami, is core faculty for VONA/Voices: Voices of Our Nation Arts Foundation, and has been named one of the one hundred most influential Filipinas in the United States by Filipina Women's Network.

Her Wild American Self
ISBN: 978-1-56689-040-3

Screaming Monkeys
ISBN: 978-1-56689-141-7